PALADIN'S HONOR

A. CARINA SPEARS

Copyright © 2021 A. Carina Spears

All rights reserved. No portion of this book may be reproduced, stored in a retrieval system, or transmitted in any form or by any means—electronic, mechanical, photocopy, recording, scanning, or other—except for brief quotations in critical reviews or articles, without the prior written permission of the publisher.

This novel is a work of fiction. The characters in this story are fictitious. Any resemblance to persons living or dead is coincidental.

Cover design and interior formatting by *Hannah Linder Designs*
www.hannahlinderdesigns.com

ISBN- 978-1-7358956-5-9

I can't drop a copy off where you are, so I'll still sign it for you and keep it on my shelf. Seeing this book in print would have been perfect were you still here to share the launch with me. Since we can't have either of those things, I can put your name next to Edgar Allan Poe's here. Maybe that will amuse you where you are. Miss you.

ACKNOWLEDGMENTS

This book has been a long journey and I could not have made it without the care and support of those around me. I would like to thank Chuck and Rick at White Cat Publications for taking a chance on my book. Special thanks to Sherry Hooker-Godoy for helping me understand military family life more, Roger Abbott for a great way to fight wraiths, Melinda M. Snodgrass for her insight on horse behavior, and Ethel Hooker for having my back. I want to thank my beta-readers Cat Moonsong, Michele Borna-Stier, Karilyn Warsinski, Wolfie-Sara, Myla Riffle, and Star Stramel for reading and helping me get the first round ready. A special thank you to LUSH the store for allowing me to experience the cinnamon and clove shampoo combination I created for my tale. Great minds think alike. Most of all, thank you. Yes, YOU, the reader. Nothing is born without faith and effort. By daring to try something new, you make my writing possible. It is in daring to try new things that legacies are born. Thank you for embarking on this journey with me.

Dedicated to Ethel Hooker.

I can't drop a copy off where you are, so I'll still sign it for you and keep it on my shelf. Seeing this book in print would have been perfect where you still here to share the launch with me. Since we can't have either of those things, I can put your name next to Edgar Allan Poe's here. Maybe that will amuse you where you are. Miss you.

AUTHOR'S NOTE

My favorite genre to read is fantasy. I love it. However, as an author, I got into writing horror first and then romance. So it was a long, roundabout journey to get to write Paladin's Honor. I like to say that I imprinted off Stephen King's "Needful Things". That's the best way I have been able to describe my writing style. There's romance in my books, but I'll make you fear for the main characters first.

This book came from the premise of "What if love came after?" In the time period when this book was written, the divorce rate had risen to 51% in the United States of America. In contrast, many arranged marriages have lasted the rest of the couples' lives. So how did they work? Why did they work? While the romance in this one isn't exactly a traditional arranged marriage, it is not an ordinary love match either. I'll let you read how it plays out.

Beyond that, I love Devon and Mirabelle as characters. Devon is an honestly good man. So many books are about "the bad boy" characters these days. Heroes have become so gritty they spit concrete. This is a call back to what an honestly good man is like. There needs to be a standard to compare to and Devon is it. If you play many fantasy role-playing games, you know that paladins are like knights but are considered "the best of the best". Originally they were the palace guards who guarded the royals themselves. In games, they tend to have divinely granted powers for healing and battle. To keep those powers, they must remain pure of heart and fixed of purpose.

Think of Sir Lancelot from the legends of Camelot and King Arthur. Now take away the downfall. Those are paladins. Devon's not perfect, but he's honestly good. Mirabelle is honest in a different way. She is true to herself.

The trend I see in heroines is hot-headed and they never listen or learn. Mirabelle is human. She isn't perfect. She makes mistakes and they carry a high cost. However, she is neither defined by them nor forever crushed under them. In time she comes to decide who she is and who she wants to be. The nicest thing is: She has more story to tell. So does Devon. This is just the beginning, and it's a great beginning to a world that is opening wide with many stories and characters coming to life in it. Did I mention that I love fantasy? Since you picked up this book, I'm thinking that you do, too. I hope to entertain you for a long, long time!

When Carina approached me about writing this foreword, I was honored. I've known Carina since 2013, and we connected over our writing of superhero stories. Not many females writing about superheroes, so we instantly bonded.

Honestly, to some extent, all authors are superheroes. We create characters and entire worlds. We weave scenarios and action, heartbreak and adventure. We give a bit of a reprieve from the everyday world for something much more imaginative. Writers give of themselves so that the reader can embark on daring adventures, can experience a first kiss all over again, can worry over the fates of characters whose lives hang in the balance, and can fall in love. The best stories of all enrich the mind, captivate the soul, and invigorate the heart. When you open the pages of a Carina story, you know you'll be immersed into a whole new world.

Paladin's Honor is one such new world, and it does not disappoint.

Paladins. The first words that spring to my mind associated with paladins? Strong. Brave. True. Warrior. Fighter. Protector of the small. A champion. Valor. Glory. And, of course, honor.

At its core, any story featuring a paladin has to have courage, heart, and action. Paladins are warriors of religion who fight battles on the field and off, within themselves and for the sake of others. They struggle to achieve just a bit more, to push themselves harder, to strive for a better world no matter the personal cost.

Devon is one such paladin, and he will fight for the sake of his Order, his brothers-in-arms, his family, and more. He has a true warrior spirit, and from the first, you will come to see just how strong and capable he is.

But, ah, beyond every strong man, there must be a strong woman, even if she has to find her way. Mirabelle is feisty, experienced despite her youth, and headstrong. It comes as no surprise that these two may butt heads on more than a few occasions!

It takes a special kind of writer to be able to create a paladin character and breathe life into him so that he isn't too good to be true. Some might think paladins a bit boring given how perfect they can be, but a skilled writer will give even paladins a flaw or two. Carina humanizes her characters, allowing them to live as real people in the readers' minds. It's the only way for a reader to truly bond with characters, and Carina does this with a quiet grace that sneaks up on the reader.

There is one other word that can and should be associated with paladins—love. The perfect marriage of fantasy and romance can feature no other hero than a paladin and a woman he vows to protect. What else can a paladin do to honor his love besides protecting her? It is, after all, how a paladin would show his love.

Sit back, relax, and enjoy the story of a world far away filled with peril and danger, love and intrigue, and, of course, a paladin and his honor.

Nicole Zoltack

I
A REUNION LEADS TO QUESTIONS

Devon dug out one of the last horse cakes he had of grain and molasses for his sacred mount River Dancer. She might be smarter than a normal horse, but she was still a horse. He didn't need her in a huff because he wouldn't let her stop and help "prune" the mirabelle plum trees growing along the path atop the hill where his best friend's family lived. River Dancer laid her ears back as he tied her to the fence away from the trees, but lipped at the treat in his hand happily when he offered it. Earning her forgiveness was easy enough.

The blossoms of the trees would soon perfume the air with a scent nearly as sweet as the fruit itself tasted. Devon hoped he might catch them in bloom before he left on circuit again. Their honey-like fruity scent always acted as a balm on his spirits. The simple celebration of life by nature helped scour the horrors of the field from his oft-weary soul. The winter had left him feeling lean. Seeing the wildlife searching for fresh browse as he traveled made him hope he could rest up and recover in good company. Although this wasn't strictly a social call, Devon didn't expect it to be unpleasant.

As a paladin, checking on the family members of the others of his

Order was part of his duties. Since his Order followed the God Rhys, the Smiter of Undead, it was all too easy for a vengeful creature of darkness to turn a family member into a lure or pawn to control the actions of a paladin. To avoid such issues, the wellness checks were important.

Of all the people he checked in on, his heart held a fond place for his best friend's family. Theovald's parents, Daleen and Alarick, had practically adopted him since the first time they met. Devon used to visit with them every other holiday while he was still a student in the academy with their son. Theovald's little sister, Mirabelle, enjoyed the stories of Devon's travels even though he rarely had news of Theo to share these days. They were assigned to different routes, but that could always change.

Raising his hand, Devon rapped upon the weathered wood of the cottage's door frame and was soon rewarded with the thumping of footsteps moving closer and the latch lifting. Alarick answered, his gray-green eyes going wide in shock under the winter- lengthened forelock of the brown hair covering his furrowed brow. The man rocked back on his heels when he saw Devon standing there. "Well, isn't this a surprise?" he said, a grin slowly spreading on his face. Reaching out, he clasped Devon's forearm in greeting. "Come on in." Turning his head, he called back, "Daleen! You won't believe it, Devon's stopped in for a visit." Devon knew that they hadn't expected him so early. The winter snows had only just melted back enough for safe travel on the roads.

Devon smiled easily at the cheerful greeting. The scent of warm dust, flour, and pastry dough tickled his nose with hints of fond memories, but his smile faded when Daleen appeared. He'd never seen her like this. Daleen's shoulders stooped. Her dark hair lacked its normal shining luster, and she twisted a dishtowel in her hands as she shuffled over. The youthful spring in her step? Gone. Even her eyes looked haunted, dark bags, marking sleepless nights. He drew up short at her disheveled appearance. "Sir Devon, we could really use your help."

Devon leaned back in surprise. "Of course, Daleen, you know I am ever at your service. How can I help you?"

"It's Mirabelle. Ever since the snows have broken, she's been away almost constantly. She barely comes in for meals, and sometimes, when I go up to check on her at night, I find she's not even in her bed! When I give her chores to do she disappears as soon as they are done, without a word."

This was a very new development. Mirabelle had never behaved like this before. Images of bright blossoms amidst dark curls came to mind. Laughing eyes that held a deep well of thought behind their twilight shades emerged from his memory. Mirabelle had been enchanted by the simple map he had sketched out of all the lands he had visited the last time he saw her. She had made her own marks upon the page as he recounted what he saw and did in each place. Her head stuffed with dreams of travel, she asked endless, breathless questions. She wanted to know about everything from the lives of the people to the lives of the farm animals in each place. Boats, carts, clothing, architecture, she drank in everything that he recalled. What could have happened?

Devon became unsettled and worried at the causes for the sudden change. Images of bandits and battles with the undead swam before his eyes. A shake of his head cleared his mind. Mostly.

He would have to find out. Ensuring the safety of this family was part of his sworn duties. Should Theovald become distracted by concern for his family while in the field of battle, it could mean the death of him. No, Devon would find Mirabelle and help mend things before he left on his next tour of duty.

Often he stopped by as Theovald's friend, but now he stepped back into his role as Sir Devon, Victor Paladin of Rhys. "Do you have any idea where she has been going to?" he asked Daleen, his voice deep and serious as he crossed his arms. A hint of cold steel came into his dark brown eyes as his mind began working on the problem.

"I've heard some other ladies from the Temple have espied her around town, often in the company of some young men and women who are garnering suspicious reputations." Daleen continued to twist the towel to near breaking in her tanned, calloused fingers. The nervous energy burned reserves the woman didn't have after sleepless nights. Devon worried she would make herself ill just before the planting season began at this rate, a dangerous thing for folks of a pioneering town. He took all this in as she continued. "No one has seen them do anything specific, but Mirabelle has stopped going to Temple in favor of spending time with these new 'friends' who aren't fit to be introduced to us, it seems! I'm worried that they will lure her into harming herself or her reputation.

The town is fairly tolerant of the high-spirited ways of teenagers, but once folks have had enough, she could find herself banned from the shops or even ostracized from social gatherings. I just don't want to see that happen to my little girl!" Her voice went up an octave and nearly broke on the last words.

Daleen was too proud to cry around guests, Devon knew, even as close to the family as he was. It sounded less and less like the influence of some malignant spirit and more and more like youthful rebellion. He sighed. Everyone experienced it to one degree or another, which was why most parents would foster one another's children as they passed their first decade of life. They would learn adult ways and an adult trade while away from the familiarity of home. Staying so long with one's parents brought on conflict. At seventeen, Mirabelle may have felt stifled.

Theovald himself had been engaged by fifteen or sixteen. Devon doubted Mirabelle had the same opportunity since her brother left home. As the last child, and after nearly losing Theovald to a vampire's fangs, Daleen and Alaric likely sheltered Mirabelle more than she cared for. Their little girl might wind up less sweet than the trees she was named for if she felt too enclosed. Young trees needed room to grow.

"Daleen, Alarick, is Mirabelle being courted at all? Is she spending any of her time with friends who are learning any trades?"

"Not that we know of," Alarick answered, his swampy gray-green eyes nearly lost under his long, brown bangs. "She stopped spending time with her girlhood friends from the Temple a while back, and although a few boys have asked after her, she hasn't shown interest in any of them. Otherwise, I would have encouraged her to consider a match. She seems wary of us and angry at the world suddenly. I do not understand why."

"Let your hearts rest easy, I will find her and discover what is disrupting your happy home. Rest assured, I will begin today after I check in with my Order. Good day to you, both."

With that Devon turned and left the cottage that had turned out to be more puzzle than haven on this visit.

2
A PROMISE OF BETTER THINGS

Mirabelle looked up at Jarick from where she sprawled upon a trio of worn rugs atop a woodpile in the abandoned woodcutter's shed. Jarick had claimed it as the base of operations for the Thieves Guild. Few went near the area since it sat on the western edge of Cemetery Hill. Despite his proclamations, the place had little enough to recommend it. It stood open on two sides with only crossing support beams to imply the third wall in the back. A partial wall in front of the beams created a small alcove meant for the storage of cords of wood. In it, a tangle of bedding on a thick nest of straw was all that made up Jarick's "private quarters". Said quarters could be easily seen by anyone who sat where she did now in the meeting spot. The rest of the room featured a couple of worn chairs and upturned stumps as a planning center. A slightly charred lantern on another stump in the center served as the only source of heat and light. Some thieves they were; they couldn't even get a table for the place.

"Patience, Miri, better things are coming," Jarick said as he lifted her chin, stroking the side of her face before rolling a strand of her dark hair between his fingers as if appraising it.

She stared longingly up at him, meeting his lichen green eyes, wondering if he might decide he needed some warming up. It felt so decadent, so bad to be with him. Her parents still thought of her as a little girl, Jarick saw her as a woman, his woman, specifically. She rather wished he would take her. It was cold and the heat of their bodies together would warm them both up and feel good. It might also ease her boredom for a time. They were still doing jobs, but it felt like they were caught in a rut.

Her eyes lit on Springer when he came in. His real name was Mitch, but Jarick insisted everyone had a false identity to use when they were working, so Mirabelle's mind went over both whenever she saw them. Springer had a long-sleeved sweater of warm, knitted sheep's wool that looked like it was tailored to fit him perfectly. The gray-eyed lock pick specialist always kept himself impeccably groomed. His short, black hair, combed so not a strand was out of place, matched his clothing. From his fitted shirts down to his leather-soled shoes, quiet as a cat's paw, he could blend into an acceptable company like he belonged.

She and Gemma both wondered why Mitch never made a pass at them. He looked far more attractive with his dark hair and flawless skin than Jarick did with his mop of auburn hair and spray of freckles. But "Black Jack" ruled the roost, and Springer seemed content to have it remain so. He nodded to Bailey, their muscle man with a baby's face and pudginess despite towering over the rest of the room's occupants, and Lee, Jarick's second-in- command. Lee exuded a musky scent like that of a wild animal about him. Bailey didn't mess with Springer, though he enjoyed throwing his considerable weight around with the others when Jarick wasn't present. Lee usually let him and watched on in amusement, but Bailey always seemed like an over-sized toddler to Mirabelle.

She watched Springer oust Cory from one of the two chairs in the place to warm his hands at the lamp on the 'table' and rolled her eyes. "I think the roads are dry enough and the weather clear enough that we can hit the next town over. There should be a sheep market coming up with the new lambs getting old enough to sell. During it, there will likely be enough folk about that we can glean some pickings from the crowd," Springer said as he turned his hands before the feeble flame.

"It's too cold to walk all the way to Heathsrow or even Mistguard. Might as well go all the way to Duskdale while you're at it. We won't get back by nightfall and it's too cold to sleep outside. Come up with another plan," Gemma said testily, tossing her short, dark curls. She moved to the other side of the lamp, putting her chubby hands even closer than his, as if in silent challenge.

Mirabelle watched Springer shake his head and hold his hands up in surrender. "No need to get upset. It's just an option."

"Well, what else is out there to do, Springer? Locally," Mirabelle asked, glancing at Jarick to make sure he approved. Springer's eyes flicked to Black Jack as well before answering.

"I can get you into most anywhere, but with it being early Spring, the pickings here are slim." She could see Jarick's mouth flatten out into a thin line. Springer must have seen it and he quickly added, "However, there is a shipment that should arrive shortly to Madame Adelle's shop.

Now that Winter's Night Ball has passed, she will have whatever fabrics she found interesting sent to her shop. Even a single bolt of the cloth she uses would fetch a good price in any of the other towns, and we can sit on it until the weather is warm enough to travel. Would that suit you better, Gemma?"

Gemma gave a half-shrug of a shoulder, almost looking down her nose at him as she did so, but Mirabelle could see that Springer's suggestion pleased her. Gemma, or Gem, liked all things feminine and expensive. The idea of bright clothing and jewels to adorn her soft, feminine curves lured her into Jarick's circle. She'd probably want to keep some bolt for herself, and Mirabelle didn't look forward to the ensuing fight. There would be no way they could ever safely wear any of the rare fabrics without getting caught. Mirabelle would have to have a quiet word with the crew to grab colors Gemma didn't like or face her tantrums later. Sometimes the best way to keep the peace was not to allow anything in that could break it.

"That sounds good, Springer. Now then, our fellows seem to have need of the lamp, Miri. So how about we generously allow them the benefit of its heat and you come warm me up instead? Seems only fair," Jarick said, pulling Mirabelle away from her perch. Mirabelle followed him to his rough love nest and if the others heard them, they'd at least understand why it was good to be the leader.

3
REPORTS, MEMORIES AND KITCHEN ENCOUNTERS

Riding back down the curving pathway of the hill to the main road, Devon quietly considered the matter. His mount blew out a mild complaint at the lack of browse for her to nip at along the base of the hill. They had pulled up short at the bottom where the pathway from the house joined up with the main road to town. He patted her neck, "Don't worry girl, we're going to be staying here a few days, so you'll get a warm stall and a nice meal soon. I know you're a little tired of the road right now. By the time we set out again, there should be plenty of new grass for you to crop." He watched her ears cock back, and she shook out her mane in response to his words. She probably only cared about "stall", "warm", and "meal" but she picked up her pace at the possibility of rest and food around the bend. After having just finished a long circuit, Devon was longing for a few creature comforts. The long pathway up to the Temple and the stables from the main road was at least a straight one and River Dancer put on a small burst of speed knowing what lay at the end.

Glancing left, he could just make out the short bridge, gleaming in the afternoon sun. Staring at its peaceful, pastoral image, he shook his head at the turn of events that had occurred since his last visit. That stretch of path from the bridge to the Temple was one of his favorites.

The buzz of insects and the calls of frogs awakening to the early scents of spring echoed to him all the way from the river he had crossed earlier at the edge of town. Tracks of animals, both wild and domestic, crossed it as he passed the bogs and lowlands that flooded with rains and brought a rich abundance of eels and rare plants to this area. It was far enough away from the wilds that no great monsters were likely to show up, yet far enough away from town to enjoy the sights and sounds of the riverlands. It was the spot that most reminded him of home.

Settling his sacred mount in a fresh stall, Devon tended to her before lifting his travel packs and heading inside. He was anxious to seek information about his friend's sister, but there were protocols to be followed, including a round in the purification chamber and a meeting with the local chapter head for his Order and the priest or priestess of the Temple.

In this case, he drew an audience with Priest Magnus and Valdesh the Younger. He performed his ablutions in record time, his hair still damp when met with them, but presentable. "I realize you may be eager to get to the dining hall, Victor Paladin Devon, but I am fairly certain our towels still work," Magnus said with dry humor at the sight of him.

Going down on one knee, Devon crossed an arm over his chest and bowed over it. "Sir, my fellow Victor-Paladin's family is concerned over the absences of their daughter. They have asked my aid in discovering what issue is plaguing her."

Valdesh the Younger frowned at his words. His mostly bald head made the brilliance of his eyes stand out all the more. He was still called Valdesh the Younger, even though he was over forty by now. His father served in the capital as one head of the order and held the title of Valdesh the Elder. Crossing his arms, his lined face looking stern, he asked, "Do you think it is related to the vampire that her brother extinguished six years ago? If it had any spawn, they might only now be receiving word and making a move."

Shaking his head, Devon replied, "I do not think so, Sir, but it bears checking into. Given the ties I have with Theovald from our academy days, I would like to look into this personally for them. If something is plaguing his sister, it would be better if I broke the news to him. Since I am familiar with the family, I believe that I may discern whether the subtle signs of an undead's cat's pawn are being employed."

Valdesh the Younger placed a hand on his shoulder. "Rise, Victor Paladin Devon.

Your devotion to your duties and your brother-in-arms does you credit. I do not see a difficulty in granting your request. Do you, Priest Magnus?"

The dark-haired priest ran his fingers over his moustache and down his short, trimmed beard. His tall, stout form belied the strong muscles beneath the layers of softness, both of the steady meals the temple served and the robes of his order. "I do not. However, you need to report in on your activities and discoveries to someone. If you see or sense any signs of the enemies of Rhys, then you should take word immediately and directly to your superior, either Valdesh here or Marsid. If it turns out to be a more mundane problem, come to Priestess Lila or myself. We may sort things out through counseling to avoid any problems cropping up in our little community."

"Thank you for bringing the matter to our attention, Sir Devon. I shall release you to your tasks. I recommend you get something into your belly before you go haring off. You will do neither your friend, nor his family any good if you grow faint in the seeking of the answer. Rhys light your way." Magnus spread his hand wide in blessing, mimicking the rays of the sun at dawn. Devon bowed his head, murmuring thanks, and walked down the corridor connecting the church to the paladin's quarters and the meal hall.

Ducking into the kitchen, he spotted one of the young lay servers and called her over. "Blessings of Rhys upon you, child."

"Blessings of Rhys, to you, Sir!" the dainty blonde child, no older than seven summers replied, green eyes looking up into his own as she greeted him.

"Do you have a name, child of Rhys?" he asked politely.

"Everyone here calls me Honey Flower, if it please you, Sir," the child said with a quick curtsy.

Honey Flower? It made sense for the Brothers and Sisters to choose it, given her green eyes and golden hair.

"Honey Flower, my name is Sir Devon. I have just arrived and could really use your assistance. Is there by chance some bread or cold sausage that I might have? I need to continue my duties for the day, and might miss dinner."

Honey Flower considered his words with all the seriousness that only a small child could muster. Her face scrunched up with concentration. After a few moments it brightened again like the sun coming out from the clouds and she said, "I will do my best for you, Sir Devon. Only wait right here, okay? I'll be right back."

"I will wait right here for you," he said, amused, although most of his words were lost to her swiftly retreating back as she headed toward the kitchens. He wanted children of his own someday, but life as a paladin did not leave him much time for socializing. His first commitment was to his God/Goddess, the mysterious and wondrous Rhys. He had never regretted his calling to become a holy knight in the service of Rhys. Saving people from the ravaging creatures of the dark was work well worth doing, but it took a strong person to be the spouse of such a warrior. The risks were high, and the dangers very real. Since he really knew very little of romance, it seemed likely that duty, not children, would be his lot for the rest of his days as it was with many paladins. Maybe not those in the service of Dido, Goddess of Life and Love, but those who followed the justice of Sigvarder, the banner of Rhys, or even the sea trails of Anjasa often led somewhat lonely, if not solitary lives.

The camaraderie of their brothers and sisters-in-arms filled the empty spaces where close family stood in the lives of ordinary folks. Devon had been a year older than Theovald and already training in the Order for over two years when Theo had arrived at sixteen. Devon had been in the field by the time he was fifteen, but the Order had not recognized him as a Victor- Paladin until he reached his majority at the age of eighteen. Thus, when a situation occurred farther North that required only seasoned Victor Paladins and higher, he wound up having to stay behind in the capital for an extended stint in the academy.

Theovald's arrival gave him something to do other than run drills. He was allowed to teach the newcomer the basics, and being close in age, they bonded quickly. Having heard Theovald's haunting tale of how he wound up deciding to join the Order of Rhys, Devon promised to always watch out for Theo's family. He had hoped to simply visit and confirm for Theo that his family was safe and well, as he always did when he passed through, but that wasn't going to be quite so simple this time around. He could only hope that he and the Order would ensure everything would turn out well. As he thought about the paladins he had served with, movement from the doorway to the kitchen caught his eye. Honey Flower returned, peering over the bundle in her arms. Standing nearly on tip-toe, the child lifted it up to drop it into his hands even as he stooped to gather it from her.

Inside a bundle of cloth, swaddled up like a baby, was a half loaf of bread, thickly cut chunks of hard cheese, and half a dozen dried eels. "In Rhys' name I thank you, Honey Flower," he intoned seriously.

Honey Flower pressed her hands together, fingers splayed upward in the half sun of Rhys. "May Rhys bless your work and your day, Sir Devon." Finishing the formal exchange, Honey Flower let out a gust of breath and gave him a beatific smile at having succeeded at the task set before her. Giving her a slight bow of his head, Devon smiled gently in return before exiting via the back doors of the dining hall. They let out into the meadow through which a path of gravel and dust led to the stables.

He gave some thought towards fetching River Dancer, or borrowing an ordinary horse for the trip into town. River Dancer's unique abilities got him through many scrapes, but taking a trained warhorse into town wasn't always the wisest course. Having just come off of a long circuit, she was prone to be antsy. A local mount would be less nervous around crowds, but were also not familiar to him. In the end he decided that if he really wanted to know what was going on at street level, he should walk it. So instead he fetched his water skin and, sighing, put on his breastplate and armor. It would go poorly if he encountered a serious threat unarmed and unarmored. It might be uncomfortable, but better that than dead. He'd had to walk in his armor for years before getting a sacred mount of his own, so it wasn't the worst hardship he'd had to endure. Topping off his waterskin, he went back out into the bright sunlight and set off down the path into town.

4
PLANS ARE HATCHED AND WARNINGS ISSUED

The base would be too cold to bother hanging out in soon so Mirabelle wasn't surprised when Jarick gathered the group together to head out. Her breast still felt bruised by the eagerness of his touch. Just proof of his love, she told herself. If his attentions were harsh and swift, at least he was passionate and told her how desirable she was daily.

It was hard to avoid slipping in the damp mud and clay as they walked through the dead growth of last year's plants towards the backs of the buildings making up the shops on the North side of town. Even Springer was having trouble keeping the burrs and seedpods off of his neat sweater. As they got closer, Black Jack raised an arm to halt them. Pointing at Springer first, they waited for him to disappear around the edge of the buildings before the next person went. Mirabelle shivered in the wind as Jarick held her back with him until the last.

When he signaled, they walked together. He rarely allowed them to be seen together in town. It made her feel a little more special. Jarick had some big plans for their tiny Thieves Guild. When he was done she would never have to worry about walking in any town where there was an active branch, and that was something she wanted. She didn't want to be afraid anymore.

Thieves weren't all that organized, but they had a code of not messing with each other. Wherever they went, as long as they handled themselves well, they'd never be robbed. That knowledge made Mirabelle feel powerful and a hint dangerous. She was no cutthroat, but she would get to walk away when trouble showed up and that was more than most could ever say.

The thought put a little swagger in her step as they cut through the closest alley onto the boardwalk in front of the shops.

She remembered when they put the boards in; she had been twelve years old. It was the spring after her brother killed the vampire that had been plaguing their town. The spring after he left. Shaking her head, she drove out thoughts of him. He ran off and joined a holy order of knights, the Order of Rhys, a couple of months after the monster's defeat. He told them pretty much after the fact, and that was six years ago. She owed him nothing.

Springer eyed a lock while Corvid gave sad eyes to a passerby and begged for a penny sweet. As the youngest member of their group, he could play off his age with people and get them to part with a few coins or some food. He was the only one of the group who could be relied upon to always bring something in. His sweet, honest face, framed by loose, short, dark hair allowed him to charm nearly everyone he came across. His short stature and lean limbs allowed him to give off a robust or hungry emanation according to whatever the occasion required. However, that gift would wane as he got older. His expressive blue eyes wouldn't carry him once he got his growth. Corvid would need to pick up some other skill set. Mirabelle thought he would do well apprenticing to Springer if he kept his air of innocence about him. You couldn't appear rough or suspicious if you wanted to be close enough to houses to pick locks.

Springer would have to impart some of his knowledge, though, and that seemed unlikely at this juncture.

Catching sight of Gemma over at Adelle's shop, Mirabelle reluctantly left Jarick's side to join her. Leech stood at the corner, lounging and picking his teeth as he acted as lookout. That had to be a first. She doubted he'd ever tried cleaning them out at all, given how bad his breath was. His teeth looked as dirty a yellow as his hair. He tried to flirt with her occasionally, but honestly, Mirabelle could hardly bear to stand too close to him. He was not, nor would he ever be, her type.

She and Gem wandered into the shop, chatting inanely about dresses and parasols as they looked around. Adelle was not back yet, and only a second string assistant minded the place. The young woman with short, sculpted hair rose from where she had been dressing a manikin to greet them. "Welcome ladies, is there anything I can help you with today?"

Mirabelle distracted the woman so that Gem could slip into the back for a few moments. Springer would need more information on the interior layout if they needed to get in and out quickly and safely later. Gem could move both fairly quickly and silently when she wanted to. So by the time Mirabelle had gushed over a red fabric with an embroidered pattern in it, Gem had returned and was gazing out the far windows as if distracted by a bird flying by. Mirabelle and Gem soon bid farewell and promised to come back after they thought about their choices.

"So how'd it go, Mirror?" Leech asked.

"Gem got a look in the back, so we should be good," she replied.

"Gem did it, huh? I bet you helped a lot," he said trying to butter her up.

"It really was mostly Gem's work," Mirabelle deflected.

Lifting his overlong bangs from in front of his eyes, Leech squinted at something across the way, cater-corner to them. "Who is that?"

Mirabelle and Gem looked up to see a man with long dark hair in full armor talking to a shopkeeper across the street. It took her a moment to recognize him. Devon! "We have to get out of here," she hissed at Gem." Too late. He turned and nearly did a double-take as he spotted her. Then he headed straight for her!

Lee looked like he might try to cut him off when Mirabelle hissed at him and gave the "scatter" password. Leech snorted in frustration but continued his forward path at a casual pace, as if he were planning on doing nothing more than crossing the street all along. Gem opened a fan and turned at a right angle to Leech and walked calmly down the boardwalk, examining shop windows as she went, but Mirabelle knew she would beeline to Jarick once she was out of sight.

Devon! Why by the outer gods was he here now? "Mirabelle?" he asked uncertainly. She looked off down the roadway, not wanting to meet his eyes. He was a paladin of Rhys, not Sigvarder, she reminded herself. It was unlikely he would divine her true purpose by showing up.

"Yes, it's me. What do you want, Devon? And why are you dressed like that?" Mirabelle asked, trying not to let her annoyance show in her voice.

"I was warned you might be in trouble," he began.

"So you thought you'd just ride in and rescue me? Is that it? Well, I'm fine, Sir Devon, as you can clearly see. So you may return to your ivory halls at the Temple of Rhys and rest easy tonight." She turned to go, but he reached out a hand and grabbed her shoulder, holding her back.

"I'm afraid such a simple answer will not suffice to remove the doubts raised as to your safety and well-being. Given the nature of your brother's work for the Order, you know what must be done. Any hint that a family member might be the subject of an unnatural influence must be investigated. I apologize if you are indeed well and my presence causes you consternation. Even so, if you are actually well then it will be of little difficulty for you to answer a few questions for me before going about your day. I can even offer you a meal and a chance to catch up on the news of your brother to make up for the inconvenience."

"Actually, I was about to meet up with some friends," she said in a haughty, dismissive tone as she shrugged off his hand.

"Then by all means, let's go meet them," he answered, his own voice taking on a sharper, harsher note that suddenly had her worried about what he already knew.

"I changed my mind, let's get these questions over with so you and I can part ways and go about our respective tasks."

"Indeed?" he said dryly, his eyes narrowing. Mirabelle took a half step back from him, uncertain of what to do as Devon's demeanor changed before her eyes. Devon had always been warm and indulgent towards her. It was easy for her to forget he was a Victor Paladin who survived battles against undead in the field. He was a year older than even her brother Theo and showed that he wasn't as easily put off or fooled as she expected. Perhaps she should not to poke the bear. If he were attempting to execute his duties, he might literally pack her off to the Temple if she proved too troublesome.

"I apologize, Devon," she said, suddenly contrite. "It's cold out and I was hoping to be out of the wind by now. Where would you like to go?" Clasping her wind- reddened hands before her, she lowered her chin and hoped he might be moved to pity. Behind him she spotted Jarick staring at them, his looks as black as the title he liked to claim. Did he think she was flirting with Devon? Good grief, he was more than five years her senior. What would she want with him, or him with her? She was surprised Jarick even had a jealous streak in him, but it secretly pleased her. Black Jack commented casually enough that the women of the Thieves Guild in other towns were often shared around as a reward to the other men for good service, and that both liked it that way. Jarick had showed no interest in sharing her for all that he talked a good game. Gemma would share her affections if a good enough bauble were offered to her, but Jarick liked to keep his treasures for himself. Looking away from him, she focused her attention on Devon.

Her words seemed to mollify him. His dark brown eyes grew less stony, and he said, "Understandable. Very well, where would you care to go?"

There weren't many options for food in the town that didn't involve going to someone's house. "Let's just go to the inn's tavern. It's only mid-afternoon, I doubt it's drawn any of the rowdy crowd yet." His eyebrows went up, and she wondered what shocked him. That she knew when the rowdiest hours were, or that she suggested a place that could circulate rumors around town that they had entered a sleeping establishment together? Guests visiting from out of town usually used the inn when a relative's home was full up, but it could be used for trysts. If he were worried about his reputation, he could lump it. She didn't want to visit with him at all and she would not go home with him as though she were a truant child. She was only a few months away from her majority. It wasn't like she had never been in the inn before. Devon must think of her as still being a child, just like her parents. 'Just Theovald's kid sister', he'd learn otherwise.

Going in, she selected a table in the middle row along the wall farthest from the stairs. That should help mitigate any rumors started by tongue-wagging busybodies. The food smelled good and although she lied outside about the cold, being in the inn's warmth made her feel more relaxed. Might as well take full advantage of the moment since he offered to pay. Flagging down one server, she ordered up some roast lamb and mash with a glass of red wine to enjoy with it. Devon cocked an eyebrow but did not question her choice. He ordered a less expensive mutton stew, which really had basically the same ingredients. The age of the sheep affected the cost. Since it was lambing season, her meal wouldn't be that expensive. Devon asked for a glass of the same beverage she was having, which surprised her. She didn't think she'd ever seen him drink, or at least nothing stronger than a small beer or light ale. Was he trying to impress her or just being amicable?

She couldn't quite decide, but as he was a friend of the family, perhaps she could afford to be a little nicer to him. "Thank you for the meal, Devon. Why don't we get your questions out of the way first before it arrives so we can enjoy it?"

He sat back in the dark wood of the booth, setting his gauntlets on the scarred wood of the table before him. "As you wish. Your family has noted some disturbing changes in your behavior of late. Want to just tell me what is going on?"

So he was playing truancy officer! This made her anger flare again. "What's to tell? I've grown up and they don't realize it. I'm allowed to seek out a life of my own. Theo took off and joined the Order of Rhys, a full year younger than the age I am now. How is it that he is allowed to make such decisions about his life and I'm not?" The server dropped off their wine, and she tried emphasizing her point by swirling the wine in her glass and taking a sip, but the momentum caused her to take a larger gulp than she planned and it was a challenge to not choke on it. She set it down on the table again, aware that she probably made herself look more like a child rather than less with the display.

Devon made no comment about it, and their food arrived, so they both set to eating. Devon paused for a moment before taking his first bite to thank the gods for the bounty. She halted in that instant, realizing her manners, but did not join him in his devotions. She had little use for the gods and goddesses these days. They had ensnared her older brother and carried him away so that he only visited a few times a year. If he hadn't joined an Order, he would probably still be toiling in the fields.

Then they would still wander along the river and meadows together, talking and exploring the landscape like they did when they were kids. She resumed eating, chewing slowly as she tried to swallow past the lump in her throat. No matter how much she tried to tell herself otherwise, she missed him.

She must have left off eating because Devon suddenly broke into her reverie saying, "Are you all right?"

Blinking rapidly, she looked up at him, his face honestly concerned, and for a moment she forgot her animosity. "Yes. I worry about my brother out there."

Devon nodded, and sat upright once more, spooning up more stew before answering. "I cannot fault you for being concerned. The life of a paladin of Rhys is fraught with danger, but take heart, I helped train him in the basics myself when he first arrived at the academy, and I have seen him fight in the field. For all that he is kind-hearted around you and your family, he fights with strength and a fierce determination in the field. Have faith in him, Mirabelle."

She took another sip of wine. Devon rarely spoke a lot, although he could tell a good story when in the right mood. That he worked so hard to reassure her seemed oddly comforting. Family friend or gaoler? Mirabelle couldn't decide which category to put him in, which only made it more difficult for her to know how to handle the situation. She nibbled on her food some more, silence being the easiest course.

As they both finished, she grew eager to get back to Jarick and the others. "Have I answered all of your questions? Are you satisfied that I am not under some dark influence?"

Devon took a last drink of his wine before rising and collecting his gauntlets. "No, but I do not feel you are in any danger tonight." Before she could come up with a retort, he paid their bill and left. What in the world did that mean? Did he really think there was some outside influence affecting her actions, or was it an excuse to wheedle at her to return home like a good little girl? That would not happen.

Hunching up her shoulders against the sudden, chill wind outside, she headed back to the meet-up site, wondering what to expect tomorrow.

5
FACING A CONUNDRUM

Devon walked back to the Temple with the wind whipping his hair against his face, causing it to slap against his eyes and cheeks in a nearly painful fashion. He shivered as it chilled the metal of his armor. It might be Spring, but the nights still had a touch of Winter's edge to them.

Mirabelle. She was a conundrum. It had been nearly two seasons since he had last seen her and if she had blossomed last year, this year she was in full bloom. Seeing her at the table ordering wine in a tavern made him look at her anew. Gone was the young girl who hung onto every bit of news of her brother, or of the unusual things Devon saw in his travels. She was a woman now, and chaffing under the pressure to be both a dutiful daughter and to discover her own calling as a woman. Devon did not think she was under the spell of some evil undead, but he thought she was under a bad influence.

The problem was that although he had a right and a duty to intervene to eliminate any unholy influences upon her; he had far less jurisdiction in simple, mundane matters such as a child's rebellious stage. Devon had already submitted himself to the Order before his hotheaded stage hit. Fortunately for him, discipline and an exhausting regime had helped to temper his hardest years. Mirabelle had no such mitigating influence.

That her actions might endanger her in the longer term, and thus affect her brother's performance in the field, did technically fall into the category of "wellness-checking" but it was a tenuous thread at best. Having arrived at the end of his current tour, he would have at least a fortnight to recover.

He could use his personal time to monitor the situation, but if he could not resolve things before he left, it could turn ugly by the time either he or Theovald returned. He did not relish his best friend discovering his sister in jail, or worse. Sighing, he leaned forward to hasten his pace as he reached the turnoff to the Temple. He wouldn't be getting much rest this break period, but if he extricated Mirabelle from a bad situation or crowd before heading back into the field, it would be worth it.

Approaching the lights of the temple, he gazed a bit enviously at the stable where River Dancer sat warm and comfortable. It wasn't far now, but somehow the very last part of a journey always seemed the hardest to him. The sound of his boots crunching on the rocks and gravel of the path echoed loudly to his ears in the cold air. His puffing breath as he crested the gentle rise came out like the steam of a dragon's breath as he reached for the door handles. Passing over the threshold to the dining hall, he smelled the promise of dinner and decided to stay and round out the stew he ate earlier. Likely he would not have many solid meals if he intended to track Mirabelle.

Valdesh the Younger caught his attention and waved him over to join him on the bench. An empty plate and mug sketched out the points of an arc above some paperwork the man had been studying. "You missed the evening service. Long day?"

Devon nodded. Valdesh held off until Devon had filled his plate and taken a few bites before prompting him for more information. Pushing the buttery baked squash around on his plate with his fork, Devon tried to decide how to best answer. "I found Mirabelle shortly before returning here. Although I do not think she is in any current danger, and none from undead, I do think that, if things go unresolved, it will affect Theovald's performance in the field." Valdesh pursed his lips to one side and grunted in reply. Upon hearing that neither he nor any of the current paladins coming in off of circuit would have to go haring off suddenly, he seemed content to allow them both to finish their meals before continuing the discussion. Once they'd both finished and moved their plates aside, Valdesh cleared his throat and continued.

"I take it you intend to pursue the matter for the sake of your brother-in-arms? You do realize we do not have any temporal authority if it is not a matter related to Rhys' domain and the immediate safety of the people?"

Devon gave a slight nod. "I am confident I can exert a counter-influence, but it will take time."

Valdesh eyed him speculatively, then spent a moment fishing out a toothpick to use. "You're one of the calmest and steadiest paladin's I know, Devon, but I am uncertain you are up to dealing with the mood swings and dangers of a young woman. Especially one who has not yet reached her majority or left home. Easier to slay the wind. I trust you to try, but if things get out of hand, you must turn it over to the local authorities. Do you understand?"

Devon gave an unhappy nod of acknowledgement and went back to polishing off the eel and squash on his plate. "Don't get me wrong, I want nothing bad to happen to Theovald's family, but if his sister gets herself into too much trouble, it is easier for me to recall him from the field until the matter is settled than to explain why we are stepping on the local authority's heels.

Understand?" Valdesh asked, his piercing turquoise green eyes boring into Devon seeking truth.

"I pledge to thee, I will abide by our Order's rules and not interfere," Devon replied at last, slightly ruffled.

"Then how do you intend to solve this dilemma?" Valdesh asked, puzzled.

"By example," Devon replied, making Valdesh just shake his head as he handed his plate off to one youngster and rose to leave.

6
SEEKING COVER

The weather turned markedly warmer the next day. Devon took it as a blessing upon his task as he headed out to the stables immediately after the early service. Soon the early service and dawn service would merge, but for now it meant sermons in the twilight before dawn when hope seemed lost and the power of Rhys was needed most.

The early service often drew those mourning the loss of loved ones, or those remembering fallen brethren in the field. Devon did not despise the notion or sentiments, but he needed to have a positive mindset for the task ahead. He was grateful to walk out into the fresh brightness of the new day when the service ended. The young grass had showed bright green shoots, which would please River Dancer as they set out on their task today. "Easy girl, easy," he murmured to his mount as he put her tack on and checked her hooves for any stones or abrasions after their long circuit.

She blew into the long strands of his hair and lipped at it, just in case he hid treats for her in it. At least that's all Devon could imagine as her motivation as he shoved her head over good-naturedly and patted his hair back down into place. She might be a sacred mount, but River Dancer preferred treats over attention. Her dappled grey hide looked like water droplets forming ripples on a river as she moved into the shafts of sunlight glimmering over the horizon. Mounting, Devon gave a light turn of the reins and a click of his tongue to get her moving.

The odds were good that Mirabelle would not set out this early, but he wanted to be in place for when she passed. His first goal was to find her. Once he observed her without her knowing that anyone else was around, he could fully discover or rule out unnatural influence. Given today's mission, he had opted to dress in a simple, unbleached linen shirt with leather eyelets and ties with leather lined brown riding trews.

The fields surrounding the Temple provided little cover, only the tall, brown stalks of last years meadow flowers with some bold clover and late crocuses adding hints of color and perfume in the under layer of growth. The bottom of the nearby hills across the way sported a few trees, but had little room for River Dancer and himself to hide.

As loathe as he was to make use of his steed's unique powers for something as unseemly as subterfuge, he did not want Mirabelle to be aware of his presence right away. If some other power were at work, it would help to see how she behaved when she did not know she was being observed.

Dismounting, Devon rubbed the side of River Dancer's neck. "I'm sending you to the Field, Dancer. Just for a bit," Devon told his mount. River Dancer turned her head towards him questioningly. "It'll be fine. Ready now?" he asked as he called upon the sacred energies to open a swirling tunnel of grey cloud towards a distant exit leading into a much greener field. "Go!" he shouted and slapped her rump. Blowing, River Dancer charged into the tunnel hanging mid-air and Devon watched it close up behind her.

The hole had no more than closed than Devon caught the long, dark, unmistakable tresses of Mirabelle as she came down the small dirt path from her home onto the wider section of the main road. Wasting no time, Devon dropped onto his belly in the patch of prairie abutting the roadway. It was not the best cover, but he was far enough back that it was highly unlikely that he would be visible.

Field training took over, and he quieted his breathing, lying perfectly still, straining his ears to pick up the faint crunch, crunch of someone walking over the sparse gravel and stone of the dirt roadway drawing ever closer. Patience is a hunter's art, and those who hunted undead needed it even more with immortal prey. Counting in his head, Devon waited until she had to be far enough away that she would not see or hear him as he pushed himself up just enough to spy over the brown growth to where she walked on the pathway.

It was surely Mirabelle, although he was struck anew at how much taller she had grown since the last time he had seen her in Fall. Her long, black hair stretched past the center of her back, its natural hint of wavy curls not deterring it at all. Honestly, had she shorn her long locks, Devon would not have recognized her at first sight when he met her in town.

Ducking back down, Devon worked his way forward on his forearms. Carefully drawing his sword, he held it over the place where Mirabelle had passed. Concentrating carefully, he watched for the telltale glow their blades gave off in the undead's presence and their powers. Despite his efforts, he could not detect any traces of malignant energies or negative forces that marked an undead. Nor did her movement imply somnambulance or possession. Sighing, Devon withdrew his hand. Counting to one hundred, he stood and looked down the pathway; she was no longer in sight. Giving a short whistle and a 'come forward' gesture with his hands, Devon called up the energies once more that linked his mount to him and watched the air boil with sudden clouds. River Dancer appeared in the expanding tunnel and crossed over to him at a comfortable trot. The mystical portal closed and dissipated as soon as her last tail hairs were clear.

Devon hugged her and gave her soft praise that got her neck arching up proudly, although she still nosed his hands in hopes of hidden treats. "Sorry, dear one, our day is just beginning." Mounting back up, he rode River Dancer into town, but Mirabelle did not appear to be anywhere on the street as he arrived. Tying his mount to a hitching post, he began asking at the nearby shops, those that were open this early, for any clues as to her whereabouts but no one at all had seen her. She had simply vanished.

7
TAKING PRECAUTIONS

Mirabelle switched off the main path to take the less used one, heading up Cemetery Hill a little way before cutting through the undergrowth that lead to the hideout. Most of the others had not arrived yet, although Gemma, Jarick, and Mitch were there. Jarick gave her a lazy hand wave and a short greeting as she arrived. Gemma just nodded and then announced she needed to use the necessary and wanted company. Mirabelle found Gemma's arm unexpectedly linking into hers and the curvy seductress' actions looked casual to those watching, but Mirabelle felt the steely insistence in her grip.

Gemma never pulled her away for foolish reasons, so Mirabelle allowed herself to get drawn along in her wake. They walked down to the screening of young trees where they had their waste pit dug before talking to her. "Hey Mirror, I'm almost out of my packets of Dido's fennel from the Temple of Dido. You still have some?"

"Yeah, but not more than a week's worth," Mirabelle replied.

Gemma looked off towards the hideout, her gaze unfocused as she said, "Jarick is talking about hitting Heathsrow today. We should stock up again if we're out near the Temple of Dido there. Neither of us need to get caught with child right now. Do you have any money for it?"

Mirabelle shook her head, "No, we'll have to 'earn' it while working Heathsrow."

Gemma turned and nodded to her. "Jarick doesn't want anyone skimming, but there're things he doesn't need to know about. I'll get your back if you get mine."

"Done."

"Now keep watch for me, because I really have to go," Gemma said, more desperately as she searched around for their rough chair made of branches that at least allowed one to sit down.

"Okay," Mirabelle said as she moved forward, not only to see the hideout better, but to give Gemma more privacy. It seemed strange to accord such little courtesies, given how much they had already seen of each other's bodies in the limited privacy of the hideout. Jarick told them all it was a necessity to get used to such things as thieves dens had about as much privacy as soldiers did in the field.

Soldiers. Devon. Mirabelle swallowed hard; Jarick would want to know who Devon was and if he was a threat to them. She didn't even know if she could honestly answer him. Devon never figured into her plans at all, and his sudden appearance took her by surprise. The dinner she got out of him had been good, but he didn't seem convinced that he should just leave things lie.

"You ready to go back?" Gemma asked as she came up behind Mirabelle, making her jump.

"Oh! Oh, yes, let's go," she replied in a duller tone.

"Hey, what's up, Mirror?" Gemma asked her, using her codename again.

"I'm worried how Jarick's going to react about the paladin talking to me yesterday." "Yeah, I was wondering what all that was about," Gemma replied looking as curious as a cat.

"Well, you can find out with the others.

I'm going to have to give an accounting anyway," Mirabelle replied. Gemma's face fell. She hoped to hear the gossip first, Mirabelle knew.

"At least I won't have to wait long, we're here," Gemma pointed out and Mirabelle looked up to see they had arrived far sooner than she had expected. The dark worn beams of the wood shed rose before them and she could see that Bailey stood outside acting as guard and Storvald was already there. Only Cory was missing from the group, probably still stuck doing chores since he was the youngest.

Jarick's eyes lit upon her as soon as she arrived. "There you are. The plan today is to hit Heathsrow and to do a bit of bump- and-snatch in the market crowd. We need to leave soon if we want to have any time to work before the market shuts down. Cory would be a huge asset today, if he can get here in time, so we'll wait a little longer. While we do so, how's about you explain what happened to you yesterday with that knight in the inn?" Jarick's expression looked decidedly unfriendly and sent a shiver down Mirabelle's spine.

She swallowed hard and looked around. All eyes were on her and she felt like a hen in the midst of a ring of foxes. "He's a friend of my family's. His name's Devon and he trained with my brother at the Academy in Sanctuary. Seems my parents put it into his head that some undead spirit possessed me, and he had to check it out."

Jarick looked incredulous, then burst out laughing. "He thought you were being controlled by an undead? That is rich!"

Laughter was better than anger, so Mirabelle ran with it. "Yeah, so thanks to my parents I had to explain that there wasn't any undead trying to hunt me down."

"So it's all over then?" Jarick asked, and Mirabelle couldn't meet his eyes.

"He... didn't seem entirely convinced, so I don't really know, but as a paladin of Rhys, he can't interfere with us." This didn't seem to quite satisfy Jarick.

"Just remember whom you belong to Mirabelle. You don't get to just stay in the inn with strange men without my say so, got it? I think a little reminder is in order." He began unlacing his breeches some right then and there.

Thinking quickly, Mirabelle moved over towards Jarick's alcove as if complying. She didn't want him "making and example" of her right in the middle of the floor with everyone watching.

Glancing over at the straw pallet, she saw that runoff water from the hillside had seeped into the straw and bedding, wrecking it. "Oh

Jarick, we can't use the bed," she began, gesturing at the mess. He merely spared it the slightest of glances as he advanced on her.

"Who said we needed it?" he replied and pushed her up against the back wall, just barely on the other side of privacy screen created by the partial wall that made up Jarick's "office". He pulled himself free of his breeches fully and fumbled to lift the voluminous layers of her skirts. He soon held them high and used his other hand to pull down her small-clothes, ramming two fingers up inside her harshly. He rubbed them against her sensitive front as he asked her, "Who do you belong to, Mirror?" His fingers continued to pump in and out, and she couldn't help squirming at the effect they had upon her body. She was so used to having to will herself to reach a climax quickly with him, that the attention he paid her now seemed exorbitant. Her face flushed with embarrassment and pleasure. Surely the others could see! It only made her feel hotter, and she couldn't bite back the moan that came to her lips. "Who do you belong to, Mirror?" Jarick repeated, ramming his fingers in faster and harder.

"You," she whispered back at last, between little hiccupping cries of pleasure.

"That's right," he said in reply, pleased with his effect on her. His fingers withdrew, and she cried out at their exit, so close to climax. A thicker part of Jarick's body swiftly replaced them. He slammed himself in deep and plunged against her body vigorously, causing the back wall to rattle loudly and shake with each thrust. "And don't forget it," he said into her ear as she cried out loudly, shaking against him as she came, barely able to stand up as the intense feeling rolled over her. Jarick commented on her reaction to his prowess, but she barely heard him as she gripped the planks behind her to keep from sliding down, his movements almost painful as she practically fell against the rough wood, out of rhythm. Soon Jarick filled her and, panting, withdrew. She gasped again at the suddenness, her body aching and throbbing around the place where he had been a heartbeat before.

It was always like this with him, though. He never lingered and was never slow in his withdrawal. It always felt so abrupt to her. He desired her and he could wring pleasure from her body, but it felt wrong at the end, incomplete. Maybe that's just the way it was, though. Perhaps if they were married and in the same bed it would be different, but since she wasn't supposed to be doing this with him at all, she could hardly ask for advice.

Straightening her clothes out, she tried to ignore the discomfort of the dampness on her legs and her panties. She needed to get some of it out of her and off of her before they went to Heathsrow, but the time wouldn't be now. Even as she thought it, she heard Jarick say, "We're done here, let's go." No time for anything else. She turned and dug into a small pouch at her side for a small tin. Pulling out one of the fine paper packets, she poured the resin powder into her mouth and swallowed it dry with a wince at the taste. She definitely didn't want a child right now. She and Gemma needed to keep on top of it. Guys never did.

8
JOURNEY TO HEATHSROW

Cory met up with them as they started off across the field behind the shops. Falling into line, they walked until the wild fields gave way to plowed ones and then turned to join the roadway leading out of town. Bailey was leaning down and whispering to Cory, who then threw knowing looks at Mirabelle, making her flush all over again.

"Boys will talk," Gemma said, coming alongside. "As long as you take care of your own business, you need not worry much.

The rest only makes you more desirable in their eyes."

Noting the hinting tone in Gemma's voice, Mirabelle said, "Yeah, I took care of any problems. Thanks." Gemma's look softened.

"Well, good. And thanks for having my back this morning. I'll be sure to have yours when you run low."

"Thanks," Mirabelle replied, her cheeks still red. "Did everyone see?" she whispered.

"No, but a couple of people probably did. Lee and Bailey were jockeying for a better spot, but most of what we saw was Jarick. I doubt Mitch and Storvald saw anything from the other side of the room, but you were loud! You've got to learn to control that if you don't want to draw attention to yourself."

Mirabelle looked down as her cheeks flamed anew. It was awful and exciting when it happened, but she didn't know how to cope with how the others would look at her after the fact. The protection that came from being the leader's girl took on a new dimension of reality and usefulness. She was with him because of that promise of safety. Real monsters existed in the world. Better to hide in the shadows with someone who might have your back. She figured that if Jarick enjoyed himself enough, she'd be safe from the more human monsters in the world.

Sighing, she looked up the path at Jarick and Mitch where they had their heads together. It would be a long walk to Heathsrow, and an even longer one back once they were all tired. The odds of bringing back anything heavier than a coin purse looked dim. How would they accrue anything if they couldn't gain the means to transport better goods? If they had the means, would it make them easier to catch? Mirabelle felt her cheeks cool down as she pondered the difficulties facing the group.

The guys slowly pulled farther and farther ahead as they covered the miles between Riverfield and Duskdale. Only Cory was left falling behind with her and Gemma. Fortunately, by that time, Cory was past sly looks and lewd gestures. He mostly wished they could take a break.

Mirabelle sympathized, but knew Jarick would not call a halt when it could cost them the entire day's take.

"Come on, Cory, I brought some water along. You can have a sip," Mirabelle said at last. Gemma gave her a sidelong glance, but said nothing. Cory looked pathetically grateful and looked every ounce of his twelve years for a change. It gave Mirabelle's heart a twinge to think what the path might lead him to, but he had the right to choose, didn't he? It's not like she had room to throw stones. The idea left her feeling disquieted as they trudged along the last three miles in silence, all of them too tired to talk.

As they came upon the mild dip in the road that led down into the town of Heathsrow, they found Jarick and the others waiting for them in the shade of a small copse of trees at the outskirts of town. "Unbelievable how slow you girls are," Jarick sneered. Cory protested, but stopped as Jarick's sneer grew. Arguing would only strengthen Jarick's words. Mirabelle saw Cory bite back his tongue and glance away, as embarrassed as she felt earlier.

"We need to get in there and get started. Stork, Bailer, Springer, and I will start scouting. Mirror, Gem, and Corvid, you take a brief rest here. Follow no later than a finger of sun from now. Stork will pluck and pass to you three. Springer will act as the 'respectable bystander' and I will create some noise if things go badly. Remember to use your false identities here. Now, let's get going." He said this last to the other older cronies as Cory threw himself under the tree, rubbing his feet. Gemma settled with more grace, but wasted not a moment after their long walk. Mirabelle fidgeted for a moment, longing to keep up with Jarick and the others and fearing being too tired to keep from getting caught later.

She didn't need to be next to him to do her part, but somehow when he walked away like this she felt like a gulf washed in between them, one she wouldn't always be able to bridge. Shaking her head, she slowly knelt down only to groan at the soreness of her legs. Walking around town or doing chores was one thing, but Heathsrow was the better part of a fourteen mile walk away. Even by cart it was a good distance.

Looking out over the tan brick houses of the town, Mirabelle couldn't help but feel jealous. The folk here lucked out and discovered decent quarry they could mine stone from. Riverfield had forests, so it used the wood at hand for its houses and walkways. Mirabelle usually loved her town, but Heathsrow was even newer than theirs but looked closer to the civilized towns she saw in books. They could use being brought down a peg, she decided as she dusted herself off. Gemma and Cory took it as a cue for them to rise. Surprised, Mirabelle said, "We should look for Stork first. He's tall enough that he should stand out more than Springer. Once we find him, Jarick will not be far away and will find us. If he needs to split us up, he'll come get us one at a time, more like than not."

The others nodded as if her impromptu speech seemed imminently logical. Mirabelle wondered if it felt that way because she was Jarick's woman or because they looked up to her in some fashion. The former seemed more likely than the latter, but as long as they made Jarick happy, it didn't really matter much.

Exhaling slowly, Mirabelle shook out her wrists. Inhaling, she stepped into her role as Mirror, member of Riverfield Thieves Guild. It was time to get to work.

As soon as Stork caught sight of the three of them, he started. Staring at Mirror first, she knew he wanted to pass the first pouch off her way. She gave him two slow blinks to let him know she was ready. Walking sedately towards him, she watched as Stork appeared to bump into a man as he turned away from a stall of wool dyes. The pair of them went down in a tangle and a thin money pouch slid across the ground towards her. She stopped it with a light tap of her foot. Gasping and pointing, she caused those around her to turn towards the spectacle as she slid her foot free of her shoe and lifted the pouch with her toes. Settling the pouch in the slipper, she wedged her foot in on top and then moved away as the two men stood.

She was across the square and Black Jack offered to help her remove a rock from her shoe gallantly, a perfectly ordinary flirtation, one that people looked away from, making it the perfect cover for Black Jack to gently slide the pouch up his sleeve while looking like he was fishing out a stone. "Good job, Mirror," he whispered to her as she nodded her thanks to the 'helpful stranger'.

Gem was up next. Stork couldn't act again so soon, so Corvid went to a grocer's stand and grabbing some eggs from a bowl, began juggling them, much to the stand owner's consternation. Shouting, the man chased after Corvid, allowing Gem to lean forward against the stand, appearing to waggle a finger and shout at Corvid, but she used her ample bosom to hide her hand as it strayed into the coins below the counter. She quickly drew back and huffed as Corvid gently tossed the eggs at the stall keeper one at a time. Resting her hands on her hips, it would take a very practiced eye to see how she secreted the coins into the folds of her belt. Soon she and Corvid were away, moving in opposite directions, leaving the perturbed stall keeper unsure of which way to look as he realized his bowl of money lacked a good portion of his morning's profits.

They did well enough that when Black

Jack called a halt, sending the word out in a chain so that none of them were together in the same place, he passed out a few coins for each of them to spend as they would.

Mirabelle was grateful when Corvid dropped a small pile into the palm she held cupped behind her back as she rested against a stone pillar. As Corvid disappeared into the shop behind her, she stretched and wandered a circuitous route over to Gem. Passing over half the pile, she walked up and down the few remaining stalls despite how tired her feet were. Even if they all wanted to eat at the same establishment, they had to avoid being seen all together at once. Mirabelle wondered if it weren't far more work to take the supposedly 'easy route' than to just perform honest labor. As it stood, it would be close to dark if not full dark by the time they got home. They needed a horse or mule or car, just something, she realized as her feet grumbled at her with pain.

Her turn to get food and drink came eventually, but she had the least time to linger and rest her feet as she was the last one. Black Jack appeared in the doorway and nodded to her as he passed and ordered a pint of ale. She begged him for more time with her eyes, but he only closed his eyes and tipped back his ale. Lingering on it, perhaps, but no slow double blink came. They had to leave and Mirabelle had to go out first.

Gathering her few other purchases, she winced as she stepped down from the tall booth seat and set her aching feet on the cool stone floor. She wandered half-dazed towards the town entrance, Jarick catching up to her once they left the main path for the shelter of the familiar island of shade trees they stopped under earlier. "You did great back there, Mirabelle. You'll go far once we go to a real city. Those nimble fingers of yours will let you climb high in the places the real Guild operates."

It was the most praise he'd given her in months. They must have gotten more than she realized if he were being so lavish with his compliments. He backed her up against one tree and rub his hands along her arms, as if chaffing the cold from them. "We could celebrate a little more before heading back," he whispered as he leaned in to kiss her. She ducked her head to the side, causing him to frown.

"I'm still sore from walking everywhere," Mirabelle complained.

Jarick smiled, "You need not be on your feet for this one." He gave her a grin. The take must have been very good if he felt frisky after everything else. Mirabelle just didn't have the energy for his attentions. He mostly had to stand back and wait for them to come to him. She and the others endured the effort.

"If we do that now, we'll never make it back before sunset and none of us brought a lantern today," she reasoned.

He drew back with a disappointed sigh, "You are right. Well, don't worry, Mirror, I'll give you more attention soon. Maybe tomorrow." Taking a curling lock of her hair, he wrapped it around his index finger, rubbing his thumb against it before letting it drop. Then he stepped back, and turning away, just walked up the road without her. Again, the sense of a gulf passed through her and she hurried despite her sore feet to catch up with him. He allowed her to link her arm through his and raised an eyebrow speculatively. She shook her head. Did he really think the only time she wanted to touch him was when he was initiating sex? He shrugged somehow, even with her arm in his, and continued on.

The others straggled in as the traffic slowed between the two cities. Most were heading home at this hour, not all the way across to Riverfield. Springer detached himself from a rock at the side of the road a good mile up from Heathsrow. "Where have you been?" Mirabelle asked a touch angrily. Springer barely spared her a glance as he held a velvet pouch out to Jarick and tipped its contents into their leader's waiting hand. A clear, faceted stone the size of her thumb and two red ones, large as apple seeds, spilled out along with six golden coins stamped with the full sun of Anjasa.

Jarick smiled broadly and slid the contents back into the purse before handing three of the gold coins back to Springer. "Now that's how it's done, Mirror," Jarick said to her, souring her mood further. However, he and Mitch began talking animatedly about break-ins and locks while she stalked on ahead, unnoticed.

Meeting up with Gemma she said, "I swear, if Mitch were a woman, Jarick would propose to him."

Giggling loudly, Gemma replied, "To be sure, but Mitch would turn him down." Realizing she was right, Mirabelle laughed along with her and the tiredness of the day slipped away for a moment. Being able to walk slower on the way back helped a great deal, and the pair of them chatted about the day and their skills as they came into town. All at once, a huge shadow loomed up from the side of the clerk's office at the edge of town, making her jump although she was too surprised to cry out.

It was Devon, and he looked more angry and fierce than she had ever seen him look before.

"You're better than this!" he hissed at her in a low growl. Then he turned and stalked away into the dark street. As she stood rooted to the spot, Gemma patted her arm and stared at Devon with eyes as wide as her own. When the men hurried to their side, they saw false fire flicker amidst boiling storm clouds that appeared out of nowhere right in front of the paladin. From its midst a dark horse, legs lost in the gathering gloom, walked out. Devon mounted and turned the steed away as the flickering lights faded with the storm into nothingness. It could have been fog, so swiftly did it dissipate. None of them pressed forward until the sound of hooves receded far from them.

Jarick grabbed her arm and swung her around harshly, "What, in the name of the outer gods, was that about?"

Gasping like a fish, she shook her head, "I-I don't know. I didn't know he'd be waiting out here."

"You'd better find out then and get him to leave us alone. Paladin or no paladin, we aren't going to put up with him getting in the way of our plans," Jarick snarled at her, practically throwing her from him when he released her arm. Tears sprang to the corners of her eyes, whether from the pain of her arm or the fear of the moment, she couldn't say. The others stepped up menacingly beside Jarick. "Solve this, Mirabelle," he said and turned away up the alley that led to the hideout. Staggering away, Mirabelle fled home on tired feet and snuck into her room to cry deep and silent sobs into her pillow there. Why did the day have to end so badly? Why couldn't Devon just leave her and her friends alone? Exhaustion settled on her like a weight, but sleep was long in coming that night.

9
QUESTIONS AND SOUL-BEARING

Mirabelle went to Temple that week just to catch Devon there, but discovered from the lay sisters after service that he had prayed and left out before dawn. So she cursed him for wasting her time listening to useless platitudes. At least her parents were a little happier. They might not ply her with so many questions now. "I wanted to catch up with Devon, but it seems he went into town for provisions, so I'm going to see if I can find him there," she told them.

"We could all go together," her mother, Daleen, began.

"No, no, I'd be too nervous to talk to him with the two of you nearby." Let them make of that what they would, she thought.

They traded the worried look that she had grown tired of seeing months ago.

Finally, her father cleared his throat and said, "Very well. Just make sure you are back this afternoon, we have some pruning to do on the trees today. I need you there to help with it."

"Fine. I'll be there after I talk to him," she said. They nodded and went out together. Mirabelle followed a few paces behind, but cut off through the field towards town, just past the front of the Temple. She wanted to get this over and done with quickly.

The rough stems scratched her arms and bits of burrs and cottony seed tufts clung to her clothes, but she didn't care. She needed to get this paladin off their backs before they blamed her. Cutting the angle did not shorten the distance that much, and it was hard to keep her anger stoked the longer she walked.

Once she merged her path with that of the actual roadway, Devon was easy to spot.

He stood against the corner of The Silver Rushes Inn, a rather hopeful name on the proprietor's part. Visitors rent only occasionally this far out. The only people who used the rooms regularly were generally trysting, which gave the place a bit of a reputation. Hence that was why Jarick got suspicious of her activities with Devon there, even though they just went in to eat.

Stalking up to him, her anger returning, she growled, "What do you think you are doing? Why, in Rhys' name, are you hanging around in town all hours of the day and night?!"

His eyes narrowed and grew stony at her words. "So now you call upon my god on Temple Day to question my doings? To speak the name of a Divine is to draw the attention of that Divine upon one's activities." He leaned in closer to her, his mien taking on a slightly angry and menacing cast. "I'm here for the same reason you are. I choose to be." As he pulled away from her and straightened, Mirabelle discovered that she had taken a half step back.

"Why don't you go back to your temple? No one wants or you here. You will only cause trouble." She was determined to chase him off.

"Trouble? Isn't that what you and your friends are causing?" Devon said as he leaned back against the support post, a faint breeze lifting loose strands of his long hair. Today he wore his armor again and looked imposing. Mirabelle had no doubt that he knew it.

Stepping closer despite her own misgivings, she snarled at him, "You know nothing, and you can't do anything. Who's to say I didn't just go out with friends and arrived back late?"

She could see his nostrils flare in anger at her words. Perhaps she shouldn't stand so close. His words were a low rumble when he finally spoke, "No one, that's why you are out here. Likewise, who will gainsay me if I wish to spend my time in town? Your friends?" He nearly spat the last words at her. Mirabelle knew Devon could not play 'guardsman' without being asked for his help. Even if he saw them do something, he could only report it... unless a shopkeeper asked him for help. With him hanging around looking like he'd love nothing more than to do just that, she and the group would have to be extra careful.

"You won't be here forever, Devon," she shot back at him. "What do you suppose will happen then?" She gave him a smug look.

"I suppose it will be the gaol then, and I will be left explaining to your brother why I didn't protect you from that fate. In turn, he will likely be distracted by the knowledge and get maimed or killed in the field. That loss may take others with him for want of his sword. Can you live with blood on your hands, Mirabelle? Have you given any thought where this path leads? I'm not here to stop you. I'm here to remind you that you are beholden to more than just yourself."

Shocked, Mirabelle just stared at him. It was completely out of character for Devon to take such a low blow. He was not pulling any of his strikes, so neither would she. "You make more of it than you should. Theo's been gone for years. Since a vampire killing Sasha, his childhood sweetheart and fiancée, didn't stop him, then nothing will. He's abandoned his family for Rhys. He didn't worry about how his choices affected us, he just wandered away suddenly on some personal quest and joined a paladin Order. So Rhys can comfort him. I can't keep living my life for a brother who's never there."

Mirabelle said a lot more than she meant to in the heat of the moment, more than she even consciously thought about herself. Devon was eyeing her speculatively, as though she stripped away some covering to her soul and instead laid it bare before him. Uncomfortable with her own words and the silence that followed, she turned from him and stalked away, taking the path home. Her anger and determination drained out of . her before she even got out of sight of town. Glancing back to make sure Devon wasn't following her, she crossed the street and rested under the shade of a trio of trees that stood there as a traveler's respite.

Lying back onto the spongy new grass, she admitted to herself how much she missed Theovald. Despite all of his tales of travel and his newfound dedication, he had never explained why he just suddenly up and left. Hot tears stung her eyes, and she tried to stop her hitching breath, but the pain, now acknowledged, begged release. This had to be one of the worst spots she could choose, but she lacked the energy to head further in towards Cemetery Hill where the tree line offered better shelter.

What if Jarick found her crying? Or Devon? She'd be even more embarrassed.

Embarrassed? Is that what it was? It's what her mind put forth, but it didn't match the sharp pain in her chest. She missed him. She missed Theovald horribly, but running with Jarick and Gemma and the rest of their little band of thieves made her feel less empty.

After Sasha died, the whole family knew that Theo blamed himself. Mirabelle wanted to help, but her father counseled her to wait a bit, to let him sort out his emotions on his own for a while. It just about killed her to do so, but she tried. Theovald mourned at Sasha's gravesite all day for weeks on end. The Temple of Rhys sent representatives to talk to the town about establishing a permanent outpost in Riverfield to help keep them safe, seeing how they were on the borders of the cultivated lands. The townsfolk agreed, and the representatives talked to her brother to let him know what happened would never happen again.

He told her about it at dinner that night and laughed. She knew there was something odd about it, but was too grateful that he was talking and laughing again to focus on it. Looking back on the moment now, she could recognize the bitterness in his voice. Having only been eleven, she now wondered if she really understood some things he tried to share with her.

A tear rolled free, unbidden, forgotten until it cooled on her lower cheek and made its presence known. She could feel others joining it. Mirabelle had avoided touching the memories, so filled with pain, worry, and despair were they. She remembered being jealous of the new Priest and Priestess. They got to talk to Theovald about what happened to him and how he felt when she, his sister, was told to wait. He claimed it helped, but he disappeared out of his room at night, she knew. Although he ate the lunches she carried up to him on Cemetery Hill, his eyes looked hollow, his frame grew gaunt and wasted, his hair lank, and his voice stayed flat when he talked to her at all. He tried to be more animated around others, but he didn't bother around her. As much as she thought it was because he didn't care about her anymore, she had a sneaking suspicion it was because he was being honest with her instead of faking at getting better like he did around everyone else.

Damn him. Damn Devon, too. If she really mattered to Theovald, why didn't he tell her what he was doing? It came completely out of the blue. He came back one morning with a handful of flowers in his grip and a fevered look in his eye, saying there was something he had to do. That was it. He returned for his things later on, after it turned out he joined the Order of Rhys.

The sense of betrayal after all of her quiet support, all of her waiting for him to come to his senses and be her brother again, left her feeling lost. He came back eventually to visit and her parents were so proud of him. She was glad he sounded more like himself when he showed up, more whole than when he left, but he still never explained. Five going on six years now and never once did he deign to give her an answer as to why.

So why did she need to explain her actions to him? Why was she beholden to Theovald even now? He picked his path; let him ride it. It didn't matter to her, so she told herself. The pain stabbing her heart called her bluff, and she rolled over to sob into the ground lest someone hear and come over. Now she felt even lonelier than she did before. She hated Theovald for leaving and Devon for making her remember. Hated them both. Why couldn't they both live their lives and leave her out of it? They only cared because the Temple told them they had to. She bet Theovald wouldn't even come home if he had the choice. Devon only visited them out of duty and courtesy towards Theovald when you got down to it. He wasn't really her friend or her parent's friend; he was Theovald's brother-in-arms. Some bond beyond their mere tie of blood connected them. Bitterness welled up in Mirabelle and stole her strength. She hated the new temple and the people who served in its hallowed halls.

What did they know about the real world? What did they know about pain? She knew. She lived out where people got hurt, killed, and abandoned. It was the way the world really was. Why not grab whatever enjoyment you could while you were alive? They were all doomed anyway. Nothing really mattered.

The day was wearing on and the tears stopped at some point. Gathering up some green leaves, Mirabelle blew her nose and cleaned her face up as best she could. She felt hollowed out, but better, more determined. Maybe she couldn't change the past, but the present belonged to her and her alone. Gathering herself up, she walked back home. Jarick could wait until tomorrow. She needed to rest up and regain her strength. They had big plans in the works.

10
SPRINGER PROVES HIS WORTH

Jarick hopped down from the woodpile. "Springer confirmed that the fabric shipment should arrive sometime today or tomorrow at the latest. I want everyone present around town, ready to go at a moment's notice. Here," he said, pressing a few copper coins into each of their hands, "spend a little so no one minds that you are hanging around."

Gemma pursed her lips at the size of the tiny pile but only replied with, "Hey, how is it that Springer seems to know all these things?"

Mirabelle watched Springer draw himself up to his full height and brush off his fine clothes in response to Gemma's surly retort. "I, madam, do not sit in this backwoods hole waiting for tidings to come to me. If you want news, you have to seek it out." They locked stares, Springer's cool grey ones competing with Gemma's fire-filled brown. Only when Jarick called, "That's enough!" did the two of them back down.

"No more of that. We need to be focused on the job at hand. You're ready, right Mirabelle?" Jarick asked her, clearly looking for support.

"Of course, Jack, whatever you need." He smiled at her use of his work name. Mirabelle was learning what pleased him best and took pride in it.

11
DREAMS INTO DUST

They were heading through a narrow alley between the Wormwood Apothecary and the stonemason shop, when Jarick stopped them all. Devon was visible across the street from them and would spot them at any second.

"Hey Miri, want to really tweak that damn paladin's nose?" Jarick asked Mirabelle suddenly, taking her wrist in his hand.

"Sure," she said. Devon had been making waves in her life. The others had to keep leaving her behind, and she thought Gemma might even make a play to replace her at this rate. If she could get a little payback in for it, she was game.

"I've got the perfect plan," Jarick said, his lips suddenly warm against her ear. Shoving her hard against the wall of the stonemason's shop, he hiked up her skirts and took her right there in the alleyway. Mirabelle's eyes flew open in shock. Any passer-by could see them if they looked into the alleyway. Then she realized the chances of any others peering into the alleyway were low. She could see the rest of the crew standing stock still behind them. However, when she tossed her head the other way, her eyes locked with Devon's and she saw him blanch, nearly doubling over with a terrible look of pain on his features.

Well, this is what he got for sticking his nose in where it wasn't wanted. It was her life, and she if she was with Jarick it wasn't his damned business. She could feel Jarick speeding towards completion again before she was ready. While she was still recovering from his unexpected attentions, he pushed Lee forward and said, "Get in there." Before she could say anything, Leech was upon her, his foul mouth covering her own. Pinning her wrists up against the wall with his left hand, he freed himself from his breeches with his right. Then she felt him enter her, his tongue slamming painfully into her mouth at the same time. She tried to squirm free, but the weight of his body trapped her, and her movements only seemed to inflame him more.

Her mind reeled with disgust, horror, and a terrible sense of betrayal. Jarick knew she hated Lee's attempts at flirting. Given a choice, she would never allow him to even lay a single finger upon her. How could he do this?

Her eyes darted over to Jarick, pleading for him to end it, but he only answered, "See? He'll leave you alone now. He'll give up and leave us all alone. It's perfect." This was his idea of a perfect plan? Jarick had always talked about how the women of the other Thieves Guilds were passed around, but she never believed he would do it to her. For all his insinuation that those women liked the situation, she definitely didn't. Leech was as greedy as his namesake, and sucked against the skin of her breast where her bodice was cut low, leaving bruise marks. He thrust into her even harder, faster, finishing swifter than Jarick did, but the sensations of him, the smell, and taste lingered. She spat and gathered up the edges of her bodice to cover the red welts left by the pressure of his sucking mouth.

She could see the others in the alleyway now, Mitch looking away behind the shops, but Bailey stared at her with a speculative look on his face. When eyes met his, he gave her a slow nod and she shuddered at the implications there. Turning away, she found Devon still standing at the edge of the street. His face looked hard as stone as he shook his head slowly in a short arc before looking down the street away from her, but he didn't budge from his spot.

Jarick sent the others back up the alley and taking her wrist led her back out and through the meadows to their camp.

For once, she didn't want to go. She wanted to pull away and run, but she knew in his current mindset, he'd chase her. Given how she had fallen in his esteem from Devon's interference in his plans, he might punish her by letting the others have her. It was better to play along for now.

In her heart she knew he had destroyed any ounce of affection or desire she had felt for him. The walk back made her see him in a very different light. Gone was the dangerous young man with big dreams. Instead, he was a young man with no prospects who would use her to consolidate his power over a motley band of followers. The longer she stayed with them, the worse her own future would become until she reaped a bitter life. He never loved her, but that was fair, because she realized now that she didn't love him. He made her feel wild, dangerous, and wanted, but she didn't really miss him when he was away and she never saw them together building a life. How could she have been so blind?

Jarick let her wrist slip free as he gained the doorway. Gemma still stood outside and held out a hand to halt her as she came up. Blearily, Mirabelle looked over at her with wounded eyes. Wordlessly, Gemma offered her a packet to avoid pregnancy from her tin. Still clutching the bosom of her dress closed in one fist, she took the powder and tipped it back with a practiced hand. A child from the events that happened today was the last thing she wanted. Mouthing a silent thank you to Gemma, she steeled herself to go into the shed and face what was to come.

Inside, Jarick held forth amidst his small court, laughing as he recounted the look on Devon's face. Mirabelle barely looked up from the floor when he called her name and said, "You did good out there." No, she didn't. What she did would make her parents weep and cause her brother to come and bloody Jarick's nose. If that were the worst he did, Jarick would be lucky. One word from her and Lee would get worse than that.

One word from any of them, though, and Theovald would wind up in jail or cast out of his Order for actions unbecoming a Paladin of Rhys. He'd do it, though, and then he'd look at her with disappointment for the rest of her days. She couldn't bear that. Of all the stupid things she had done, if she caused her brother to lose his faith, it would be the worst thing of all. Finally, she interjected her own words into the conversation the others were having. She didn't raise her voice, but its tone cut off Jarick's speech as sharply as a crack of thunder.

"I have to go," she said.

"What?! Why?" Jarick asked, perplexed.

"Because I have to stop Devon. If word one of this gets to my older brother, he'll kill you." She turned, still clutching her bodice tight, still feeling Lee's fumbling, awful touch upon her skin. No one spoke. No one stopped her. An air of finality hung in the air as she walked away from the lot of them. She knew she'd never return there again.

Her steps were careful as she walked along the edge of the hill. She blanched as she entered the same alleyway, but she needed to find Devon quickly and he might still be at his post across the way if she were lucky. Yes, some luck that would be. She thought at herself bitterly. The things you consider lucky when you run with thieves. He wasn't there as she stepped out. Looking up and down the street, she saw him walking slowly towards the front of town, probably headed back to the temple to report.

Despite her abhorrence, she stepped backward into the alley and took the time to adjust her bodice laces to make it look less like bandits had just ravished her. Yes, wouldn't want it to look like what it was. Her mind taunted her with how stupid the enterprise was for the entire walk. It wasn't that far, but it was far enough to give her mind plenty of time to torment her. Devon had stopped at the last shop and turned to watch the road, or so it appeared. He looked startled when he noticed her coming through the crowd towards him, but continued to wait for her, his face looking grim.

She gave him the barest glance and walked past him, her shoulders in a defeated slump. No word passed between them, yet he fell into step beside her, just a half step behind. She waited until they were several carts-lengths away from the bustle before mumbling, "Don't tell him."

She stole a sideward glance at Devon's face; he returned her gaze impassively but did not speak. Setting her eyes forward, she repeated,

"Don't tell him. Don't tell my brother what happened. I don't want him to come here and hurt anyone or get into trouble over me. I won't see them again, just... don't tell."

The man beside her made no reply, his face an unreadable mask. Mirabelle cursed herself a fool. He probably had to report what happened to her to his Order. If he thought it would hurt or be able to be used against Theovald, he'd have to. His silence was deafening and condemning. Mirabelle's head hung ever lower as she trudged on. Her heart settled into her shoes and she felt like she kicked it with every thought and step. How could she be so blind? How could she be so thoughtless as to think what she did wouldn't affect her family? She thought she was being initiated into the mysteries of adulthood. Now she felt like she threw a precious treasure into the river. She could have at least waited for love before giving away her first time, but she thought she loved Jarick. The truth cut her soul and made her choices look even stupider than they already did to her.

They traveled all the way to the pathway to her house, and she turned to go up the path automatically when Devon gently took hold of her shoulder and stopped her. She picked her head up and realized how far they had come at last, then looked over at him puzzled. "Go to the river and wash up first," he said at last.

The words made no sense at first, and then she realized. He was providing her with a way out. She still smelled of sex and reeked of Lee's bad body odor. She never wanted a bath as badly in her life. This way, there would be no questions. Devon offered her a steadying hand as she approached the marshy section of rushes. His mailed feet sank in even farther than hers did, but he did not complain. Once she made the sandy embankment at the river's edge, she waded under the shadow of the bridge. Turning to watch the roadway, she saw Devon cross to the slightly more solid ground just before the road where he stood guard, studiously not looking at her.

After everything else he had seen, she was grateful that he wasn't watching her now. Never again would he look at her and see the little girl he once told tales of his travels to. No, he probably wouldn't want to visit any longer than he had to, to make sure their family was safe. More things she never treasured while she had them. Welcome to adulthood, Mirabelle. Where no one will ever want to know or hear about you again. Her mind jeered at her.

As long as he didn't tell, she didn't care, but he promised nothing to her and she knew she was lying to herself when she said she didn't care. There was no going back to the way things were, but she didn't have to make things worse. She could at least try to be better.

Once clean, she made sure her clothing was reasonably scrubbed. Easier to say she fell in the water trying to get a pretty rock than to explain the scent of Lee's unwholesome body on her. When she walked back up to the roadway, Devon helped her climb back out. He looked at her now, a swift and cold appraisal. "We need to wait for that to dry," he said and leaned back against the edge of the white stone bridge, fitting action to word.

"Won't they get worried?" she asked, gaging the height of the sun.

"More than they already are?" he asked pointedly, and she stopped talking to him, feeling a touch of heat grace her cheeks at that barb.

Time slipped by and the music of the frogs and crickets grew as the shadows lengthened. Lost in her own thoughts, she didn't expect to hear Devon's voice break the silence. "As long as you keep your word, your parents need not be told."

"What about my brother?" she asked.

"I don't know yet," he answered. "Come," he added, offering her his hand. She took it reluctantly, and he led the way back to her home. He held only her fingertips and slowed his steps on the hill, whether for her sake or because of the armor she didn't know, but she took what cold comfort she could that he at least accorded her that much honor. She wouldn't blame him if he didn't want to help her at all, no matter how difficult the terrain.

He let go before rapping on the door. This bewildered and amused her despite the seriousness of everything. It was her house, she could have walked in. A moment later the door opened and her father's eyes opened wide in surprise. Turning to Devon, he said, "You did it. I don't know how you found her, but thank you for bringing her home, Sir Devon. Can we offer you some food? We still have some left from dinner."

Devon shook his head, dissembling. He just moved aside so

Mirabelle could enter. She missed his next words with her father as she reached the dining area and nodded to her mother across the way in the kitchen. Her mother nearly dropped the plate she held upon seeing her. Mirabelle took the opportunity to escape up the ladder to her loft room. She was hungry, but hardly felt like she deserved to eat. If she went down, then there would be questions. Questions she was too tired and upset to answer. Devon must have taken his leave at last because she heard the door latch.

She heard her mother come over to check on her, so she feigned sleep. The ruse soon became the truth, and she slept at last.

12
DEVON'S SLEEPLESS NIGHT AND DILEMMA

Devon begged off the invitations to eat, saying he had to get back to his duties, which was only half true. He deserved no credit for Mirabelle's return. In fact, he feared he may have precipitated today's turn of events.

What had happened shocked him. He ran a hand through his hair nervously, the images still flashing before his eyes. That the ne'er-do-wells did it to punish Mirabelle for his disruption of their plans hurt deeply. He knew that things would end badly eventually, somehow. It did not ease his fear that he may have caused Mirabelle to be mistreated so. Guilt hung heavily upon his conscience. He would have waded in, regardless of the rules, and given them what for if she had called to him for help. She never did. When she went off with them afterward, he stood there, dumbfounded. He did not want to believe it, that she could have been a willing party to what he saw. It took him several minutes to collect himself and to move out of the street.

Staring out at nothing, his mind raced, trying to make sense of it all. When he blinked, the world into focus, he realized they still directed his gaze at the same alley where it had all occurred. Blanching again, feeling nauseous, he turned and used a single hand on the shop walls to help guide him to the edge of town. He needed to get away from all of it, but now was the perfect time for the miscreants to strike. If he left his post, then all of this would be for naught. He still had a job to do, he needed to see it through.

Taking up position at the corner of the inn, he waited, his gaze sweeping the street listlessly. Still caught up in his thoughts, his guilt, and wondering how he would explain his failure to protect Mirabelle to Theovald, he missed seeing her familiar form. Coming up the street amidst the few late shoppers finishing their chores for the day was Mirabelle herself.

Gone was the spitfire girl he knew. She barely took her eyes from the ground long enough to acknowledge him at all. Whatever else may be true, he knew upon seeing her that what happened had not been of her choosing. He cursed himself for his failure as he fell into step as an honor guard come too late. When she finally spoke, out of earshot of anyone else, he expected her to berate him, to ask for reprisals against the men who had hurt her, but she only begged him not to tell her brother. Not because he would be angry with her, but because she didn't want what happened to hurt him.

Here were signs of the Mirabelle he knew.

Worried about her brother instead of herself in what was probably the worst moment of her life. His throat ached, and he did not answer. What could he say? What comfort could words bring to such terrible moments as this? It pained him to realize that her request would spare him from having to explain his own culpability in the matter.

He owed her better than that, but the choice to tell Theovald or not should be hers. There was still the matter of his report. If he struggled for words now, he dreaded having to dance around the truth that would be recorded in the archives. He couldn't lie, but it would be a challenge to word it so that Theovald or someone else would not infer what Mirabelle did not want known.

The fields were painted gold and green in the late afternoon sun, but Mirabelle trudged before him, eyes fixed on the dirt of the path. She looked like she were walking to the gallows. The wind shifted, and he caught the scent of the yellow-toothed one that had thrown his body against her second. Devon pinched the bridge of his nose, shaking his head as if to clear the suddenly vivid memory away once more.

She shouldn't return home in this state, he realized. As they finally came up to the path to her house, he stopped her. "Go to the river and wash up first."

She looked at him then, the flat, dull look in them turning to confusion, then a flare of hope. Her pathetic look of gratitude just stung him more. Offering his hand, he tried to be of better service than he was in town. It should never have come to this. He should have figured out a better way to solve the situation, gone about it differently. Something.

Instead, once he made certain she was safely on the solid strip of land under the foot of the bridge, he crossed back over the waving green rushes. Taking up a post near the head of the bridge, he watched the roadway for her so that none would spy upon her as she bathed. *Such a good guard you are, Devon, unless it matters most.* His thoughts struck daggers into his conscience. He saw Theovald's family nearly as much as his own. Was it really too much to ask to keep Mirabelle safe from harm? He hated himself for failing her, Theovald, her family, and his duty.

So caught up in his recriminations was he that he missed the sounds of Mirabelle walking back through the rushes until she had nearly reached the roadway.

Galvanized into action, he reached out and helped her cross the last few steps up onto the roadway. Trying not to make her any more uncomfortable than she already was, he gauged her appearance quickly.

Her dress front was too wet for him to drop her off home without question. Sure, she might fabricate a story, but better to avoid lying if possible. "We need to wait for that to dry," he told her flatly and leaned against the stone of the bridge to stew in his own thoughts of failure more.

"Won't they get worried?" she asked him as she held up a hand to check the sun's distance from the horizon.

"More than they already are?" he snapped back, his voice a sharp whip. It was the tone he was tearing himself apart with inside and failed to modulate it in time. She looked stricken at his harsh words and dropped her eyes with the air of a defeated dog. He looked away. The less he wanted to hurt her, the more he seemed to. Life played cruel jokes sometimes.

The shadows grew long and Nature's choir sang before he glanced over at her and judged her dress was dry enough to pass with little question. He wanted to make up for his harsh words to her, but wasn't sure how. She was worried about her family's reaction to her, so he started with addressing that. "As long as you keep your word, your parents need not be told."

She looked up at him, her eyes filled with pain and worry, "What about my brother?" she asked.

"I don't know yet," he answered, finding it hard to look directly into her eyes. Determining how Theovald would react if word reached him was beyond Devon's ability to divine. Even if he omitted the details in his report, the perpetrators and their lackeys might still boast and have it spread. "Come." He walked back with her, holding onto her hand as little and lightly as he could. Given what she had been through, she may fear any touch by a man. He did not want her to fall as night stole towards them, so did his best to find a middle ground. She did not flinch or pull away, so he held out some hope that she might recover from her ordeal in time. A visit with the priestesses of the Temple of Dido would likely help more.

The walk back to the Temple was the longest he had ever made. It felt like someone moved it further away each time he looked up. Visions of the day replayed over and over in his mind. He searched for how he could have handled things better, to avoiding having it come to this. He raised his hands, rubbing his eyes with the heels of his palms, trying to get it to stop. There were so many things he had faced in the field, violence, death, sorrow, grief, but this ate at him worse than all of it.

It wasn't his place to stop her from making what choices she would with her life, but it was damnably hard to see her get hurt. Even being there didn't give him the whole story; his brain only provided speculation and mockingly passed out blame. There was no way he could bring himself to ask what had transpired to cause things to fall out the way they did, so dwelling upon it was madness.

Very well, he would treat it as a field situation. Everyone in the unit shared part of the responsibility for losses in the field. How each individual worked in relation to the others in his or her unit often decided the success or failure of a campaign. Once done, review helped, but taking action to fix what needed to be fixed and dealing with the fallout was better.

When he looked back up, he stood in the pool of light from the dining room halls. It felt like a sign. "Goodness comes with the dawn," he recited as he went inside.

13

DUTY IS THE HARDEST THING

"**G**ood, you're here," Valdesh the Younger said as Devon approached the hallway to the private cells the paladins had assigned to each of them. He planned to get out of his armor, but it looked like that would have to wait.

"Come down to my office and we'll get your report out of the way before dinner. Then I can eat without getting a nagging feeling that I've forgotten something."

"Yes, Sir," Devon said, straightening. Despite the dread he felt on the walk back to the Temple, now that the moment had arrived, an odd, unexpected calm settled over him. They went into the long room that served as Valdesh's office. There were a pair of banners done like the shields of their Order on the sandstone wall behind the dark wood of Valdesh's desk. Trios of simple, armless wooden chairs made up rows on either side of him as Devon stood before Valdesh, hands clasped behind his back, awaiting questioning.

Valdesh the Younger took up his spot behind the desk, lighting the candle in a small lantern upon the tabletop before taking up parchment and pen. "All right, Sir Devon. What are your observations today?"

"I believe the matter has been settled, Sir," Devon answered honestly, focusing on a point between the two banners. "I need a few more days to be certain, but I don't think there will be any need for me to continue my observation."

"Oh-ho, well done, then. How did you do it?" Valdesh asked, his pen scratching away.

"I can honestly say, I did nothing, Sir," he said, his voice heavy with regret.

"You will look at me when you address me, Victor Paladin!" Valdesh shouted at him. Devon started and looked up. He hadn't realized his gaze had even dropped.

Valdesh stared at him with his piercing turquoise green eyes. Devon wanted to shudder under their intense gaze, but fought to remain steady. "But you wanted to, didn't you? What really happened out there?" Valdesh asked, setting the pen aside.

Swallowing hard, Devon replied, "The matter was not in the sphere of our authority under Rhys, and as I was not asked to help, I did not interfere with secular affairs." He found it hard to continue to meet Valdesh's gimlet gaze, but by the end of his words, he saw the older man's look soften.

"You did your duty to both the Order and to the local guard by not stepping in where you had no authority. Sometimes this is the hardest thing we face." He picked up his pen again, "If you have this nearly wrapped up, then I will have an assignment for you shortly. You are due for a long tour, are you ready for it?" Having reported to Valdesh throughout the entire time, Devon knew the man was concerned that he had not taken a true rest.

Clearing his throat, Devon answered, "I think being on the road may be the best respite I can receive Sir." Valdesh tapped his pen on the desk and tipped his head to the side, eyes narrowing some.

"That bad? Well, she may not appreciate your efforts now, but in time the fences may mend. Very well, Sir Devon, I will send out a carrier bird tonight and see what answer comes out of Sanctum. Go. Attend service, eat, bathe, shrive your soul if you need it, but start preparing yourself for your next journey. Go with Rhys." Dismissed, Devon looked outside and saw that if he truly wanted to attend service, he would not get to change or wash.

Sighing, he shook his head. He would have welts from the straps at this rate. Taking himself to the Temple, he sat closer to the back to spare anyone from having to deal with the scent of his sweat. One of the lay sisters ran the service, which had an opening hymn followed by a pair of readings from the Book of Rhys. Devon had hoped the words of Rhys would soothe him, but the sister's voice did not carry well and he wound up alone with his thoughts and they were filled with Mirabelle and her tormenters.

He sang the closing song fervently, attempting to drive off the darkness in his mind. Entering the field so distracted was dangerous, such concerns could and likely would get him killed. He had only a few days to clear the shock from his system.

After the end blessing, he went to the dining hall and ate what would fill him up the fastest. As soon as his hunger was assuaged, he went to his room and finally stripped out of his armor. His shoulders were feeling the cut of the straps after sweating in it all day. Frowning at the depth of the marks, he gathered a set of lighter linen bedclothes and headed off to the purification chamber.

Walking around the large shallow pool set in white stone, he collected a set of towels and a scrubbing gourd from one cabinet. Then, setting them next to one of the large wooden tubs lined up in the alcoves opposite the purification pool, he went to the other cabinet. Should he use the salt scrub? He didn't plan on keeping vigil, and although he dearly wanted to free himself of the images plaguing him, the lavender cleansing salts were probably not ideal.

Moving to the next shelf, he checked the baskets until he found a small round of soap filled with star anise. It not only purified, it protected from negative forces, and called upon the Divine for aid. This was what he needed.

On the lowest shelf was a pot of hyacinth hair wash. It was the blend used by the paladins of Sigvarder, but as it helped with grief and death, to allow one to let go of what could not be changed. That was what he needed right now. Until he picked it up in his hand, he didn't realize that it felt like someone had died.

He stood there for a moment, staring at the jar in his hand, and then it hit him. He was mourning. He'd just never felt this way without having lost someone close to him. What happened today hit him as hard as having seen someone die. Flipping the bar over a few times in the air, he watched the spinning star pattern in it and hoped Rhys could fix things somehow. Rhys, Smiter of Undead, Bringer of Hope, and Lady of the Dawn, have mercy on me your servant, grant me hope to see things change for the better come morning's light. May it be.

He went to his tub and set up the woven modesty screen before turning the water taps. He watched, but there was a little steam. Most of the hot water must have been used up, and he had let no one know he'd need more heated. Slumped over the tub, he gave a half-hearted swish of the water with his hand. Despite the lack of steam, the water remained reasonably warm. He might not soak as long as he had planned, but he wouldn't be freezing while he bathed, either.

Climbing in, he felt the rising water embrace him and gave himself over to the simple enjoyment of its touch. The warmth was enough to ease the knots forming in his muscles and he sunk low despite the sting as it hit his welts. It passed quickly. The images threatened to begin again, but he grabbed the soap and inhaled deeply, focusing on Rhys.

He hummed the hymns he knew as he scrubbed himself down, calling back the memories of his childhood in Laguna. His family lived close to the stone walls of the canal, only a street away in fact. The city had cobblestones everywhere, with a line of small trees on each side of the street to offer a hint of green. He loved all the colors of the stones on the sides of the houses, the pattern on the roadway, and seeing the new catches brought in on the riverboats each day.

Using the strongly scented hyacinth hair wash reminded him of the year he felt called to serve as a paladin of Rhys. Ever since he turned twelve, he felt more and more drawn to the services at the local temple. Theirs was more dedicated to Anjasa, what with all the travel and trade, but whenever Rhys came up, he listened intently. The name tolled inside him like a bell. His parents noted his increasing interest and did not dissuade him. At fourteen, he announced he wanted to join the Order of Rhys and was accepted for training.

The flowers bloomed in profusion from the suds then, and he seized upon the memory of the feelings he had that day. They were amazing and so strong, so clear, that he knew that serving Rhys was his destiny all along. Have faith, Devon. Rhys will guide you through the dark to a still brighter day.

He set the memories aside as he rinsed himself off. Climbing out, he felt better. Drying off, his welts had calmed down and might not even bother him when he tried to sleep. Once he restored everything to order and donned the light-weight sleeping clothes, he returned to his room and settled down for the night. Unfortunately, sleep fled from him.

His mind stopped looking backward and instead sped forward. What if Mirabelle still felt beholden to those wretches?

Valdesh was sending a bird tomorrow to get him a new assignment. If it all started up again, he wouldn't be able to stay and sort it out.

What if she contracted an illness from this? She might not seek treatment for fear of having to explain how she contracted it. Such things could devastate if left unattended.

Scenario after scenario chased themselves around his tired brain until he groaned and pulled his pillow over his head as if they could be physically blocked out. Finally, he gave up and dressed enough to go down to the chapel. There he caught the late service again, and he wondered if his frequent attendance to the morning service bespoke a warning from Rhys. His thoughts took a darker turn by the time he returned to his bunk. The matter was not closed yet. He had to visit Mirabelle in the morning. Somehow, his mind accepted this as a plan and allowed him to slip off into a troubled slumber filled with dark dreams.

14
PRUNING GRAPES AND PROBLEMS

Mirabelle let the chickens out and scattered some feed to them before checking on her father's horse and the few sheep they had. Whereas before she rushed and bolted away to visit Jarick and the others, now she lingered. She had no desire to see them again, ever, but to do that she could never leave her home again. The very idea of coming across any of them in the street made her queasy. Instead, she looked at the stained hooves of the horse and the shaggy condition of the sheep entrusted to her care and felt ashamed that she neglected them these past months.

Apologies on her tongue, she began working on them in a more serious fashion, attempting to make up for abandoning them for so long. Once their bodies were treated for fly bites and abrasions, she mucked out the stalls, taking time to fetch buckets of water and rinse the floor clean before bringing in fresh, sweet straw for them to bed down in.

They seemed more forgiving as they settled into the cleaner accommodations. Satisfied, she went out and washed off her arms before setting up the tools for the next task her father set for her: pruning the grapevines. It was hard, but repetitive work, leaving her mind free to wander, and it only had one place it wanted to go. She kept saying yes to Jarick's request and then discovering in horrific detail what it entailed.

Tears flowed down her cheeks, and she had to quit for a while when she realized they would not stop. She sobbed silently behind the animal shed, blowing her nose on the inadequate square of cloth she brought with her in case of something like this. Just when she was certain the tears would never stop, they slowed, and with little coughing hiccups, she found she could rise again. She scrubbed at her face with a sleeve and stumbled back out to the vines. Taking the cutters in hand, she imagined chopping bits off Jarick and Lee as she cut away the old growth on the vines. It helped a little, but did not take away her fears of seeing them again.

She was so intent upon her task that she didn't hear Devon ride up on his horse. Something on the edge of her vision made her turn, and she saw him dismounting, tying his dappled mare to the bushes that stood near the pathway before the fruit trees.

Mirabelle wiped her brow and wondered what he was even doing there. Hadn't he done his duty to her parents already? She paused to try and remove any traces of her tears; she would not let him see her being weak. He didn't even try to go to the house where her parents were working on cleaning the cellar. It needed to be touched up before readying it for the next round of canning this year. Instead, he walked straight over to her.

"Sir Devon," she said coolly, congratulating herself on keeping her tone level.

"Mirabelle," he replied with a nod of acknowledgement. "I spent some time considering the matter last night." He seemed at a loss what to call what he saw her do. She didn't want to have this drag out; it was already painful enough.

"What was your ultimate conclusion then? As you can see, I have a lot of vines to get to today." She turned away and squeezed her eyes shut tight for a moment, biting back a curse. That line sounded so much like an innuendo that he couldn't fail to notice.

He coughed into his hand, no mail or armor at all today; she guessed he didn't expect to be attacked anymore. "There are side effects that could develop that I could help you with before...you wouldn't have to let anyone else know what happened if you asked me for help." He looked rather nervous and fidgeted with his hands, examining them as if they had something on them.

"There won't be any offspring from what occurred. Is that all you came here for?" she asked acerbically. When his shoulders pulled back suddenly, his head coming up with bewilderment in his eyes, she realized she had guessed wrong. Whatever he offered his help with, that wasn't it. Now he'd have even more fodder to despise her with. Mirabelle looked away from him and crossed her arms.

His voice was soft when he spoke to her again. "I just thought that the yellow-toothed fellow didn't seem to be very scrupulous with his health, and he could, possibly, injure your own because of it." Mirabelle's eyes looked at him from over her shoulder. Disease. Oh yes, Lee could have something the way he was, and trying to get it handled without word getting to the ear of some talkative old biddy might be nigh impossible. She didn't want to admit that she wanted his help, but now that he brought it up, it would be stupid for her to refuse. She could hardly fall farther in his opinion.

"What... what do you need to do?" she asked, licking lips, her mouth gone dry in worry.

He looked relieved. She didn't understand why, but she just accepted that he would help her. "It's relatively simple, a special prayer to Rhys' while I lay my hands on your head. It takes almost no time at all, but once done, you'll be safe as long as you don't..." his words trailed off.

Anger rose in her that he would think she wanted anything to do with Lee or any of them now. "That's over, so let's get this done, all right?" He only nodded and stepped closer. Now she felt nervous. It seemed crazy, but her heart filled up with fear as he came closer with the grapevines at her back. Get a hold of yourself! She told her mind to stop, but it did not care to listen. She shivered as he touched her, nearly flinching, but whatever she expected to have happen, didn't.

He held his hands over her hair, barely touching her at all, and murmured a prayer she had not heard before, and after a slight tingling around her head, there was nothing else. Then he stepped back. "There, if there was anything wrong, it's gone now, and since you said you dealt with any other possibilities, I'll go. If you are all right, that is."

All right? She was anything but all right, but she was surprised he could bring himself to care. Paladins tended to be above reproach, and now she was anything but above reproach. "I'm as good as I can be. Thank you for your kindness," she said and sketched a light curtsy before turning back to hack at the grapevines. Devon seemed to stand there for long and long, but he finally went down the hill to his horse and rode away.

Tears sprang up from Mirabelle's eyes once more and she wondered who she was crying for herself, or him.

15
THE REST FOR THE FAITHFUL IS DEEP

Heading back to the Temple, Devon's mind analyzed everything. Although he was reassured that Mirabelle would not return to running with that gang of thieves, and that she was safe from diseases of any kind for the moment, his spirit remained unquiet along with his mind. So much so that he discovered River Dancer halted in the middle of the road, looking back at him. He didn't need to give her much guidance, but had gotten so wrapped up in his thoughts that he stopped giving her any signals of where to go at all.

Patting her side, he reassured her. "Don't worry, girl. Once we get out on the road, it will be better." Would it, though? He thought the same thing last night when he took his bath. Then he thought that this visit would solve most of the trouble. Yet, here he was, feeling distracted rather than accomplished. Mirabelle's parents had their daughter back. She would be safe with them, but it did not make him feel better.

Perhaps it was the look in her eye when she spoke to him. She had recovered her tongue and fire enough to grow sharp with him, but when she realized he didn't come to discuss potential children... he shook his head and moved River Dancer into a trot. She looked as stricken as he felt the day before. Her eyes held a sickening woefulness he would never have willed on such a bright spirit.

He wished there was something more he could do for her.

The Temple looked welcoming after so many days of worry and effort. It finally felt like a homecoming. Maybe he would talk to one of the Divinities or Great Victor Paladin Valdesh the Younger. It was surprising how much the man took after his father over in the capitol city of Sanctuary. Devon had met him and many other paladins on his various circuits. He went home to visit his family at least once a year, but it was less home to him now than the Temple of Rhys and the time he spent with his brothers and sisters-in-arms.

Arriving at the stables, he tied River Dancer outside and stripped her down and gave her a good currying before setting her up comfortably in her stall. Heading inside, he greeted Honey Flower and Happy Story, who were sweeping up the dining hall. Once past them, avoiding the piles of dust while trying not to bump the benches where they were stored atop the long wooden tables, he took the hallway to the Temple proper, looking out the tall windows as he passed. Silverlight was shoving Trenton around playfully as Trenton tried to brush out his mane.

Somehow the very ordinariness of it all helped to lift his spirits. Entering the chapel, Devon took time to visit each of the stained glass stations and honor each of the gods and goddesses who guided and protected him on his journeys. Although the Temple of Rhys naturally focused on the Book of Rhys, they had days set aside to celebrate the gifts and aid of the others in the pantheon. Unfortunately, he often missed the special festival days while out on circuit, so he paid his respects now.

Before Sigvarder's azure dragon, he prayed for justice to find the thieves who hurt Mirabelle so. Moving to the red moon and mortal blossoms of Dido, he prayed for healing for Mirabelle's heart and for the well-being of her family. Coming to Anjasa's green songbird and golden sun coin he prayed for a safe journey for himself. Before Rhys' violet stars, he gave thanks for his calling and asked for protection for Theovald and the other paladins of his Order. He dropped his gaze and was about to turn away when his eyes lit upon the black and white half moon of Quinn and Zsofia, the guardians of all knowledge and wisdom. Help me know what to do, he prayed. To his surprise, inspiration hit him. Perhaps there was one more thing he could do after all... but it would have to wait until morning.

Devon slept better that night than he had in most of a month. Arising, he found a missive outside his door. Valdesh had an assignment for him. He was bound for the Northern loop and would meet up with Marsid and a party of new recruits, and veteran Victor Paladins. They would look to season the new members, which meant some pressing into the unsettled lands.

Rolling the message up, Devon blew out a breath he didn't realize he was holding. So, it had to be today then.

Devon went about all the proper preparations and made sure he had everything ready before heading out. Today would mark a turning point in his life. He just hoped that he was ready to face it.

16

AN UNEXPECTED PROPOSAL

The day dawned bright through the window behind Mirabelle's head. She dreaded waking up even more than sleeping. Her parents were full of questions that she didn't want to answer. Her world had become limited to this hill and the pathway to the river. She didn't dare go into town for fear of running into any of her so-called friends, and she hardly wished to visit the Temple with the pious fools who did not understand what the real world was like. Even she hadn't realized how cruel it really was. This was her life, endless chores and a hopeless, listless emptiness that gnawed at her during the day and gave her fearful dreams at night.

Despite her mother's attempts to engage her in conversation, she kept her answers short. They had no reason to complain though, she figured, as she did any chore they handed her meticulously. It was less to please them than to fill up the time. When she ran out of chores, the memories came back to haunt her. Better to scrub her fingers to the bone than keep reliving the event over and over.

The morning sun burnt off the dew and the sheep were soon grazing with their one horse on the hillside. The chickens were clucking merrily as they scratched the ground and peered about in search of interesting bugs or bits of grain. The vines were all trimmed and starting to grow while the trees of her namesake were covered in buds that would soon perfume the air.

She hated them the most. They were sweet smelling and welcome by everyone. She had nothing in common with them anymore. Her very name mocked her. In the past few days, even her father stopped calling her "little plum". She missed it, but knew it was for the best. She didn't deserve even that little kindness anymore. Nothing would be the same again, and it was her fault. She would probably have to tell Theovald. Somehow she doubted she could hide what happened from him. If Devon didn't tell him before she did, since he never promised that he wouldn't.

The gloom in her heart dulled the color all around her and turned even bird song into cacophony. It was in this mood that she wandered down the path towards the river. She thought about lying out under the serrated willows and just staring up at the golden light as it filtered through their delicate leaves. Sometimes that helped, but she passed by them, planning to stare off the bridge into the river. This idea held a strange attraction to her, but the sound of hooves behind her broke her from her reverie. It was Devon.

Turning around to face him, she saw the burgeoning packs. With him riding out in full armor, she knew he was leaving.

"I suppose I should wish you a safe journey," she said, knowing she should say something.

He tipped his head at her as he reigned in his mount. "But you do not wish to?"

Her hands balled up into fists. His words were too close to the mark. "Of course I do, you help keep my brother safe," she said instead.

"Ah. I have put some thought into the matter of safety and come to the conclusion that there is a way to provide more protection to you and your family than Theovald is able to give alone," Devon said to her, his dark brown eyes unreadable.

This piqued her interest. "So what plan or scheme did you come up with?"

"I offer myself to you in marriage," Devon said.

"What?" Mirabelle replied, shocked. "Just like that? You don't even know me. You haven't asked me or my parents or anything."

His horse danced, shying away from her loud outburst. He reined the animal in gently and calmed her. "I am asking you now. If you agree, then I shall make my intentions known to your parents. But you are clearly not one to listen to them, so if I am to have your hand, then I needs must ask you for it. You surely would not have it be otherwise."

Mirabelle considered his words. He was right. If he had approached her parents first, she'd never have listened to them. But this was no kind of proposal, either. "Why do you even want me? You've seen for yourself that I'm a soiled woman. I've been with other men and you're a follower of the Divine of Innocence."

Devon looked into her eyes, his brown ones holding something unfathomable to her. "Naivety is never knowing what is bad. Innocence is knowing what is bad and choosing what is good. I've seen you, Mirabelle. You are choosing the path of innocence."

Somehow his pious words, spoken gently, made her blush as if she were a maid. No one at the Temple ever spoke about Rhys or innocence like this. He continued, "Mirabelle, I know you as a woman who is high-spirited and strong-minded. You are someone who truly knows what she wants and can gain what she desires without needing the help of anyone. I need someone with that independent spirit, for I will be away for long periods of time." He frowned, pausing for a moment as if to gather his thoughts. "Any wife I have must be able to care for herself and our household; I would have to have a woman I could entrust with the full running of it.the wives of paladins are no fainting flowers. You have the traits I require in a wife and if you wed me, your family will gain double protection since your brother will often be home when I am not and others will still check in on you. It is a good arrangement for all concerned."

Arrangements, conditions, qualities, had this man no passion in his soul? If she agreed, the town would never speak ill of her behind her back no matter what she had done back when she was with the Thieves Guild, but would she be consigning herself to a lack-luster marriage and some dull marriage bed? Would it be worth it, to have the freedom to do as she desired when he wasn't around? Was she seriously even considering this?! This cold-hearted thinking must be contagious.

"Well, I don't know, I can't make such an important decision on a moment's notice. I need some time and some space to think it over fully," Mirabelle said, sounding nearly bored with it all.

"I am going on circuit for the next 6 months I will expect your answer upon my return," Devon told her, his voice gravely serious, as his eyes bored into hers while he steadied his mount.

This was a turn. "What? No jewelry, or flowers at least? Most men would try to actually court the girl they wanted to propose to," Mirabelle retorted sharply.

"I am no gardener to give you flowers. I am no jeweler to bring you wrought gold and gems. I am a paladin. What I offer you is faithfulness, for paladins know how to keep vows. I offer you steadfastness; when I am not on circuit or performing services for my Order, I will be at your side. I would give you my strength; there is no trouble you can face that these shoulders could not bear. I offer you my protection; you need fear no one nor anything if you accept me. And I pledge that neither you nor any children we have shall ever want. I cannot make you rich, but even were I to die in battle, the church will provide for you and for our children. It is part of their pledge to us who serve as paladins."

Devon turned his horse to go. "So you see, you will have plenty of 'space' to consider the matter. And if you do not choose me, there will be no hard feelings or regrets."

Incredulous, Mirabelle called after him, "Don't you care about me at all?"

Turning his head towards her, he replied, "Of course I care. You are the sister of one of my brothers-in-arms. You deserve better than what those… ruffians can offer. But I am also practical. I will not pin my hopes on you unless you accept me. I will not pine for you and you will not hurt my feelings by rejecting me. You may consider the matter solely based upon your own requirements and expectations. Now I needs must leave, I have dallied long and long in putting off my rounds. I shall see you six months hence."

"Don't you want anything from me?" she asked, still confused by this unorthodox courting style of his.

Pausing his mount, he called back, "You may light a votive candle in Rhys' temple and pray for my safe return if it pleases you." And with that he rode off slowly across the stone bridge as Mirabelle pursed her lips and looked pensively at this strange man and his unexpected offer.

The months passed and Mirabelle spent a lot of time at home helping her parents with the fruit trees and fields, spending time near the bridge by the river in her spare time, reading or fishing. She stayed away from town most of the time, just to keep from being pressured by Jarick or the others, but after a couple of months they seemed not to care. He had moved on and it looked like Gemma was his new woman.

Mirabelle felt nothing but relief. Jarick was passionate, but the things the group expected of her were not the sort of things she wanted to do. She was only sorry it took her this long to realize it. But of Devon's offer she could make neither heads nor tails of. So she tried to put it out of her mind, which made it the thing that haunted her day and night.

She knew her parents wouldn't object, and neither would her brother since Devon was a paladin and a friend of his. So it was truly up to her. A few other boys, from temple and around town, brought her posies during the spring. Even so, she couldn't help but see them as young and unseasoned and too much like Jarick in various ways. She told herself that she wanted more than to be a soldier's wife who never knew when her husband would be gone. Stubbornly, she refused to visit Rhys' temple. She still considered the clergy there to be out of touch with the real world in the safety of their hallowed halls. Devon knew the real world and the dangers that were in it. He might serve the temple, but he was no fool.

Devon.

If she didn't care about him, why couldn't she stop thinking about him? But it was utterly ridiculous, she told herself. If she told any of the girls in town about his "proposal" they'd laugh themselves silly. It just wasn't the way things were done. *I see in you the qualities I would want in a wife were I to take one.* Mirabelle certainly didn't bother with what everyone else thought, and it seemed that Devon didn't either. Or did he? Argh! That man! You didn't get accepted into an Order of Paladins without being considered of the highest quality and stature. And even offering to marry her. Surely it could not sit well with his commanders that he would take up with a woman with a reputation like hers. But it didn't stop him. He did what he wanted, not what anyone else thought he should.

Was he really as staid as he seemed, or was there an impulsive, passionate side to him waiting to come out? My duties keep me away for long periods, I would need a wife who is independent and can keep a household together with her own wits and wisdom. You could even take up a craft or profession if you wanted to fill the time. He did not despise her spirit. In fact, it sounded like he knew exactly what he wanted and had been searching for it for a long time.

And he slipped up. He mentioned her specifically at the end. She ran the conversation back over in her memory. Yes, she was sure, or at least pretty sure he switched from some idealized version of a wife to her. But why? Was it from talking to her brother? Her parents? Or did he like what he saw of her in the alleyway?

Now she felt her cheeks burning. Two men taking her one after the other in public? Was that something he found attractive? Or was it her body, her wares clearly laid out to see that made him decide he wanted to sample them? Maybe the chaste Paladin Orders were not exactly as they were billed to be. But that made her think of her brother and lead down corridors of thought best left alone.

The season began to turn. Summer offered its first bounties as the moons turned red-orange in the night. Cool midnight breezes promised yet cooler weather to come. Her dreams of Jarick turned faceless and then into Devon, but he remained chaste even in her dreams. She often awoke to the stifling heat of morning wondering if she should indulge herself in a fantasy as she sought release and whom she should imagine if she did.

Summer began to wan and the Harvest Fairs were on. Here Mirabelle hoped to find some distraction from her dilemma, perhaps discover a less cool-tempered suitor from amongst the men there. She tried talking to them, but all of them seemed like boys to her now that she had met the steadiness of a man. And yet, still she didn't know if she even truly liked him, much less loved him. What if Devon was as cold in the bedroom as he was in his speech? She'd die. She couldn't live like that, and what might get overlooked right now while she was unattached as high spirits would not be tolerated once she took a husband, particularly one so highly regarded in his profession.

Mirabelle tossed herself down in a pile of hay and tried to puzzle things out again. Her thoughts chased each other round and round until she dozed off. "Mirabelle, dear, it's time to go home. I hope you didn't sleep the whole Fair away," her mother said. Mirabelle looked around and up at the sky, sure enough, the stars were beginning to make an appearance. A quick check of her person confirmed that all her belongings were intact and her body. It was in cautious of her to drift off like that with so many strangers attending the Fair.

"No, of course not! I got to visit some of the stalls and watch the quilt judging earlier. Did you see some of the new designs? Rings! I would never have thought to do those, so clever," she replied and her mother agreed. They were still nattering on about the fine details of the new crafts shown off when they came across her father and headed home with a new sheep in tow.

The last few weeks before Devon's return were upon them and Mirabelle attended temple services with her parents. A summer staying away from town had left her feeling a bit stir crazy, and the idea that maybe listening to some holy writ might give her more insights on Devon decided her. Sitting between her parents, she tried to see the place through his eyes and failed. It still seemed some sort of ecclesiastical cage where those who could not handle reality ran off to imagine how the world would be perfect if only they prayed enough. But it was pretty to look at. The sand-colored stone held more subtle carving and artwork than she realized as a child. And the brightly colored glass of the votives flickered with a few dancing flames off in the corner. She always loved the colored glass there and in the back of the high ceiling of the temple wall. Here the violet stars of Rhys, there the azure dragon and silver crescent of Sigvarder, the red mortal blossoms and full red moon of Dido, and the yellow and green songbird and gold sun coin of Anjasa. Other smaller discs held images of the myriad of gods, but this temple was dedicated to the four top Gods of the Paladin Orders.

Yet these scenes and images that distracted her in her childhood held no especial meaning now. Memories, yes, but they told her nothing of why her brother left their family to be sent far away, nor why Devon allowed himself to be sent here. And they certainly held no clue as to his actions, nor any reason for his proposal.

Mirabelle slouched back on the bench and tried to focus on the reading about Rhys. "... and in the hour before dawn, when it seemed all hope was lost, Rhys appeared to them once more to give them courage. Not as a man as before, girded for battle, but as a woman to give comfort to their weary souls and to give encouragement as a mother does for her children. So it is that Rhys reminds us that we can hope to change ourselves and our lives, and that hope springs forth in every breath from every breast. And take heart they did, and rose together to smite the creatures that had crept in from the outer darkness. And when it was done, she gathered the fallen to her bosom to be taken to her kingdom, to serve forever as her personal guardians and protectors, and the rest she laid her hands upon and blessed them. And 'lo! From that day forth they were endowed with special powers and became the earthly hand of Rhys, the first paladins, that evil might not undo the good in the world, but rather that hope might be carried to all corners to those in need," spoke the priest. Then the preparations for the blessing of the paladins and the small meal to be shared to break the fast of night began. There were no new paladins or worshipers, so there would be no anointing in this ceremony.

As the priestess and priest began their intonations, Mirabelle suddenly realized that these well-known tales and passages weren't of some glorious history. Those men in the tale died. Even if they were taken back by Rhys herself/himself, they lost their lives facing down the undead. A cold chill crept down her back. It always seemed like it was something in the past, but if that were so, Rhys would not need paladins anymore.

She had always worried about her brother, but the reading gave form to her amorphous fears, and Devon faced the same ones. She had the strangest temptation to turn in her seat, to look for him, but she knew it was weeks too early for him to arrive. Her mother noted her fidgeting. "Is there something wrong?"

"Um, no mother. I just need to use the necessary soon," she replied. This seemed to satisfy her as Daleen patted her hand. Then they all rose to form a double ring around the altar space to receive a thin trencher of bread with a bit of herb and meat along with a small sip of juice or small beer, which it would be depended on the season.

Alarick spoke up as they wandered back home, "It was nice to have you with us at service today, Mirabelle. You've seemed so pensive the past few months, not like yourself at all. Is there something you need to tell us?"

Startled, Mirabelle answered, "N-no. There's naught to tell." She caught her father glance towards her stomach. Oh, no! Did he think she got pregnant, and that's why she stopped going to town and spent so much time alone? She could feel her cheeks heat up. Fathers! "I'm fine, really, I just realized that maybe I should start behaving more like a grownup instead of a kid. I'm just not sure what I want to be, yet."

Her father let out a little snorting breath of a chuckle. "Well, you know, I think the orchard will manage itself all right today if we go into town together. I believe they are cracking the seal on the last ice storage this afternoon, and they will be making fresh ice cream. How about we head down together and have some? I find it's easier to tackle problems with something good in your belly."

"Oh, can we bring them some mirabelles and apricots as along for them to mix in?" Mirabelle asked excitedly.

"That might be a good idea. I don't think the champagne grapes are ready yet or they would probably blend in nicely. They might even trade us some free ice cream in exchange for the fruit," Alarick replied, rubbing the short beard on his chin.

Daleen nodded, "Seems we will stop by the house after all. We can change out of our seventh day clothes and wear something lighter for the walk into town. Autumn may be close upon us, but today promises to be quite warm."

Soon, they were changed and with a half- bushel of fruit they headed off to the market square. It was the first time Mirabelle bothered to have a real conversation with her parents in months, nearly a year, she realized, and it felt good. It wasn't until Mirabelle saw them without the worry lines on their brows that she realized how concerned they had been for her. Yet they had not tried to truly stop her. They deserved more from their daughter than she had been giving them, but she tucked away the thought for later. They all laughed and chatted about the Fair, the farm, their plans for winter, but none mentioned Jarick and his gang, nor Devon's visit.

The last couple of weeks ticked by with both great speed and an agonizing slowness. A sense of anticipation built up in Mirabelle. She had no answer to Devon's proposal but hoped to talk to him and learn more about him. Of course, the day of the six-month mark came and went without him appearing. Travel times varied, as did weather conditions on the road. Yet she could not easily repress the fluttering in her stomach, and her breast, if she were honest. Devon was not uncomely, but she did not study him with an appraising eye when he was last there. Was he as handsome as memory suggested? Her mind invented new torments that were not completely quelled even as they harvested the apples and champagne grapes on the farm.

But after the second week, when Mirabelle went to the temple, there was an announcement at the end of the sermon. The priest, grave faced, said, "Children of Rhys, word has come to me skeletons raised by the foul hand of some powerful dark magic user attacked that the nearby town of Duskdale. In the battle, two of Rhys' paladins fell."

The priestess chimed in with, "Let us have a moment's prayer for the fallen that Rhys will gather them safely to her bosom and grant them respite from their long fight. And let us pray as well for those still out in the field battling to protect the good townsfolk of Duskdale." Mirabelle let out a gasp, drawing her parent's stares, but she did her best to mumble along with the prayer of protection and the closing hymn, mostly by rote memory, for most of her brain remained stunned by this news.

Devon might be dead.

Given the time frame, it was impossible that he could fail to be there either as part of the initial engagers or the support team called in to back them up when he had to pass right through Duskvale on his way to Riverfield. Mirabelle barely waited until people began filing out before hurrying to front to catch the priest and priestess as they helped direct the removal of the remains of the meal. "Priestess Lila, Priest Magnus, please, do you know the names of the fallen paladins?"

They turned to her, a bit startled, but Lila answered, "Do you wish to pray for them, child?"

"Um, it's, actually..." Mirabelle began as her parents approached, but she couldn't keep the secret from them any longer. Drawing in a deep breath, she plunged onward, "Paladin Devon made an offer of marriage to me before he left. I've been waiting for his return to discuss it. Please, can you tell me if he's okay?"

Daleen and Alarick made noises of astonishment, but Mirabelle could not spare a moment to address them yet. "Please," she pleaded.

The priestess glanced at the priest and some private message passed between them. Priestess Lila took Mirabelle's hands into hers and said, "I am sorry, daughter of Rhys. The missive was brought by bird and by necessity was brief. I cannot tell you the names of the fallen, but I promise we will pray for Victor-Paladin Devon and the other paladins every night. As a Victor-Paladin, he is field-seasoned. It does not promise him safety, but he is no novice at the ways of the enemy either. Go home and rest, daughter. It is the best thing you can do right now. And pray for his safety."

"Why didn't you mention this to us sooner, Mirabelle?" asked Alarick, but Mirabelle barely heard him, her eyes fastened on the iron of the votive candle rack. "You may light a votive candle in Rhys' temple and pray for my safe return if it pleases you." Was this it? Was this Rhys' punishment upon her for making light of his worshippers and disparaging the clergy?

Distractedly she asked, "Father, may I have a coin for the votive candles?" Out of the corner of her eye she saw her parents exchange worried looks, but her father fished out a coin and gave it to her. "Thank you, father. I'll head home on my own, if that's all right."

With a heavy sigh, he responded, "Very well. Your mother and I will be waiting for you at the house."

Mirabelle watched them go as she made her way over to the votive candles.

Dropping in a coin, she gathered one of the wooden tapers and lit it from the tall, ever- lit candle of Rhys and knelt down on the coarse cloth of the kneeler. Clasping her hands together, she silently begged for Devon's life.

Please, Great Rhys, she thought, don't punish Devon for any shortcomings on my part. He is a good and worthy soul who is doing his best to serve you. Please don't let him die out there. Please... don't let him be dead. For your glory, she concluded.

Lacing her first two fingers across each other in the sign of Rhys, she bowed her head as she rose. Then she headed out the door towards the path that would take her back to her house. She held her tears until she passed the last of the clergy and cried most of the way home.

17
UNDEAD IN DUSKDALE

Devon's sword lashed out, flashing with a silver-violet glow as he stabbed under the arm of the man in front of him, who stood impaled upon a skeleton's saber. Damn them, where did they all rise from? Even if every man, woman, and child who ever passed away in Duskdale were raised, and that wasn't even remotely possible on the cemetery's sacred soil, it wouldn't account for this horde of monsters!

Kris' eyes were staring down at the blood pouring out of the wound in his gut. Ducking down low, Devon came up from under the young paladin's arm even as Kris staggered back and fell, his hands going to the blade sticking out of him. Don't take it out, don't take it out, he willed at the young man but could not spare further glance or breath as the unnatural creature he wounded was still up and moving, using a fluid grace that it never had in life.

Devon's eyes flashed with an angry coldness at the sight of so many of his brethren downed by these puppet creatures. They weren't here by accident. Some greater undead both raised and commanded this host, and it had to be close by to command so many. And given the number of skeletons present, it had been following their company for some time, gauging their strength. It had to have been adding to its numbers night by night, planning to wipe them out by simply exhausting them. And they hadn't sensed them. Damn them, damn every one of these beasts to the dark gods that powered them.

Swords were a poor choice against creatures that lacked flesh, but the light of Rhys blessed their weapons. "There is no night so dark that the sun does not dispel it in the morning's dawn," he intoned. The creature flinched away from the spoken words of holy writ, and Devon brought his sword down hard in an angled stroke from its collarbone to its opposite hip. The blade sliced through as though the thing was made of nothing firmer than dry, rotted kindling. The creature fell apart, its spine severed. Devon drove a third swift strike across its neck where it lay on the ground and drove the steel-rimmed heel of his boot against its jawbone. Dispatched at last, he quickly rushed across the clearing to the aid of their commander, Great Victor-Paladin Marsid.

Beset on three sides, Marsid took some strikes on his shoulder pauldrons, but appeared mostly unharmed so far. Roaring a wordless battle cry, Devon picked up all the speed he could and slammed hard into the one on Marsid's left and drove it straight into the two nearest skeletons behind it. Despite their unnatural speed and grace, skeletons lacked the physical solidity that flesh granted. They landed into a pile with another couple of their fellows and Devon slowed not the slightest but brought his sword up high and brought it down square on the breastbone of the topmost one and cut down, the light of his blade actinically bright as it passed through the first and second easily, the acrid smoke of the burned bones rising to Devon's nose. He felt ground beneath the tip of his blade and turned the edge such that he could walk the blade diagonally across the other pair on the right before they could extricate themselves from the pile.

The rattling chatter of the jawbones of the two he couldn't get to give warning that they were coming for him. He'd angered them. They'd tear him apart slowly if they could.

Even the ones he'd wounded were not fully incapacitated. He could feel the teeth of one close around the metal, protecting the tendons to his foot from harm. Although their jaws were easy to unhinge, the magic that imbued them gave them a fierce bite strength and he heard the metal shriek under the force. He drove his sword into its forehead even as he felt the metal begin to pinch his foot.

Grimacing from the discomfort, he sensed movement behind him and turned aside just as Marsid cleared his pair and charged the two coming up to menace Devon. Taking a moment to catch his breath, Devon looked up to see the firelight glint off of a field of white coming through the trees. Looking behind him, Kris lay with glassy eyes. Barton lay a few feet beyond him, struggling faintly. A group of skeletons were ripping the flesh and armor off of Barton to prep him for violation by their master. Shock and disgust washed through him, but there was no way he could get over to his fallen brothers-in-arms.

Casting a glance about the campsite, he saw Trenton rising. The man moved with a slight limp where an enemy blade had struck through the chain on the side of his leg armor. "Trenton! Can you tend to Barton?" Looking up at Devon, he turned his head to where Barton lay. Eyes narrowing, he nodded and shouted at the monsters "Let him go!" Then whispering the sacred words of Rhys, light flickered down his hands onto his leg and although the blood remained, the wound had closed. Testing it, Trenton managed to stand and prepared his blade to rush the unnatural creatures.

Slightly relieved, Devon turned back to the oncoming phalanx. One of them held a thorn blade high and called to the ones behind him with the thin whispering screech and jaw clacking that made up their language. Whirling the blade in the air in a fine arc, the monster turned its empty eye sockets towards them before lowering the blade at him and Trenton. Rhys help them, for they were outnumbered.

18
A DREADFUL TRUTH

"Did you know anything about this?" Mirabelle heard Daleen ask Alarick as she hung laundry. The sound carried farther down the hill than one might expect. She slowed her steps.

"No dear, Devon did not approach me about it." Her father's reply came from the grape arbor and after a moment she could see him move down the line some and resettle the bushel basket, he was filling. Usually suitors talked to the parents first so they would know the person's intentions were honorable, as opposed to the intentions of men like Jarick. Mirabelle blushed as she thought about it. She had felt so grown-up and it was fun, but she knew even then that she and Jarick would never wed. Now she wondered why she ever wanted him. To upset her brother, she realized, and her parents wound up casualties of her anger at Theovald. It seemed a poor reason to give away the first explorations of her body, if not her heart.

She had thought that she loved Jarick. She tried to believe she did, but while it was exciting to be with him, when he wasn't around, she found she didn't miss him as much as she thought she would or should. And knowing she wasn't causing a strain on her parents' minds and hearts easily decided her once she was away from him. That and the fact that Jarick would let his second just have her like that. That didn't sound like love, either.

Head over heart. Now she sounded like Devon as well! By Rhys, she hoped he was okay. She didn't make her steps quiet, but she didn't announce herself either as she came up the path to the house. Her mother's back was to her so the laundry would not flap into her face with the wind blowing as it was. Listening, she heard her mother say, "Well, it explains why poor Mirabelle has been so quiet and solitary lately. But I had no idea she fancied the man at all. We've only known him a few years and only had short visits before this."

"I can't say I am displeased at the prospect, but I wish Mirabelle would have come to us with it before now. Perhaps we could have done more to help cushion this blow if we were aware of the arrangement," her father replied.

Crossing over to where her mother was, Mirabelle said at last, "There is no arrangement, father, he made an offer and asked me to consider it while he was away."

"And?" her father prompted and her mother turned to her, laundry forgotten.

"And... I don't know! I would ask him questions, find out more about him. But now, now, he might be..." and she couldn't go on. A choked sob escaped her throat and her mother pulled her into a hug and her father came over and joined them both. Wrapped in the warm circle of their arms, she sobbed again, unable to control it anymore.

With gentle care, her parents led her inside and sat her at the table. Handing her a handkerchief, they bustled about and brought her some broth and fresh grape juice. They told her that they still loved her no matter what and to not give up hope as Rhys watched over those designated as his worldly protectors. But their kindness seemed to only to open the floodgates of her heart, and she keened as openly as any child. A part of her mind chided her for such hysterics for a man she hardly knew and shared not even a single touch or kiss with, but her heart would have none of it. For whatever reason, his quiet strength, his certainty about things, or that he continuously believed in her value even when faced with evidence to the contrary, he had burrowed his way into her heart. He got past her defenses and thoughts and objections without even being there! What kind of man did that? Could do that?! Devon, you had better make it back safely, she thought fiercely.

Finally, her tears wound down. It had seemed like they would never end. The little hiccups subsided, and her mother urged her to drink as she retrieved the broth. Daleen had set it on the edge of the hearth to keep warm when Mirabelle was not up to eating it right away.

"Well, you had said you were maturing and taking life more seriously," her father Alarick said at last. "It seems you were wrestling with some heavy questions. Growing up doesn't mean you have to do it all alone. It's okay to come to us when you need to. We'll always be your parents, okay sweet plum?"

"I know," she said quietly, staring at her hands where they gripped the handkerchief as though it were a lifeline. "It's just that he's so quiet; I don't know what's in his head. Then there is the whole marrying a soldier, whether he works for the temple. And look! I haven't even accepted or rejected his proposal and I already get to know how bad it can be to fear for a husband's life while he's on the road."

Her mother sat down in the seat cater-corner to her and taking her hands into her rich olive brown ones said, "Darling, there is no promise of survival in any profession. The truth is, we are all mortal. Some just face it in a clearer fashion than others. Remember how old man Truant was just checking over his property two years back after that spring storm and got hit by a widow-maker branch? No one realized something had happened to him until he didn't make it back for mealtime. And then there was that young boy, Mizzel, wasn't it dear?" This last was directed at her father and he nodded his head. "Mizzel was chopping wood outside and lost his grip and badly chopped his own leg. Even with everyone trying to help, they couldn't get him to the temple in time for them to heal him. You were pretty small when that happened so you might not remember him. But accidents occur, death comes. But I assure you, the paladins are better trained to deal with danger, and better armored against it, than most. The bigger question, daughter, is can you cope with a man being gone for months at a time? Can you deal with being alone for so long?"

Her mother inclined her head and her look became more serious.

"Marrying a paladin brings with it a measure of prestige and respect, but that respect will quickly turn on you if you... share your affections with any other man when he is away. While a normal soldier's wife might be forgiven, a temple-wife will not be. Even if you are not married to a priest or priestess, the attitudes of the townsfolk will be the same. Bear that in mind as well as you think about this offer."

Mirabelle sighed and looked down at her hands again. "Mirabelle!" her mother snapped. "I mean it."

"I know, mother. Believe me, I've thought about it," Mirabelle replied wanly.

Apparently satisfied, her mother added, "We've met and talked with Devon in the past. I would say that my impression of him is of a serious and grounded man. He would never betray you or deliberately do you harm, but he may not match your... youthful exuberance." Mirabelle was certain that was a euphemism for something else, but her mother went on. "But he may be a good grounding force for you, and you may be an uplifting one for him. It's up to you. We just want to see you happy with the person you choose. Did you see any other boys you fancied at the Fair?"

Running her hand absently over the uneven surface of the table's dark wood, Mirabelle replied, "No, they seemed to be exactly that, boys."

"Well, perhaps you know what you are looking for better than you think. Go to sleep, darling. Tomorrow should make things look brighter." It was rather early, but Mirabelle felt wrung out and sleep seemed like the wisest course.

"Thank you, Mom, Dad," she said as she climbed the narrow steps to her upstairs loft room.

"Don't mention it, sweet plum, pleasant dreams," her father called up even though he had remained mostly quiet during the whole exchange, whittling in a corner. No matter what, she still had her parents, and they loved her. That should be enough. Or so she hoped.

19
LIGHT A VOTIVE FOR ME

Dawn came and Mirabelle helped with the chores around the little farm and orchard. When she finished at last, she asked if she might be excused to see if there was any news at the temple. Her parents raised no objections, but Mirabelle feared and hoped what news lay waiting at the end of the long walk.

Arriving, she looked around for the priest or priestess, but found neither. She waited for a time in one of the pews near the front, and eventually someone came to check on the eternal candles. "Please, can you tell me if Paladin Devon has returned?"

"Oh, you must be the girl I heard about," said the middle-aged woman before her in the soft pinkish orange robes of dawn. "I am afraid the company is still in the field and no further word has been sent. I promise I'll let you know if anything arrives. You live up on the hill just on the edge of town, right?"

"Yes, that's right," Mirabelle answered. "Well, if word comes while you are away, I will make sure someone comes to get you, all right?"

"Okay." Turning away, Mirabelle caught sight of the votive candles. None were burning. A streak of heat and cold shot through her. When did they update them for the day? How would Devon stay protected if they didn't let the light stay lit? Walking over quickly, she lifted a taper with shaking hands. She fumbled three times just trying to get it lit and to stay lit long enough for her to light another votive. She lit two to make up for it. She hadn't thought about the candles when she came down. Her money was still at home, what little she had saved up. She'd bring some tomorrow, she decided. Kneeling down, she prayed softly, "Please Rhys, forgive me that this flame went out. I will keep it lit for Devon, if you only bring him home safely." With that, she rose and left for home. The trek never seemed longer.

Day after day, she went, and the word was the same. No news, no one had ridden ahead. It was if the ground had swallowed them all. Duskdale wasn't that many days away. But three passed, then four, soon a week. Each day, Mirabelle lit an extra votive and dropped in the coins for them. And each day her visits and prayers became longer and longer.

She found on one of her visits that someone had laid down a finer cloth over the kneeler. It was softer and kinder on her knees, which were becoming chaffed from the normally coarse material. And she realized the clergy were less lofty and far more kindly than she gave them credit for. So she thanked Rhys for their kindness as she prayed for Devon into the night.

To no avail.

At last she caught herself nodding off, and the clergy came and covered her with a blanket and bade her stay when the night was full dark outside. Her parents arrived in the morning and the clergy spoke gently to them and promised to look after her while Victor-Paladin Devon was away. They looked concerned, but Mirabelle just bowed her head and prayed harder when it looked like they would ask her to come home.

Ten days passed, then eleven, and hope flickered and died in her breast. She had already brought a dark lace mourning veil with her. At least two paladins were dead. It wasn't wrong per se, but she knew who she was mourning. And though Little Mercy and Honey Flower both tried to bring her food, she kindly turned them away. Eschewing all but a little water, she kept vigil as best she could at the small shrine. After midnight, she poured more of her dwindling supply of coins into the box, and lit yet another taper. It marked twelve days since the news came. Mirabelle felt hopeless and lost in her grief.

20
ASSUMPTIONS AND WHERE THEY LEAD

Reaching the Temple of Rhys at last in Riverdale, Devon wondered if a finer sight ever existed. He and the other paladins took their weary mounts and selves into the side courtyard to the stables there. The young clergy would be happy to tend to and spoil their sacred mounts. Devon was certain his steed, River Dancer, would be happy in no time. But as he tied his mount up and prepared to set her up with some hay and water, the Priest and Priestess of the temple came up to him together, heedless of the horse apples on the ground.

Something must have happened.

"Please follow us, Victor-Paladin Devon. Little Mercy can tend to your mount, you are required now elsewhere," and Priestess Lila gestured for Little Mercy to take over Devon's duties. What could be so pressing? Was Kris or Barton's family members here wanting word of their children's fates already? He wasn't ready or fit for delivering such news, if so.

"Priest Magnus, Priestess Lila, I'm in no condition to give report to anyone. Please, let me bathe and remove the scent of horse and sweat off of me," he asked, neglecting to add the scent of death from the list. They had tended to the wounded after the battle but stayed armored as much as possible the past week, knowing that a greater undead lurk beyond their sight, gaging their strengths and weaknesses. With a full Temple of Rhys here, not just a shrine as at Duskdale, the Divinities could invoke Rhys' protection at the borders before nightfall and keep the town safe until Rhys' sun rose, and the undead were forced back to their lairs.

"I'm sorry, Victor-Paladin, please believe me the matter is personally urgent to you and should be addressed immediately," Magnus said to him as he strode up to the doors of the temple and held it open to him and Lila. Important to him personally? Did something happen to Theovald's family? Did Mirabelle come to harm? Concerned now, he loosened the chin strap on his helmet and lifted it off in deference before entering, but followed quickly on Lila's heels. His eyes made out little in the dim interior after the brightness of the noonday sun. A few candles burned at the altar, beneath the colored brilliance of the stained glass windows above. Shadows of clergy moved about in their duties, cleansing the wooden pews, freshening the flowers, and praying at the stations of the gods. On his left several pinpoints of light danced, and the colored glass shone as his eyesight adjusted. A figure knelt before them, and to this place the Divinities ushered him. Puzzled, he blinked several times, trying to make out the person in a dark lace veil before the votives. He heard Rhys' name whispered over and over from her lips, as one does when too drained and weary to repeat the litanies anymore. He couldn't imagine who it was at first, and then his brain finally stripped away the veil and recognized the silhouette. This wan form was Mirabelle?! Looking up he saw there were no less than twelve votives lit, possibly one for each day past the time he said he'd return. So this was all for him.

Shaking his head, he announced from behind her, not too loudly lest she jump, "You know, you need only to light one. And you are supposed to pay for each one you light with a donation."

She gasped out a sudden breath and turned dark, haunted, sleepless eyes towards him, rimmed red from crying. "I have paid for each one, every single day you've been gone since the news came that you might not return," she snapped back, her voice rasping from long hours of prayer he guessed.

A foolish, easy grin spread across his face, chasing away some of the darkness from the long nights on the road. "So may I assume your answer is yes?"

She tried to rise but her legs would not hold her up and she sank down to the cold stone of the floor and steadied herself with a hand against the railing of the kneeler. He waited patiently as she swallowed and tried to recover her voice. "It's yes," she said at last. With care, he reached an arm under hers and helped to sit in a pew where she could rub feeling back into her legs.

Waving the Divinities over, he asked Priest Magnus and Priestess Lila, "How soon can we arrange a wedding?" Mirabelle gasped and stared at him in surprise.

"It should not take long at all for you, Victor-Paladin Devon. We are grateful you are still with us," Priestess Lila replied warmly, nodding to him and sparing a smile towards Mirabelle.

"But what about my parents?" she asked. "We shall go to them next, after your legs have recovered. Would you like me to retire for a bit and wash the road dust from myself before we approach them?" Her reply of "yes" was so quick and harsh she ducked her head and a touch of blush rose to her pale cheeks.

Chuckling, he said, "Then it will be so." Rising carefully, he stepped close to the Divinities and said, "Can you make sure someone brings her something to drink and perhaps a bit of salted bread to restore her? I see she has been mourning my demise, if a bit prematurely."

Crinkling appeared around Magnus' eyes as he attempted to keep his features schooled. "I'm sure we can have one of the junior clergy assist her. She has been here praying more hours than the clergy these last few nights and we have worried she would make herself ill were her heart over-wrought much longer."

"Her heart need not fear more tonight, but your good selves must call upon Rhys' protections tonight and likely for some time to come at the borders of this town. We who have survived know we are yet trailed. The fiend without will have to build up again, but I know he will make his presence known to us in time. Fortunately, Riverfield is about to have a great host of paladins present as both my company and Theovald's will probably attend. So at that point I suspect the creature will give this up as a bad cause, at least until we are separated once more in the field. But for now, it is enough. We are safe under Rhys here and good things have come with the dawn," he finished.

"Goodness comes with the dawn," they replied in unison. With that, Devon went to the bathing chambers to make himself presentable to Mirabelle's parents. His fellows were already there making use of the bathhouse and cleansing pools and they hailed him as he entered, concerned for what drew him away so suddenly.

And the reality of it all hit him as he looked back at them and he sagged against the doorframe as he replied, "I'm going to get married."

21

FOR EACH TEAR YOU SHED

Mirabelle was surprised with how quickly preparations went once she said yes. Recall notices went out and her own brother was expected to arrive in a mere two to three weeks. Honestly, if it weren't for the fact they were waiting for him to arrive, she was certain that Devon would have had them hitched within a week!

This was insanely short. Most girls spent a whole season contemplating and planning their nuptials. But since Devon was a soldier first, it was tacitly understood by the church and at least some community that things needed to move apace as he may have a little time before being recalled to the field. And being that he was a soldier for the Temple of Rhys' they moved swiftly to assist, clearing away the normal decorations of the season for those used for the rarer investiture ceremonies and rushing through the appropriate paperwork. Mirabelle wondered if she were marrying the man or the temple. What exactly had she gotten herself into?

The question repeated itself in her head as she saw Devon come out of the temple doors into the sunlight. His dark hair lay unbound and long from the months in the field still. His face was not uncomely, but had some lines and hard planes of maturity. No fresh-faced boy was he. But he also carried himself with a confidence and surety of purpose, an intensity that none of the boys of her age had. She must have looked unsure of what she saw, for he asked her, "What is it? Do I have something out of place?"

He twisted and turned a bit to examine the lay of his outfit; the tabard lying overtop of which should have hidden a multitude of sins even if something were out of place. But his gyrations gave her a greater look at his form in a way she had not bothered with before. He did not move with any stiffness, and his muscles were firm and taut. And if he was not thin, he wasn't carrying much extra weight either. A slight softness existed around the middle that would likely make it pleasant for her to snuggle up with him at night.

She giggled with a slight nervousness at the line of her thought and waved lightly at him, "No, your attire is fine. I was just noticing how long your hair has grown while you were away."

"Do you not like it so? It has become uneven, I will grant, but it shall be shorn before our wedding day. Would you care for it to be cropped short?"

"No, somewhere in-between would suit, I think."

"Then it shall be so, my lady."

My lady. And she was to be his lady. His words were very true and yet she had never heard him address her with what was normally a common appellation to ordinary speech. She turned away from him, feeling suddenly shy. It made no sense, after all he had seen her at her worst behavior and seen enough of her body that it hardly mattered that she had not been completely naked. He had no surprises coming on her end. But although she had been with Jarick, and unexpectedly Lee, she had known them, known what she was getting into with them. Or at least so she thought. But she didn't know this man she was about to be bound to for the rest of her days. And as harshly as she had spoken to him in the past, now she didn't know how to bridge that gap. Given Devon's nature, there wasn't likely to be much help from him on that quarter.

Thinking for a moment she turned back and said, "How about we go for a walk somewhere?"

"Very well, my lady. Where would you like to stroll?"

"I thought we'd go to a place you enjoyed. If this is to be the town you put down roots at, what place appeals to you most?" She congratulated herself on turning things around to be about him. His choice would probably tell her something about the man himself, even if his words were less than forthcoming.

"That is simple enough. I like the bridge over the river where I left a single man and returned an engaged one, although I knew it not," he gave her a tiny, slight smile and his look softened in a way she had never seen before. She exhaled and could not seem to draw in enough breath.

So she was the thing he loved best about the town.

"I thought you told me you weren't pinning your hopes upon me," she asked, cocking her head to the side as she took his proffered arm and linked hers through. She didn't know what he had used to wash with, but it had a sharp, clean scent to it. A vast improvement over the scent of horse and sweat he had arrived with, although she was too glad to see him at the time to be concerned with the matter.

He looked down at her with a mild amusement in his features. "I did not."

Infuriating. Devon wasn't a huge conversationalist. "Then why did you say you liked the bridge the way you did?"

"Ah, because it is the pathway that led me to you," he replied. He may not say many words, but she could not find fault with the ones he chose.

"So do you love me, then?" she asked boldly, once they were far enough away that there would be no one to overhear their conversation. Some things need to be discussed privately.

"You've said yes, so I feel safe to do so," Devon said. "So, yes. But what of you?"

Mirabelle realized that although she had thought of him often and feared for his life, she never told him how she felt. "I think I may, but I hardly know you in truth. That's why I wanted to go for this walk with you. To get to know who you really are." They had wandered farther down the road as they talked and neared the fragrant shade of the serrated willow trees. The trees liked to be close to water, but not too close. It was probably why they were sacred to Anjasa. They were often the first true sign of land for those on long sea voyages. Perhaps that is why the fishermen made their lures in the shape of its leaves, Mirabelle thought as Devon diverted her to the shade of one. The river flashed in the distance, barely visible from here, but the white of the stone bridge gleamed brightly.

Here he helped her settle against the sturdy trunk of one of the large willows before kneeling down to join her. He tried his best to be gallant; she had to grant it to him. Casting about for a time, he found a stone and turned it over and over in his hands as if trying to gather his thoughts. "Mirabelle, I know not what to tell you that I have not already. I am a man of faith and a faithful man. I pledge to you that I shall never betray you, and that your trust in me is well placed. But what decided you at last to accept my troth, if I may ask?"

Mirabelle looked up into the gold and green of the willow's canopy. Perhaps it was a good place to speak the truths of the heart. "I hadn't decided. Even up to the day you were meant to return, I hadn't decided. Then I thought you were dead, and I couldn't imagine not getting the chance to make that choice, of a world where you weren't in it. And the longer you were gone, the more it pained my heart, I thought it might be love, but I'm not sure what it is."

He let out a sigh and touched her under the chin lightly, drawing her gaze to him. She suddenly felt like crying all over again. How cruel to be told your wife to be wasn't sure if she even loved you. But he didn't seem upset with her. Calm as ever, he whispered her name, "Mirabelle." Her eyes welled up at the gentle way he said her name. A sob racked her, and she bowed her head lower than the surrounding willows, and Devon rose quickly to wrap his arms around her. Settling once more beside her, she felt him lean her against his strong shoulder as she cried. It should be him crying, not her. The world was so messed up even as things were so right, it was all wrong.

"Mirabelle, my Mirabelle," he crooned gently into her ear. "Love is a seed we plant together. A great tree such as this willow is not grown in a day. Although love can spring up quickly, like a vine, if it has no good foundation, it will choke itself and fail. That you opened your heart to the possibility of loving me is enough. I will do my best not to grieve you or bring you pain or sorrow. And for each tear you shed, I will try to give you twice as many joys." He whispered sweet words to her, each a pledge, a promise, and at last he held her and rocked her until she tired of tears and felt only the warmth of him comforting her. His heart a steady beat in his chest. She grew drowsy and realized he never once kissed her during all of it. He could now, but he did not. She wondered why as she drifted off to sleep against him.

22

SAVORING THE SWEET

When she awoke, the sun lay low on the horizon behind them. Surely people wondered where they were, but he hadn't moved. He sat still and at her stirring he looked upon her with bemused tenderness. "All done, now? We should get back before the night settles."

"Why didn't you wake me?"

"You needed to rest. A heavy weight has been resting on your shoulders all this time. It is time you let me carry it for you. There is no trouble you face that these shoulders cannot bear."

Gazing sleepily at him as he helped lift her up she asked, "Is that not what you said to me before on the bridge, before you left?"

"Indeed, it is. As I pledged it, so it shall be. I uphold my pledges, my dear lady Mirabelle." In the gathering dusk, his voice sounded different, deeper, huskier suddenly. And he gathered her into his arms once more and held her tight. He buried his face in her hair and breathed deeply as though he were trying to capture her through scent alone.

At last she asked him, exasperated, "Why don't you kiss me?"

He let go of her then, slowly, and she was sorry for the loss of him. In truth, she felt some stirring towards him as he held her locked in the circle of his arms. "Why should I rush these sweet moments of discovery? You said yourself that you hardly know me. Should we not savor these tender beginnings?"

His eyes glittered in the faint light and she felt a little ashamed for expecting him to rush at her at the slightest provocation as Jarick did. It was an unkindness at best. Finally she said softly, "You have the right of things, I didn't mean to raise my voice as I did."

Chuckling, he replied, "But then you would not be Mirabelle. Do not worry, my hide is thicker than that. But come, we must not linger here after dark." And he set a nearly punishing pace back to her house, soon to be her parents' house only, she realized, and bade her goodnight. She did not hear his footsteps retreat until the door was latched and locked for the night.

23
BEGGING AN EAR

The walk back to the temple proved a long one for Devon. He'd said a lot of things back there, trying to comfort her. But he remembered every one. He vastly underestimated the number of tears women shed compared to men. His own mother was a very solid and practical woman, as were his aunts. Since he left rather early for training, he never had much time for visiting with girls closer to his own age back then. Now he felt more than a bit perplexed.

He counted every sob she made, every tear that fell, and wondered how he could make up for them all. And these were his burden to bear. Somehow, he had won her heart and she couldn't understand it yet herself.

As he walked up the road, he ran across Priestess Lila as she headed along the main road towards the town's border. "Hail, do you desire an escort while you do your work?"

"Do you think I would not have asked for one before I left the temple had I thought so?" she asked, her eyes twinkling. Devon flushed and stuttered, trying to find the right reply for the Divinity. She did not leave him floundering long, "Enough, Victor- Paladin Devon. I would not mind some company as it is a long walk these days for me. The path can be uncertain in the dark, which it will be by the time I return."

Nodding acquiescence, he inclined his head to show that he would follow her lead. She stepped lively enough as she moved ahead. The bridge lay not so far ahead and Devon struggled within himself whether to confide in the Divinity, but as they shrove the Paladins, he finally decided to lay his dilemma at her feet.

"Priestess Lila, I find myself in difficulty and would beg your ear if you are willing," he began.

Her voice was colored with amusement as she cut in, "You may have more than my ear, the rest of me comes with. What grieves you tonight, good Paladin?"

The wind left him as he realized he had no clear way to state his issue. They continued a good few paces before he raised his eyes from the dust and stone of the roadway and spoke. "I gave my vows to the temple and Rhys some time ago, but now I am about to do so again with Mirabelle. I thought such a marriage would prove beneficial to both parties, but now that I have her agreement, I am perhaps not as certain of what duties await me. Not the consummation, don't think that," he said rapidly and went on, silently cursing himself, "but how to... make her happy. I don't think she is so sure of herself, and I don't know how to help her with these doubts."

"I think a man that realizes he may not know everything before going into a marriage is wiser than he realizes. But a moment, good Paladin, and I will consider your plight." Backing away a step, Devon's eyes scanned the open fields of rushes before them as Lila stood before the bridge and intoned a greater prayer of Rhys to guard the town from any intrusion from spirits and undead until dawn. His thoughts wandered to those of his friend, Theovald, and the spirit of his lost love buried in the town. Did blessings such as these keep spirits such as hers away? Or did it keep only ill- wishing ghosts at bay? If she were at rest on the hillside, within the borders, would she be trapped inside until dawn? Would darker undead be trapped thus as well? His hand clenched tighter as he gazed around the landscape, bathed in the blood-red rays of the dying sun as Lila slowly dropped her hands, the incantation over.

She seemed to look him over appraisingly as she turned around. "Expecting trouble to come so soon?" Her eyes flickered across the same fields empty of aught but darting dragonflies and the first mosquitoes of evening. "A chill wind blows from the Abyss, but we stand bathed in the light of dawn. What darkness should we fear?" He relaxed a bit at her recitation of the words of scripture from the Book of Rhys.

"You are right having called upon Rhys, we must have faith in the god's protection and goddess sides of Rhys."

She bowed slightly and stepped beside him, waving at the newly interested mosquitoes. "Were these little vampires subject to Rhys' powers, I would be much happier. Let us head back and I will answer your question as best I might." Devon fell into step beside her, attentive.

"How old are you now, Victor-Paladin Devon? Twenty-two?"

"Twenty-three this name day past, Priestess Lila," he replied promptly.

"Ah, twenty-three. And Mirabelle is about to turn eighteen in just two days, yes?"

"Yes, it would so seem," he said, coughing into his hand. Why did the subject of Mirabelle unnerve him so?

The Priestess spared him a brief smile, "It is a volatile time in a young woman's life, that age. You've come offering stability, but doubt, for either of you, is completely normal. Has she implied that she does not desire the match? It will be quite a sudden life-change for a girl who knew you hardly at all a year ago and little more now."

Devon nearly tripped on nothing at the thought, "No, she... she is unsure of her own heart. I tried to give her what assurance I could, but I pledged to give her twice the joy as the tears she sheds, but I didn't know how many tears a woman could shed!"

Now the Priestess laughed outright. "Oh Devon, that is a tall order but if anyone can fulfill such an oath, it is you. Why not use the opportunity of her name day to show her your quality? I'm sure we can supply a reasonable stipend for you to offer her a proper gift for one who is courting."

Inspiration fell upon him like the blessed rays of Rhys' dawn light.

"Actually, if it please the temple, I believe I have something in mind, but it will cost much of what I have in reserve as well as whatever gift the temple would bequeath to me for the occasion of my wedding."

"Oh? What did you have in mind then, Devon?"

He told her, and her eyes crinkled with delight. "I believe that might just work."

24

OF TRIFLES AND FOOLS

The next day, Devon went through sacred ablutions even though it wasn't required again so soon, then asked for absolution and blessing by Priestess Lila before joining his brothers and sisters-in-arms at the breaking of the night's fast. Many wished him well, and tried to engage him in conversation, but his answers were brief, his mind caught up in the task before him. He'd faced armies of undead and perspired less he realized, rubbing his sweating palms on his trousers. He sighed. He went not in his regalia, but in more ordinary clothes, the sash of star- violets across his chest proclaiming his position. Somehow, facing his fiancée seemed a difficult task, and he desired some hint of Rhys' shielding about him as he set out again for her house.

The sun was well up by the time he reached the turnoff for the hillside cottage where Mirabelle lived with her parents. He found the three of them working side by side, shaking free the fruit of her namesake onto clean canvas tarps as he arrived. Clearing his throat, he announced himself and moved to aid them as they worked, filling the baskets with hands both deft and gentle. When that was done they moved to the champagne grape vines and collected a few bushels of those. By the time Alarick called a halt, Devon's hands were thoroughly sticky and his back offering complaint. Farm work called on different muscles than riding and fighting.

Daleen and Alarick called him into the cottage with them as Mirabelle shyly joined him at the washing bowl. She poured from the pitcher for him, as he did in kind for her. It rang in his soul as an odd echo of his morning bathing at the temple. Something delicate and faint called to his mind but was lost as the two of them were called to eat. Fresh grape juice from the sweetest grapes Devon had ever tasted graced the table as cold cuts of roasted boar were served out on rounds of brown bread with thin slices of sharp cheese. Devon could not deny his hunger, but it only mirrored the others at the table. The long morning chores led to healthy appetites all around, and none stood on ceremony about having seconds.

"So what brings you here today, Devon?" Alarick finally asked at last.

"I was hoping to spend some time talking to Mirabelle alone if that is all right," he responded.

"Certainly, why she is as safe with you as with her own brother," Daleen chimed in as she set a pair of wooden containers before them, wrapped up in traveling hand kerchiefs done up with bows. Mirabelle stuck her tongue out to the side at the comparison of Devon with her brother Theovald. Devon was amused but reminded of how young she was. "Take that with you and we will see Mirabelle this evening," Daleen added at last.

"Of course," Devon replied getting up. He offered his hand to Mirabelle, and she accepted it gratefully, stacking and scooping up both containers with one hand. They went out together into the bright, crisp afternoon sunlight hand in hand together as they walked slowly down the path.

"So where are we going today, Devon?" she asked once they were well out of earshot.

"Actually, I had something I wanted to talk to you about, so I thought we'd go back to the serrated willow grove if you are amicable."

Mirabelle sighed, "It seems the place I've wound up spending most of my time this summer. I suppose it's as nice a spot as any."

"What I had to talk about is for your ears alone," he added. She cocked her head speculatively at this and seemed to regain the spring to her step.

Once they arrived in the shade of the grand willows once more, Devon took the food boxes from Mirabelle while she arranged herself and then joined her. The thought that they were sitting exactly where they had the day before when she cried herself out was not lost on him. "So what is so important and secret?" she asked him at last.

"I'm not sure how secret it is, but I am curious what life you had dreamed of having before I came along. Where did you imagine yourself being and living when you were younger?"

This seemed to catch her off-guard, and she paused, tipping her head to the side as she laid a finger along one cheek. "Hmm, it's been a while since I thought about it. Not since I spent the night over at Mandy's house in town. Well, I always wanted a farm of my own, but without so much hill. It was tough to climb up it as a child after visiting temple. It was fun to go down in winter, but terrible to go up at the end of the day.

"I guess I've always wanted something a little like my parents' place, with fruit trees and vines, but I wanted some actual grain fields as it seemed to be hard to afford flour and stuffing sometimes as the winter stores ran low and prices went up. Trading works well for us in the summer, but everyone has their own store of preserves by winter so we didn't have much to trade then.

"I wanted a large kitchen with good light so I could have herb boxes in winter, and a large hearth so I could bake and cook at the same time. I've always loved my loft bed. It's been my escape since childhood, but I probably would have to have a ground floor bedroom as well for having babies or for when I get old. And I need a good sitting room where I could do crafts with family or friends." She laughed ruefully at this last and shook her head. "I guess that would be you, unless you don't do crafts?" She looked over her shoulder at him as she finished.

Clearing his throat, he answered, "Well, I have little time for them, it's true. Most of my crafts involve care of my weapons and armor and my horse. Unless you count my martial training as a craft, some do. But aside from that?" He pondered momentarily. "I have made handles and pommels for blades and knives in the past, bone or wood, sometimes with leather wrappings. I made them up as gifts when I was fresh into the academy and wanted to thank some of my friends from there. I think I made an antler handle for one of your brother's knives, come to think on it."

Mirabelle sat up in surprise, "Oh, I think I know the one you mean. He still takes it with him. He mostly uses it for eating, I think."

"Oh, well, I'm glad he likes it then." They sat together in silence for some time. "Why don't we see what my mother sent us out with?" Mirabelle asked at last. "Very well." Opening their boxes together, they found a layered trifle of custard, freshly whipped cream that had fallen slightly, and fresh mirabelles. Devon looked it over and wondered if there was some message hidden in the piece. Did Daleen think he would sample her daughter's sweetness before their wedding date? Or was it nothing more than a timely, seasonal treat? Devon couldn't escape the realization that love made him a fool for Mirabelle-and a fool was the other name for a trifle. Sighing, he dug out the wooden spoon set in a clever side section and tasted it. It was good.

His eyes found Mirabelle's as he swallowed the first bite, and she had the same look of pleased surprise that he did. "It's very good, isn't it?" He nodded in agreement. "My mother is very good at cooking, but it's that the mirabelles are at the height of their season right now that makes them so sweet. There is a season to everything, don't you think?" she asked, shyly. Devon murmured agreement. "Then don't you think it's the right season to taste of something sweeter than this?" she asked, and darting forward swiftly, she leaned him back against the bark of the willow and kissed him soundly. He blinked rapidly, surprised, and then let himself experience the kiss. He meant to speak up, but when he tried to open his mouth, she pressed her lips over his and he gave himself over to the moment's joys.

He had to admit, her kisses were sweeter than the trifle made of her namesake.

25

RHYS AND SHINE

Devon woke up for the early devotionals and after the pre-dawn service roused some of his fellow paladins he had spoken to the night before. The idea sat better with them in the evening than in the first rays of Rhys' light, given the groans that rose from some of his cohorts.

"How are you a follower of Rhys' when you don't want to greet the dawn?" he chided them playfully.

"Because we fight undead at night. Dawn is when you go to bed knowing the job is done and you're safe. How can you be a paladin of Rhys and not know that?" Trenton shot back, but his mood belied his words.

"He's right, you know," Catkin added. "Glad you made it back in good time,

Catkin," Devon said, giving her a small, warm smile.

"I'm not so sure I'm glad to be back with this special project you've got cooked up for us. You are so going to owe us for this," she chided, but she winked back at him as she geared up, not in her usual armor, but a temple field-hand's uniform. "So, when do we start?"

Devon looked down at her, "Right after breakfast."

The group trooped down to the main hall and gathered with the priests, priestesses, and lay folks, many of whom were similarly dressed as the paladins. The junior clergy ran out platters of food for them, each taking a table. Little Mercy was their server today and filled with giggles as she ran back and forth. That she and the others would make a game of chores was nothing new. But every time she got near Devon, she giggled harder and could barely keep her step and the food off the floor. That Happy Story, Red Sunrise, and Honey Flower were all grinning at him off and on only meant there was something up and everyone already knew about it, except him.

Glancing back at his plate, some prankster had set a single mirabelle plum in front of his trencher bread. Somehow the morning meal of bread, nut milk, and fresh fish seemed particularly engrossing to everyone around him suddenly. Giving it a sardonic look, he opted to just run with it rather than fight the tide. He asked for their help out of the blue. He could take a little ribbing in exchange. Snatching up the fruit, he popped it in his mouth and swiftly divested it of both skin and flesh, setting the pip on the edge of his plate. The fruit was incredibly sweet and called to mind the kisses Mirabelle gave him, her lips touched with the juice of the fruit of her namesake from the trifle they shared. He closed his eyes, chewing thoughtfully. He wasn't really that big on sweets, but he could come to love this fruit if such were the memories it brought with it.

When he cracked his eyes open, the activity at the table had stopped dead. "What? You put a fruit in front of me and expect me not to enjoy it?"

"Just didn't know you liked mirabelles so much," Trenton said from beside him. Meeting his look squarely, Devon admitted honestly, "Neither did I." Trenton took a deep breath in and let it out slowly, shaking his head and patting Devon on the back.

"Looks like you do have it bad, Devon. Didn't really expect that out of you. But I wish you happiness in this new journey you are embarking on." Raising his glass he called out, "To Devon!" And the hall rang with several answering cries of "To Devon."

They stacked what dishes were left onto trays before trooping out to the stable yard. Each of them fetched their magical steeds, if they had them. The others mounted more ordinary horses, and the priest and priestess hitched up a pair of donkeys to a cart in which various tools and implements were being loaded. Devon hadn't expected his request to include the Divinities and lay people, but he was grateful.

Clicking his tongue, he got his mount moving down the path from the temple and hooked a left onto the main road leading into town. It must have looked like a parade, so many folks riding through the small town at once. Several shoppers and shopkeepers came out to observe the spectacle. Devon waved to a couple early on, then did his best to imitate a statue, keeping his eyes forward. He wasn't terribly comfortable being the center of so much attention, and it would undoubtedly be worse at the wedding. The very thought made beads of sweat trickle down his neck. Well, he'd have to soldier on, that's something he did well enough.

Soon they were clear of the town and passing through the fields on the far side. As they reached the last outskirts of town, in a sparse and narrow patch of field bordering a dense wood, Devon called a halt. The rest fell in line and Devon suddenly felt sheepish. As they weren't on campaign, he wasn't actually "leading" this band on the project. No one took it amiss, however, as they all dismounted. They soon gathered about the cart, seeing what tools were on hand to determine how to best tackle the task at hand.

"So what are we going to do today?" Catkin asked as she gathered the reins for her steed and Trenton's.

"Well, I'd like to clear enough of the woods over there to have a decent field, and we must get the wood cut up for building," Devon replied.

Storm, a paladin who had arrived in from rounds the night before spoke up, "Wait, wait, you can't use green wood like that, it will shrink on you come winter."

"Actually, we're going to magically season it," Priestess Lila said. Storm looked duly impressed. Sure, you could use magic for such mundane tasks, but it was a pricy endeavor. "You lot get to saw down trees, Magnus and I will carry the timber in the cart to the mill and back as the loads are completed. One of the priests from the temple of Sigvarder will use a seasoning spell on the wood while we are in town. Valdesh is talking to the local stonemasons and a carpenter about the hearth and layout. He will join us presently. Scarwrist and Wayland will be in charge of digging post holes for the frame to be anchored in once he arrives with the plans. In the meantime, you will be helping to dig out stumps." Scarwrist's reptilian fringe rose and fell dejectedly at the news. "What Scarwrist? You didn't think it would all be battles and fishing, did you?"

"N-o-o, Priestess-ss-ss," he responded, the words sounding odd and hissing from the lizardman's mouth.

"Very well then, the rest of you may grab tools and get started, if you aren't cutting, you are digging. May Rhys bless the works of our hands today and keep us in touch with the simple beauty of the soil and the goodness of honest toil." Her blessing was brief, but there would undoubtedly be a longer one once the house was completed.

"Ambitious, don't you think, to raise a house so shortly before your wedding?" Wayland asked Devon as they carried tools towards the edge of the forest.

Devon's brown eyes met Wayland's gray- green ones. "Many hands make the work go quickly."

"Well, that they do. I suppose roping the wedding guests in as they arrive could get things done in time. Not a bad plan there, Devon. You're a more canny fellow than I gave you credit for." Wayland gave him a slap on the back as they set down their tools. Devon wasn't sure if his words were the compliment Wayland thought they were. He hadn't set out to create a workforce in announcing their wedding, but he couldn't deny the efficiency of such. His brows furrowed as his mind took the notion down a different branch. Perhaps he should ponder how to better use the skills of townspeople in the defense of their own homes against the undead. The horrors of what happened at Duskdale were still fresh, and fewer deaths to monsters would be desirable all around. Perhaps he should ask Scarwrist what his people did to defend themselves. Maybe the new paladin had fresh ideas.

"Hey Scarwrist! How about you join our group?" he called and saw the ridge of the lizardman's neck rise in response. Soon the blue and green scaled paladin made his way over to the tree he and Wayland were sizing up.

"What is-ss-ss it, Paladin Devon? I mus- ss-t ss-say, I did not ex-s-pect to dig holes when I joined Rhys-s' ranks-s."

"Being a soldier is all about digging holes," he replied, smiling as he watched the golden, slit-eyes of the tall reptilian paladin shift in the light.

"I had heard as-ss much about ss-ss- soldiers-ss, but I did not expect it to be the s- same having joined a holy order of paladins- ss," Scarwrist said, his black, forked tongue flickering out from a lip slit designed for it. It flashed out far enough that Devon saw it turn from black to purple, to a light blue towards the back. He'd never really seen a lizardman up close enough to see such details before. They had a range of colors, but then, so did humans.

Scarwrist had hints of yellow on his scales near where they turned into horny ridges or actual horns. The rest was a mottled pattern of blues and greens along his neck and tail where Devon could see, moving into pale blue bands like those of a snake's belly on the front. He wondered how closely related lizardmen were to the much less pleasant snakemen of the Northwest or the more mysterious nagas of the Eastern Islands.

"Since your part doesn't start just yet, I wondered if you could tell us how the lizardfolk deal with undead normally. With that, he and Wayland marked where they would notch the tree and a bit higher on the opposite side where the cut would be made to insure it would fall where it should.

Scarwrist's tongue flickered in and out a few times and he cocked his head oddly, before turning so he observed them with one eye and then the other. Finally he answered, "Ss-so, you truly want to know? You may not like the ans-sswer. We do not have the same ss-ss-sensibilities-ss as you do."

"I have borne many things, and as Zsofia and Quinn say, 'All knowledge makes us wiser, although not all knowledge makes us happier,'" Devon quoted.

Scarwrist's head snapped up at this, a sudden, bird-like action. "I am ss-surpris- ssed you know the words-ss of the god and goddess-ss of the Half Moon. Then again, you have us-ss engaged in ss-skilled trades- ss, eh? Perhaps-ss the wisdom is not beyond your grasp." As

Devon and Wayland set the saw into place, Devon saw Scarwrist puff out his throat, the colorful yellow and green throat flap extending as the cavity swelled with air. The lizardman's voice became deeper, more resonant and was easily heard above their sawing.

"My people live in the ss-swamp or near water. These places-ss are destructive to the undead. Water and fire are both antithetical to their kind, although fire is faster." Devon noted that Scarwrist hissed his syllables less when speaking, using his throat cavity in that fashion.

"But it does not mean we are ss-safe. They are drawn to the ss-stagnant energies and death of ss-such places-ss." Scarwrist paused, looking down, his throat deflating as some heavy memory probably crossed through his mind. It was a look most paladins wore at one time or another, although the lizardman's face was different, the look of pain was recognizable.

Gulping in more air, he continued, "They come and ss-seize our children when they can. These are our treasures-ss, rather than gold or jewels-ss. And through them they force us-ss to do battle with their enemies. Often times-s, the young are killed anyway, no matter what we do. Not just one hatching, but the offspring of many years-ss. It is terrible. And ss-so I came to the drylands-ss to ss-seek the blessings-ss of Rhys-s. My people shouldn't ss-suffer under the hand of ss-such tyrants-ss as these." Conviction rang in Scarwrist's words, and a clawed hand curled into a fist as he finished speaking. Devon and Wayland paused, taken aback by the realization that the lizardfolk were preyed upon as badly as or worse than the so-called "civilized," races of men, elves, dwarves, and the like. "I'm sorry, Scarwrist. I promise, I'll try to help the next lizardman I see," Devon replied, Wayland nodding beside him.

"I thank you, but beware if you do. Many of my kind will betray you becaus-sse they are already thralls-ss to ss-some undead master." Devon and Wayland exchanged a grim look. It wasn't a new story for paladins, but the breadth of the implications were staggering.

The first trees fell and Scarwrist and Wayland started in on digging out the roots, leaving Devon to spell Catkin and Trenton. A little while later, Valdesh arrived and called Devon over, a shovel in his hand. "I have the plans here, but as the homeowner, you should decide where the doorway will be and be the one to break ground there."

It made sense. Devon glanced over the plans, rubbing his stubbly chin with a gritty hand. Backing up, he tried to picture in his mind how it would all look once done. At last, he walked forward with the shovel and buried it into the ground. That it hit no large rocks was a good omen. He turned the shovelful of soil over and tamped it down as Valdesh came over with a small flagged stick to mark the spot. Pulling out a measuring line, Valdesh quickly laid out the dimensions, having Devon tamp in markers at all the corners and put a set of blue flagged ones inside the larger outline of the house where the hearth and chimney would be. "Good, good," Valdesh said after rising with a groan. "I'm not so used to getting up and down as much anymore. But now we have the layout. Looks like Wayland and Scarwrist are up to their eyeballs in that root hole way over there. Since you aren't partnered up, do you want to dig the corner post holes yourself? Nothing like the feeling of knowing you have set up the foundation of your own home. You will know exactly the strengths and weaknesses of it this way."

Devon looked at the older, grey-haired paladin. His words seemed to bespeak more than just the foundation of the house that lay before them. Devon knew he would have plenty of time to consider the advice as he worked. "I would be very pleased to do the honors," he replied. He dug down a good three feet into the sandy soil, Valdesh using a measuring stick to insure they were both deep enough and each one even. Seeing how much sand there was here made Devon worry that it might not make good crop soil. Looking around, he noted how very sparse the wild plants were.

Originally, he only saw it as a good, open stretch to put in a house and farm. Now he saw it for its potential shortcomings and silently cursed himself a fool for not taking more time to make his decision.

"What's eating you, Paladin Devon?" Valdesh asked at last, his eyes narrow and speculative. Devon realized he must be scowling.

Smoothing his features, he replied, "I'm just wondering what kinds of crops will grow here. Will only that stretch near the trees be any good for growing?"

Valdesh slapped the drying dust off of his hands and smiled. "Good soil doesn't just come to be overnight, Paladin Devon. Look at what you have and add what is missing."

"You do?" he replied. His family was more city oriented and fishermen rather than farmers. It's part of why he found Riverfield so charming.

"Indeed, you add what is missing to the blend, with a good helping of manure to hold it all together." Valdesh laughed as Devon gagged, sticking out his tongue. "Now I know why I haven't taken up farming before now!" Devon replied. Storm and Marsid were hauling back the first of the downed trees, soon followed by Catkin and Trenton. The Divinities helped them load the first ones, then moved the donkey cart closer to where they were cutting while Valdesh went to the field across the road to check on their mounts. Devon smiled to himself to see all the effort going into helping him get his house together to share with his soon-to-be bride. Wiping the sweat from his brow, he wondered what Mirabelle was doing for her name day.

26
MIRABELLE CHOOSES HER PATH

Mirabelle had the day off from chores and went into town with her mother to pick out a new dress. They both knew it would likely be the same one she would wear at her wedding. "Mother, I've never seen a paladin's wedding before. Do they wear their armor, or do they wear their order's tabard and sash, or something else?"

Daleen spoke, paused and let her breath out in a rush, "You know what? I'm uncertain myself. I suspect it's their choice but probably the armor or the trappings of the order, similar to what they wear at the investiture ceremony. I take it you and Devon haven't talked about the details yet?"

Mirabelle looked down to hide her face as her cheeks burned with blush, "No, the temple seems to be handling the ceremony. I figured we just had to handle the food and invitations." They walked onto the wooden planks of the seamstress' shop, lifting their skirts as they went across the slatted boards. Her mother lightly rang the bell outside as they entered.

Adelle Maron herself was in the shop's front, huddled amidst the partial mannequins that held both men and women's clothing in various stages of completion. Adelle was quite a talented seamstress, and had some following in the capital, but she said, "I can't think there, I need a peaceable atmosphere to create" and thus Riverdale gained a semi-famous denizen. Although she had grown older now, and was probably in her fourth decade like Valdesh the Younger-who was himself likely older than most of the paladins who came to him now, her dark blue eyes were still sharp in a face still handsome despite the lines. Setting her pins and swatches aside, she rose with regal grace. "Good day, Daleen, Mirabelle, to what do I owe the pleasure of your visit? Or do I know already? Were you coming to me for one of my creations for your big day?"

"Well, yes, Adelle, we were hoping you might have something already made that might suit the occasion, and yet be useable on temple days, if not more regularly," Daleen replied smoothly. Mirabelle was surprised her mother wasn't intimidated by the woman. Adelle's proud bearing and powerful, commanding presence cowed her.

"I'm glad you aren't reaching too high, darling, for my creations are often booked months in advance. These here are the culmination of three months work, and as you can see, they are only half complete. I should have them ready to ship off in time for the Winter's Night Ball in the capital, but only if I am not distracted." She spun round quickly on them. "There is also the matter of some thefts from my shop early in the spring. Little came from the constabulary, but I have my own suspicions."

She drew herself up and looked down her nose at Mirabelle, making her squirm. "However," she added, her tone softening. "We all have our phases and we all suffer the follies of youth, as long as that is where such things stay. Your wedding is an occasion of note in the town, and will be of some note among the Temples of Rhys, at least in a few small ways. I cannot spare myself, especially with such short notice for a work of moment, and I would not put forth a piece I did not have utter faith in. Thus, I am sparing for you my younger apprentice, Collette. She is young, but you may trust her instincts. She has permission to pick through some of my older prototypes. As you are young, some pieces might be useable with some altering. This, young lady, is my gift to you. You must still pay her, but you will have her undivided attention to your particular needs. I am confident she will perform marvelously for you and rise to the occasion." She said this last to Mirabelle, but then nodded to Daleen.

Mirabelle didn't know what to say to this. She and her mother had really planned on having a dress made if there were no suitable ones already available, but it seemed unwise now to even hint at such. "Thank you very much, Adelle, for your generosity," Mirabelle said instead. This seemed to strike the right chord with the woman. "Yes, yes, of course, darling. I believe you've made a wise choice for your future. Seems only fitting to send you out on that path on the right foot," so saying, she lowered herself once again amongst her mannequins and resumed her work. Speaking around the pins in her mouth, she added, "Go ring the small bell over the door to the back room that should bring Collette out."

Mirabelle and Daleen wandered away from the woman in her nest of fabric, embroidery, and lace and made their way towards a narrow doorframe. It stood beside the long, green leather seats framed by wood-paned windows running along the dark green wall of the shop on the left side. The bell pull was easier to reach here. Set just a few inches above the ledge of the chair, it sat firmly attached to the dark red-toned wood of the door frame. Collette did come flouncing down the hallway in only a few moments, pausing as she encountered the two of them there.

"Oh, I thought Adelle was calling me, can
I help you?" she asked, her bright azure eyes all eager innocence.

"Yes, I'm Daleen, and this is my daughter Mirabelle. She's getting married shortly and today is her name day, so I thought we'd get her a dress. However, Madame Adelle has clarified that we should consult with you on the matter. We'd like something formal enough for a temple wedding with a paladin, but functional enough to wear on less formal occasions if possible."

Most of the townsfolk knew each other, but Riverfield was growing large enough that not everyone recognized every single name and face. Collette may not have recognized her, but she must have told Adelle about the visit from the two women who bought nothing back in early spring. From that, Adelle probably put two and two together and recognized the girl who used to be enchanted with the lace and trappings of her store when she visited as a child. Adelle had nearly called her out on it, too! While Mirabelle had been away, the gang had clearly carried out their plans and robbed the shop. Maybe she could protest her innocence before a paladin of Sigvarder, and prove that she'd changed, but it would cause more people to look at her askance. Having that when she was trying to leave the past behind her could cause her more trouble in the future. Mirabelle was deeply grateful that Madame Adelle was willing to be forgiving.

Had the seamstress once done something she had regretted? Mirabelle wondered. Looking back at all that she knew and had learned, she admitted to herself that people could change. They did it all the time.

Even her brother's experiences differed from hers. He fell in love first and told her all about how wonderful it felt to be in love with Sasha. In the beginning, Mirabelle was jealous of the way Theovald would talk about how graceful, witty, and charming she was. The way he went on and on about her hair being as golden as ripe fields at sunset would set Mirabelle off on a fit of giggles. Sometimes he got mad or frustrated with Mirabelle, but he didn't stop talking to her.

When she finally talked to Sasha about how she felt like she was losing her brother, Sasha just smiled at her and told her she was gaining a big sister. That changed it all for her. The future looked certain and bright... and then the vampire came.

Theovald lost his first love to the monster, but took the fiend down in the end. He was only a desperate young man trying to save someone he loved. Everyone praised him, but when he came back from that place he was forever changed.

She studied the pattern on the runner carpet and twisted the toe of her shoe lightly on it.

Theovald.

He left after Sasha died. He might have saved her soul, but not her life. At first he had been despondent, barely talking to the family, and slipping away at night. Yes, she knew but didn't tell on him. She kept hoping he'd come out of it and be his old self again. Then there was suddenly something he had to do, and he wandered away to join the paladins of the Order of Rhys. She was still scared what might be out there and felt safer when her brother was around, but he just left her. And she cried, then got angry at him. And... oh my.

Her heart sank lower as she realized what really attracted her to Jarick. She wanted to get back at her oh so pure and holy brother for abandoning her. He left her to the monsters, so she decided to run in the shadows to snub him. Then what Jarick did, giving her to Lee like that, right in front of Devon! Ugh! It was horrible, and stupid, and yet Devon was still here. It spoke of his quality, but what did all this say about hers? She wished she could take the whole thing back, but would she be here now if things hadn't gone as they did? She didn't know. But did he think he was saving her? Did she need saving?

Mirabelle lifted her eyes enough to steal a guilty look at her mother where she chatted up Collette. Her family knew she was mixing it up with a bad crowd, but didn't stop her. Maybe they saw how well that worked with Theovald. But whatever he did at night, it wasn't this. Was she really a bad person? Looking further back, looking at her life, she decided no; she wasn't. She may have done something stupid, but she spent most of her life being kind to her parents, her brother, everyone. And that was the real Mirabelle. The real Mirabelle was worthy of marriage to a paladin and deserved a good life.

For so long, she had been just reacting to everything, not looking past the moment. Not seeing where she could wind up or what she wanted for herself, but now the future came calling. It was time she set her own hands to the reins of her life and turned this horse the way she wanted it to go. She'd show Devon just how good a choice he made.

"Are you crying?" Collette's voice rose and made Mirabelle's head jerk up suddenly.

Scrubbing at her cheeks, she said, "I'm just overwhelmed by Mistress Adelle's generosity." She heard some shifting amidst the fabric of Adelle's nest behind her to her right.

"I was just explaining to Collette that we probably wanted a simple print with a bit of embroidery at the hems so it would look nice but be functional after the ceremony," her mother said.

"No. Let's take his breath away," Mirabelle blurted. Her mother looked stunned, but Collette clapped her hands together with glee.

"Are you sure about this, Mirabelle?" her mother asked, her brows creasing in puzzlement.

"Yes, mother. Devon's going to look resplendent in his armor or in the formal temple vestments, I should match him, not appear a drab bird in comparison. The temple is going all out on our behalf, and his, to be fair, and everyone will attend since it's a rare event to get to be a part of a paladin's wedding. Let's make it worthy of their memory. I want to start off on the right foot, appearing as his equal partner in this, not somehow inferior to him. Can you help us do that, Collette?" She added the last as she turned towards the bright-eyed blonde girl. Collette was already rubbing her hands together in anticipation.

"Oh, oh yes! I'll go over to the temple today and be sure to find out exactly what he's choosing and match the patterns and colors. It won't be exactly alike, as you aren't joining the Temple after all! This is a wedding, not the investiture of a layperson, but you're right, it is close in ceremony. Everyone will be there. I promise, I won't let you down!" Collette grabbed her hand, nearly bowing over it in her excitement. If it weren't so cramped in the hallway, Mirabelle was certain the girl would have jumped up and down for joy. And here she thought she was the one getting married!

A bemused smile reached her lips even as the tears dried on her cheeks. She didn't even realize Adelle had come up behind her until the older woman's shadow fell across her. Turning to look over her shoulder, Mirabelle saw the woman give a small nod of approval, "Did I not tell you Collette would be full of vibrant energy? Collette, dear, you are welcome to go through my prototypes from two seasons ago. I think there are some pieces there that will help, given your theme. As for you, Mirabelle, I'm sure you will make a lovely bride. You are correct; you are stepping forward into a new life with a man of high station. Impress upon everyone that new status and doors will open for you that were previously shut. Just realize, what you choose your appearance to be like is what you will have to do your best to become, so choose wisely. It is a rare second chance for a woman to come into her own via ceremony rather than having to swim upstream to create that path. Hearing you now, I believe you can do this. You will come to my shop later when you do decide to have another dress made, yes?"

Mirabelle turned to face the woman and realized she was offering an olive branch in full. "Yes, of course Adelle. It's the least I could do." Adelle's chin rose and her eyes narrowed some but softened at the edges. "It's settled then. If you make a good enough impression, you may be find families in the capital willing to foster some of your children… at least among those who are related to the servants of Rhys. Riverfield is not the farthest point on the frontier any longer. Show them what you and your hometown have to offer," Adelle added, her gimlet gaze sharp and shining.

Children? Did this woman think so far ahead? Taking a deep breath, Mirabelle stood up straight and did her best to take her place among the amazing women in her life like her mother and Adelle. "I will," Mirabelle.

Looking back on her childhood, Mirabelle realized that she would finally be the person she had always dreamed of being. She breathed in the mantle of adulthood and mentally prepared herself to become an upstanding member of society. She would shine and be a proud of whom she was.

"Then I leave you to it Mirabelle, Collette, Daleen." Adelle nodded to Mirabelle's mother as an equal before returning to her nest of fabric once more. The woman didn't smile much, but you knew when she approved. "Let's get started!" Collette said and drew them by their elbows over to the far side of the shop. Mirabelle did not understand what she would end up with for a dress, but she looked forward to seeing Collette's creations.

At least two hands-breadth of sunlight had gone by the time she and her mother walked out of the shop. She felt a bit dazed after the whirlwind of fabric swatches, colored stones, glass beads, and mother-of-pearl buttons. Her mother had pursed her lips at the increasingly exotic, and thus expensive, items, but Collette had laughed at her expression and promised that if they used some prototypes as a base, the cost would be less. That seemed to provide Daleen with a measure of relief, but now Mirabelle felt thirsty and her stomach gave a small growl of hunger.

Daleen laid an arm around her shoulder and said, "How about we stop for a soda water before we go? It's been a long day already."

Mirabelle looked up into her mother's smiling face, catching a warm look in her dark blue eyes. Mirabelle realized she couldn't remember the last time either of her parents had hugged her without being worried about her. It was before she got into a relationship with Jarick, and long before her vigil keeping at the Temple. She had not realized how much she missed it until it was there again. On impulse, she wrapped one arm around her mother's waist and hugged her tight.

"I'd like that." Together they crossed the street to the apothecary's shop.

Pazel Wormwood ran the town apothecary shop and his family was actually known for their shops in the various towns from here to the capital. Pazel himself was behind the counter. His blonde hair was going grey at the roots, what was left on his head at least. He had added a few more wrinkles the past couple of winters, but his pale green eyes were still bright and his hands were steady.

Mirabelle realized he might have been handsome in his day with those unusual eyes of his. To her he had always been the funny shopkeeper and potion maker with a quick quip or greeting for every guest who walked through his door.

"Ah, little Mirabelle! Well, not so little anymore perhaps as you are getting married soon. Ah, you littles grow up much too fast these days. What can I get you and your lovely sister, today?"

Mirabelle couldn't help giggling and she caught her mother coughing into her hand and suspected she nearly did the same.

Daleen answered for them. "We'd like a pair of soda waters, please."

"Ah," he replied, nodding sagely. "Thirsty work looking at dresses. Would you like it flavored or plain? And what flavor if so?"

Mirabelle gasped. "How did you know we were looking at dresses?"

He shook his head, bemused. "When a woman goes to Adelle's most fashionable shop just before her wedding day, what else could it be? It is directly across the street, you know." His eyes twinkled with delight as Mirabelle dropped her face into hand, her fingers resting on her forehead as she realized how obvious it must have been.

"I would like raspberry syrup in mine if you still have some," Daleen went on smoothly.

"I'd like mirabelle in mine today, if you don't mind," Mirabelle added, blushing.

Pazel reached down into his special, magically cooled chest and pulled out a couple of chilled glasses for them, filling them with soda water and flavoring before setting them back in. "If you get any sweeter, your new husband will want to eat you up!" Mirabelle's newfound experiences over the past year brought new meaning to the man's innocent words, and she flushed all the more.

"Ah, now, now, save the blushing for the big day! And don't fret. I have not met a paladin who has a truly mean bone in his body. And those who follow Rhys are warmer than those who follow the god of Justice, Sigvarder. It will be all right." With that he pulled the pleasantly chilled drinks out and set them on the glass top of their filigreed metal table. Most places had wood, but Wormwood's had painted metal tables and chairs. He explained that the glass tops were much safer for setting potions on and easier to clean. But Mirabelle always thought it exotic and a special treat to sit at them.

Sipping at her beverage, she realized that this would be one of her last moments with her mother as nothing more than one of her children. Soon she'd be setting up her own household. Or would she? She paused and stared off into space, trying to picture life with Devon.

"What's the matter, Mirabelle?" Daleen cocked her head to one side, her own drink forgotten in her hands.

"I realized... I don't know where Devon and I will live after we get married. You don't think he expects us to live at the Temple, do you? Or worse, move away?" She shivered at the thought.

"Haven't you talked about this with him at all?" her mother asked.

Mirabelle rubbed her shoulders with both hands, suddenly chilled by the thought of moving away. Devon wasn't a local boy, he might have property elsewhere. "Well, he asked me about what kind of household I dreamed of having when I was a kid, but that's not the same thing at all." She looked at her mother, unhappiness pulling her face down into a frown.

"Well, then that is something you should definitely talk to him about. Where is Devon today, anyway? I did not think he would miss your name day."

"I don't know. Maybe he's planning to stop by after dinner? He might have some duties to attend to at the Temple. I really never asked my brother what he had to do when he wasn't riding circuit or on holiday with us." Mirabelle looked out of the windows of the shop, scanning the street for any sign of Devon, but there were few people walking about outside. Maybe he was in one of the shops selecting a gift for her? She wondered what he would choose. Then again, he might just give her another pledge and nothing. Or would he kiss her again? That sent another shiver of a different kind across her skin.

"Are you okay, Mirabelle?" her mother asked.

She rubbed her hands more briskly over her upper arms to cover it. "Just the soda water, I think. I must have drunk it too fast."

Her mother chuckled at that. "Well, let's get home and make you a proper name day dinner. We should be sure to make enough for Devon in case he comes to share the meal with you instead of visiting after we're done."

Mirabelle ducked her head, realizing her mother was right, if he showed up he'd probably like to stay and celebrate her name day with her. "Yes, let's do that."

27
NAME DAY

They called a halt to the work when the sun was a good four hands-breadths above the horizon. Most everyone was tired, and the Divinities had to make preparations for evening vespers and bless the evening meal. Given how much work everyone did, Devon expected the kitchen would be picked bare. Wiping the sweat from his brow, he realized he had the additional responsibility of visiting Mirabelle still. He didn't hold out much hope for his well-being if he missed it. They rode back together and cared for the mounts before adjourning to the bathing chambers. Trenton and the other guys razzed him while throwing cleaning sponges at him between groans of soreness or relief from the hot bath. A hint of noise from the behind the wall between their bath and the women's bathing chamber got Wayland's attention.

"You don't think Trinity trotted in there, do you?" He looked genuinely puzzled as he stared at the side wall.

"You don't expect her to get curried down like a horse by the young lay-servants do you?" Trenton asked dryly.

Splashing as he returned to the stairs that also acted as a seating bench, he replied, "Well, no, but wouldn't her hooves damage the stone? And one slip in there and she would probably break something."

"I'd trust her to manage herself safely. She runs courier for groups all day long. I'm sure she's dealt with worse," Marsid said from under the small towel he had over his eyes.

Wayland threw up his hands, "Okay, okay, I'm just not used to centaurs in bath houses. Sounds kind of like a bull in a porcelain shop to me."

Devon finished up and toweled off saying, "Best hope she can't hear you comparing her to an ordinary beast of the field through that wall." Wayland suddenly looked wary, much to everyone's amusement. "Guess you'll find out at dinner if she brings a lance."

"At least you'll be there to take the strike for me," Wayland countered.

"Alas, no. It is my lady's name day and I'll have my head on a pike next to yours if I miss it, I wager."

"A sad pair we'll make as we stand before Rhys laid low by the women in our lives." Wayland set his hands on his hips and shook his head sadly as Devon dressed.

Devon waited until he had buckled his belt and had his boots on before playfully adding, "I didn't know you and Trinity were courting." Wayland sent an arc of water his way, but Devon swiftly ducked out the door and heard it splash down the inner side of it as he set off down the hall to the back entrance. From there he headed to the stables. Mouth-watering aromas rose from the dining hall, and he was sad to miss it. He only hoped that he wouldn't wind up missing dinner altogether. Saddling his mystic steed, River Dancer, he headed out towards Mirabelle's house. The dapple grey snorted at him for dragging her away from her own dinner, but trotted along amicably enough at the promise of a treat at the end.

He rode halfway up the path but tied River Dancer up there rather than riding all the way. If he took her along any further, he'd have to tie her to the fruit trees or grapevines. That would probably end badly both for the plant and the horse, not to mention his standing with his future in-laws. River Dancer might be a mystic steed, and thus smarter than the average horse, but as the breeders warned, that doesn't make them 'good' nor would it stop them from giving into temptation if left to their own devices. "I'll bring you back some when we leave, okay?"

River Dancer snorted and pawed at the ground irritably. "How about a nose bag for now?" This seemed to get her attention as her ears cocked forward.

He had a small amount of emergency grain and rations in his saddlebags, so he used the grain now to placate his long-suffering companion. He only hoped that he wouldn't be stuck eating his emergency rations tonight. She really was a good and steady mount, unlike Trenton's cocky, vain Silverlight. That horse was too smart by half. He was a handful for Trenton and acted just like him, much to Trenton's annoyance some days. Devon smiled as he patted River Dancer before finishing his walk up the familiar path.

Knocking on the doorframe, he tugged at the base of his tunic, trying to even it out. he was in such a hurry to get here that he didn't take as many pains as he probably should have with his appearance. Reaching a hand up reflexively to rub his scalp, he realized he hadn't cut his hair yet either, and he probably had a day's growth of beard on his chin now. Well done, Devon! He chided himself. But the door opened and burst in on his musings.

"Ah, Victor-Paladin Devon, we hoped you might stop by tonight. You're in time to share a bit of food with us if you like. We're on seconds, but there is plenty left," Alarick said. His brown hair sun-touched from his harvesting efforts.

Victor-Paladin? Devon wondered if he were interrupting or if they had expected him before now with such a formal greeting. Stepping in, he sketched a half-bow from the waist for both Daleen and Mirabelle. For once, Mirabelle seemed happy enough to see him. Perhaps Fate arranged things so he couldn't be in good standing with both her and her parents at the same time. However, Daleen seemed pleased enough to have him join them. He did his best to shove his wayward thoughts to the back of his mind as he sat down and found a setting already waiting for him. A fine baked ham lay on the cutting board before him with a mix of roasted vegetables in a thick gravy made from the ham drippings and a fresh apple pie lay steaming on the sideboard.

"Well, dig in, good Sir. We can't have our daughter's future husband wasting away to nothing before the wedding," Alarick said, settling back into his own chair. "Don't you have anything you'd like to say, Mirabelle?"

"Thanks for coming over for my name day," she said at last.

Devon paused and finished his meal prayer silently before meeting her deep blue eyes. "I am grateful to be here for it. I hope you will pardon my lateness."

"Nonsense, we were busy all day ourselves with preparations for the wedding. Did the Temple keep you busy all afternoon?" Mirabelle asked him.

"More like I kept the Temple busy today," he replied before applying himself to his food. After a full day of back-breaking work, the meal tasted like it was mana from the hand of Rhys herself. He made noises of appreciation, but couldn't bring himself to stop and converse just yet. They had a light repast at the height of the day, but it had burned off long before now.

Mirabelle finally burst out with, "Are we going to stay in Riverfield once we wed or will you be moving us away to wherever you are from?" Devon blinked rapidly, taken aback. Daleen and Alarick were leaning in, so the topic must have been on the table before he arrived.

Swallowing, he told her, "The answer involves your name day present. I hoped to surprise you, but if the matter has been bothering you, I can answer you best by showing you."

"You can't just tell me the answer?" she asked in an exasperated tone.

In reply, he stood and wiped his mouth with the cloth napkin provided and set his plate aside. Turning to Daleen, he said, "The food is excellent. I hope I might return to finish it, if it pleases you, but as I arrived late, it seems it is the hour of presenting gifts. Since this gift can't come to Mirabelle, may I have your permission to bring her to her gift?"

Daleen looked at him speculatively, but seemed to have already guessed the answer. "Ask your bride-to-be, Devon. She is the one who would have to go out with you, but I'll not object. Let me set your plate near the fire to stay warm. Will you be long?"

"It may take some time. Likely only a hand span, but no less either," he replied. At Mirabelle's a-hem, he focused his attention back to her and could hear her foot tapping under the table. Not a good sign. He needed to pull out his best courtly manners. "My dear lady, would you be so good as to accompany me to see the gift I have secured on this occasion of your name day? Although I fear it will have to suffice as your bridal gift."

Curiosity proved stronger than her temper and her foot slowed, then stopped. "Where is this gift at?"

"Come, I'll show you." With that, Devon crossed over to the door and held it open for her. She walked through, arms crossed, ready to be unimpressed. He sighed. Her moods tended to be mercurial, and he likely read her signals wrong. Hopefully she would like the home he was having built as it was not a gift he could take back.

"Okay, we are outside. Where have you stashed this wondrous thing? Is it a boat to carry us away down the river?"

He had to laugh at that. "No Mirabelle. I'm not stealing you away without warning from everything you've ever known. Does that set your heart at ease?"

"No, it just means you'll give notice first," she replied tartly.

"I come to join you here. I believe I mentioned something to that effect long ago when first I proposed to you."

Spinning around to face him beneath the trees of her namesake, she said, "No, I'm sure where we would live never came up."

Reaching up, Devon plucked a couple of ripe fruits from the tree over her head. "Then allow me to rectify that. I come to join you, Mirabelle. If your heart is here, then here is where we shall remain."

Her arms came free slowly from their tight hold and dropped loosely to her sides. "Can't you just speak plainly from the outset? Why all these games?"

"I do not mean to play games with you, I only wished to surprise you. Have no fears, Mirabelle," Devon said as he gathered her into his arms. He felt her stiffen in surprise, but then shiver at his touch. "Are my arms about you unwelcome?" he asked, pushing them apart slightly.

"No, it's just, you haven't come to me before like this. I'm usually the one throwing myself at you."

"Waiting makes it sweeter, does it not?" He leaned in close again, raising his hand to rest against her neck as he murmured against her dark tresses. "Do you think I do not desire you, Mirabelle? Nothing could be farther from the truth." He breathed in. The scent of her, the hearth fire, and the sweet blossoms rose along with his desire. To keep control of himself, he broke off their embrace.

Confused, Mirabelle asked, "Why did you stop?"

"Because, you'll never meet my paladin steed, River Dancer if we stand here all day."

"Oh," she said, surprised, and looked down the path to where the dappled mare stood. She had managed to get free from her nosebag as the ones the paladins used were designed to breakaway at need and was merrily chewing away at the few tufts of grass she could reach.

Going up to her Devon retrieved her fallen nosebag and untying her said, "This is Mirabelle, I'm going to marry her so be on your best behavior, okay?" The big grey mare snorted and looked around at Mirabelle, her ears twitching. Mirabelle came up slowly, moving at an angle towards the horse's side so she could see her. Raising her hand out, she let the dappled mare sniff her. The animal gave a deep whuff sound, then turned her head back towards the branch she was tied to and gave a little toss of her mane, a ripple moving down her chest and withers, making the few flies attempting to bite her take to the air.

"She's lovely. I've only ever seen one true paladin's mount up close, and that's my brother's gelding, Noble Heart. But he never keeps him in our stable when he visits. So I've only met the animal a few times. He said there were rules about it." As she spoke, she reached a hand out to gently stroke River Dancer's withers, and Devon kept an eye on River Dancer to make sure things went well. The magical mounts of paladins were smarter than average horses and had the ability to be sent to and summoned from the sacred, secret pasturelands where they were bred, but they were still animals and required careful attention. Battle-trained, they were formidable in the field. If they didn't like someone or felt threatened, the person in question could become badly injured or killed.

However, River Dancer tended towards a very placid and steady temperament. She didn't have the vim and vigor of Trenton's Silverlight, nor the sleek lines and speed of Catkin's blood bay,

Dayspring, but she was solid and didn't spook easily. Given the creatures he faced in the field that was a real blessing.

"Want to really win her over?" Devon asked.

"Sure, what do I need to do?" Mirabelle replied.

Handing her one of the fruits he plucked, he said, "Pull out the pip and offer her the fruit. Just keep your hand flat like you would with an ordinary horse. They may have magical properties, but most of these fellows are greedy guts, that's why I tied her up away from your fruit trees."

Mirabelle giggled at this and bit the top of the fruit with her teeth, expertly peeling back the flesh and removing the pip with a minimum of mess. Devon's thoughts took off in an entirely unwholesome direction watching her, so he turned towards his mount and closed his eyes as he duplicated the process. It took more force of will not to imagine other things as he worried the fruit with his teeth. The scent of mirabelles filled the air and his mount bumped him with her nose, sniffing eagerly. Opening his eyes, he said, "Not yet." To Mirabelle he added, "See what I mean? She'd like just about anyone who gave her treats." He had Mirabelle hold hers out first and River Dancer quickly lipped it up and had it gone in short order. His mount turned to him, looking at him hopefully while trying to act coy at the same time. Laughing, he gave over and offered his treat.

"Forgiven, now?" he asked the horse. She blew out her lips and checked his other hand in search of more. "See? Greedy, lovely beast."

Untying the reins, he said to Mirabelle, "We must ride double a ways, is that okay with you? It's unfortunately too far to walk and get back before dark."

"I can probably manage that okay. Are you going to tell me where we're going?" she asked as he mounted and helped pull her up behind the saddle.

"To the other side of town," he answered. Clicking his tongue and pulling gently on the reins, Devon got River Dancer moving at a gentle walk down the hill. "Are you comfortable? I'd like to get River Dancer up to a trot on the main road if that's all right."

"Yes, I'm fine. Your saddle's actually shorter than I expected it to be, but there's plenty of room for me. I won't slide off, I promise,"

Mirabelle said from behind him. "Very good then, my lady. Let us go riding together." Devon got River Dancer moving at a good pace and felt Mirabelle's arms slide around his waist as they rode on. Although perfectly natural, his thoughts had not completely recovered from their earlier imaginings and suddenly he was very aware of her body right behind his. He just hoped her hands wouldn't stray with the horse's jouncing step and betray his thoughts all too well to her. They weren't married yet.

He thought fortune was with him when they reached the edge of the shops and passed them without incident. As they rode past the last farms, the clear framework of the house showed in the golden afternoon light. Devon dismounted stiffly, and heard Mirabelle gasp and say, "It's so big!"

Panic filled him as he realized she must have noticed as he pulled his leg over to dismount. Stammering he said, "I... it's... I didn't mean for you to notice."

Puzzled, she asked, "How could I not? You brought me out here to see it, didn't you?"

Devon rocked back on his heels. Did she really think he brought her out here alone to expose himself to her before their wedding? Or worse, ravish her on her name day? "I... I swear to you I did not bring you here with any form of ill intention!"

She moved her head back a bit as if trying to focus on him better. "Devon, what are you talking about?" Then realization seemed to dawn on her and she sputtered with laughter, startling River Dancer with the sudden noise, making her shift and dance in place. At last she gulped enough air to say, "Devon. I was looking at the house!"

Finally, he understood that he had been his own undoing. Flustered and flushing, he bowed his head, his hands clenched at his sides in shame. He heard Mirabelle dismount and felt her wrap her arms around him from the side. "Hey, it's no bad thing to have a desire for your bride-to-be, my paladin." He glanced over at her, tears welling up in his eyes, and looked away again. Her voice softened when she spoke to him again. "Hey, there, there now. You didn't hurt me and you didn't offend me. After everything you've gone through for me, do you truly think I would be upset by so simple and ordinary a thing by you? You are still a man, my paladin, and you are allowed to be human. Worry not about it. Why not show me this place that I am certain was not here yesterday."

Swallowing hard, he took the avenue of escape she offered and found his voice choked and thready when he tried to speak. "The other paladins and I, along with half the Temple, came out to begin work on our future home. I've purchased the land, and based on your description, we had an architect draw up plans. I hope you will like it. It is ours and my gift for you."

His voice grew stronger by the end. He tried to surreptitiously wipe his cheeks, but she still saw. "I think it's lovely, Devon. And where they cleared the forest away, we can plant fruit trees, the land is already good for it. Thank you, my love." With that, she leaned up and kissed his cheek. That she called him "her paladin" would have been enough, but she finally accepted his love for her and admitted her own for him. Reaching down his hand, he raised her chin and kissed her fully on the mouth, allowing his soul to speak to her through that kiss. Facing her fully, he continued to press his lips against her sweet, full ones and let his hands pull her against his taller frame, heedless of what may come. They stood there, lost in a glorious embrace for untold amounts of time. When he finally came back to his senses, the sun was resting on the horizon and River Dancer had wandered into the field in front of the frame of the house to graze.

Pulling away felt almost painful, so tender and perfect was the moment they had lost themselves in. Her sigh at their separation echoed his thoughts, and he stayed poised over her, his brown eyes searching her blue ones, memorizing the scent of her body, the softness of her skin, the way her black tresses caressed her face and cascaded over her shoulders. "Mirabelle," he breathed her name as softly as the breeze that blew past them.

"Yes?" she answered, her body still where it pressed against his.

"I think it is time we went back, your parents will wonder."

"You're probably right," she answered, yet neither of them attempted to move away. Devon knew she would let him do whatever he desired to at that moment, nay, she would gladly and willingly join him if he asked, and that knowledge stayed his hand.

Lowering his arm, he took her hand and led her to where River Dancer stood cropping grass and silently helped her up behind the saddle before mounting himself. They rode back silently, lost in their separate thoughts but their bodies touching as he rode back. If this was what lay ahead of him, he finally believed that married life might suit him.

28

THEOVALD'S SECRET

The next two weeks were a whirlwind of preparations. Devon and the other paladins worked on raising the house during the day, and he polished his armor at night. Duties to the Temple, greeting new arrivals for the wedding, and dinner with Mirabelle and her parents filled his so called "spare time" and he often fell into his bed having barely finished a single piece of his armor each night. It took him two to finish shining his breastplate. For all of his effort, he knew Mirabelle was even busier as all the other preparations fell on her, well the ones that weren't being handled by the Temple.

His visits with Mirabelle were brief and often filled with questions that he did his best to answer, but truth be told, sometimes he had to guess. Organizing a wedding had to be as hard as setting up a new barracks.

This morning brought in the one guest they had been waiting for and when Devon saw him enter the dining hall, he immediately stood up and strode over to him, clasping him in a congenial embrace, slapping him lightly on the back.

"Theovald! You made it. I thought you'd be at least another week!" Devon exclaimed, happy to see his friend for the first time in at least a year.

Theovald hugged him back before pulling his helmet off, freeing dark blonde hair that hung down to his shoulders after months in the field. "Well, we hit a patch of good weather and after that fracas you had in Duskdale, things have been exceptionally quiet." Theovald threw an arm over Devon and walked back to his table, taking a spot next to him and loading up a plate with ham, eel, eggs, and fresh slices of brown bread. Happy Story brought fresh cider around, and Red Sunrise gave him an open salt to use. Theovald nodded to the boy and said, "You've shot up a bit since the last time I saw you. Won't be long until you get to pick your adult name, will it?" The little freckled face lit up, a quick smile touching his lips.

"It will be awhile yet, Sir, but Priest Magnus says if I don't study harder I might have to call myself rock." The boy looked fairly unrepentant at the admission.

Smearing some honey butter on the bread, Theovald told the boy, "Well, if that happens, go with Cliff. It still means rock, but sounds more impressive."

The boy laughed and gave a jaunty wave as he resumed his duties, dark red hair bobbing between the rows of tables. "I forget you grew up here and still know everyone," Devon said at last, eyes following the young lay members as they made a game of bringing drinks and clearing tables.

Downing some food with a big gulp of cider, Theovald said, "Yes, I enjoy coming home and seeing everyone. The kids here are shaping up, but it's up to us to keep them safe."

Turning his head towards his friend, Devon asked in a low voice, "Is there something you suspect?"

Theovald slowed his chewing and finally stopped. Meeting Devon's gaze, his normally sky-blue eyes took on a grey cast that he got when serious or worried. "Something happened last year. I turned in a report, but there were a few details I left out." That wasn't like the Theovald that Devon knew at all. His friend's eyes scanned the room as if there were more to see than the paladins, the young lay clergy, and the usual members of the Temple. "I'll tell you about it later."

After Theovald finished his meal, they went out together to the stables, grabbed their mounts, and began riding towards town. "So what is it that you felt you couldn't say in front of everyone else in there, Theovald?" Devon asked, his voice heavy with concern.

Sighing, Theovald nudged Noble Heart closer and said, "That encounter we had up in Battleforge the end of last summer, we..." His words drifted off and Devon looked at him askance. Theovald was the more eloquent one. "I saw Sasha."

That got his attention. "Her ghost, you mean?"

"Yes." Theovald wouldn't look at him, but studied the mane on his horse rather studiously. "When at last the dawn was just cresting the tops of the mountain and the light crept across the tops of the trees but didn't yet reach the bottom, she took out the last few shades that lingered.

Devon could see why he might want to keep that out of his report. Sasha's ghost might be benevolent, but she was still undead. If anyone in the hierarchy ordered her to be put down, it would drive Theovald mad. She was the reason he became a paladin, Devon knew. "Have you seen her since?"

"No." The golden head bowed lower. "Neither have I, but I have wondered if she might be around." Devon nudged River Dancer into the lead. Noble Heart was a good steed, but if Theovald didn't pay attention, the horse would prefer to head towards a field or even back to the Temple rather than through the noise of town.

"The thing is, a greater undead, a Lich orchestrated the attack on Battleforge. And he wanted me, but didn't get me. The odds are good he's going to come after me or my family." Now he raised his head and looked Devon dead in the eye. "And that means you and my sister and parents."

Devon nodded. "The attack in Duskdale was by a greater undead. We've been having the Divinities use shield prayers at night at the borders of the town. It's highly unlikely an attack will come while so many of us are gathered in one place, but it isn't impossible either. I'm more worried about afterward. If someone goes missing soon after a celebra- tion, everyone will assume they lingered a bit. And in the course of a couple of days, a lot can happen."

Theovald's scowl matched his own. They'd both been in the field long enough to know the truth of what could and would happen to such an unlucky soul. What Devon saw at Duskdale was nothing. That was a greater undead having to rush. Just the thought of what such monsters would do if they had the chance to take their time turned his stomach. It was hard to believe such creatures were once men.

Now Theovald thought he had one stalking him? Given that he took out a vampire before he even became a paladin, it was entirely possible. Paladins were always targeted, though; it came with the job. However, where ordinary folks were often victims, paladins could fight back, and effectively. Saving others from the terrors of the night was their entire mission.

The pair quieted as they entered the town proper, and seeing some activity going on that was clearly related to his upcoming nuptials broke Devon out of his brooding. There were always dangers. Life was a risk, but it didn't mean you shouldn't enjoy the good side of it while you could. Forewarned meant forearmed, and he would make sure the Divinities here knew that the town should be under special watch.

Once they reached the edge of the fields and the new house came into view, Theovald whistled and said, "Looks like I don't have to worry about you taking care of my sister. That's a fine looking new home. Guess I'd better worry about a proper wedding and housewarming gift. Maybe I'll get you two a good winter quilt so you won't get cold when the weather turns."

Devon flushed at him and Mirabelle sharing the same bed. Having been friends for a long time, Theovald caught on quickly, "Oh-ho, I take it you don't expect you'll be needing a quilt to get warm."

"I won't always be there," he mumbled back.

Theovald sighed heavily. "Yes, that's true. That's what worries me. Maybe between us we'll keep them all alive."

Devon regretted weighing down his friend with worry again. "Instead of a quilt, perhaps a blessed holy symbol of Rhys for the front and back doors?"

His friend managed a slight smile, "Maybe. Maybe both. Faith won't keep you warm in winter."

"You're too generous, Theo." "You're marrying my sister, Devon."

"You're not generous enough then, Theo," Devon shot back, and they both busted out laughing. How he missed their academy days sometimes. Riding back into town Devon asked, "Do you want to visit with Mirabelle now or wait until dinner?"

"I still need to get those gifts for you two, and I'd like to get cleaned up, shaved, and my hair cut before coming to see my parents. My mother will never let me down if I arrive for dinner looking so shaggy. I will catch up with all of you later."

"Okay, my friend." They shook hands and Theovald quickened Noble Heart's pace, leaving Devon to his own thoughts. He reined River Dancer around to head past his new homestead and into the woods beyond. The house was mostly done, a few pieces of furniture were arriving and the locksmith was creating locks and keys for the doors. For all that Mirabelle may have once run with the thieves of this town, it did not mean she would be safe from their predations. Not to mention that Devon wanted neither thieves nor undead bothering his new wife in their new home.

The woods were a mix of birch, ash, larch, maple, alder, bull laurel and oak. The yellow tops of a few tall willows were in the mix, but the serrated willows were not in attendance. They preferred to be closer to water. A few black alders, white spruces, and pines struggled here and there, while mushrooms, serviceberries and a few wintergreen plants nestled at their roots between patches of ferns growing over any spot where one of their fellows had fallen.

He supposed they could gather acorns and see if they were edible or not. Further north, where the oaks were mixed in heavily with pines, the nuts became so full of tannin that they were bitter. You could boil them repeatedly to get the bitterness out, but he rather doubted Mirabelle had that kind of patience. The maples might produce sweet sap, but although he knew some of them were sweet, he couldn't really tell which kind were which. Paladins were rarely in the same place long enough to need to worry about them as a source of sustenance.

Riding through, he wasn't certain what he was looking for, but chided himself on not bothering to explore the woods close to the property ahead of time. Then again, there hadn't been a great deal of time to worry about such things. His life usually involved an unvarying routine of riding circuit, reporting, attending services, and getting supplies to start all over again. There were moments of action, but much of it was quiet and contemplative, even on the road. Ever since he arrived in Riverfield this time around, his whole life had taken a side trail that made him wonder if he'd ever get back on his old path again.

His head moved in automatic sweeps, his eyes watching for telltale signs of disturbance by man or beast. Deer tracks he noted and glossed over, rabbit and birds and well. Finally, he saw it, bits of bone sticking out of the leaf cover. The telltale curve of a human skull lay nearly hidden by the gold and brown leaf litter of fall, but there was no mistaking it for anything else. Dismounting, he pulled his sword from his pack and wished now that he had Theovald with him. Instead, he gave a command to River Dancer, and the horse came alive, ready to fight.

Devon no more than held his blade towards the pile, before it lit up with a violet glow, warning him of the presence of the negative energy of the undead. Before he could even draw it back for a strike, the ground erupted beneath his feet and from under the hooves of his horse. He could hear River Dancer screaming a challenge even as she slid sideways off the skeletons pouring out of the ground beneath them.

The damned things were well hidden here, beneath the leaves and below the canopy of trees, from nearly any hint of sunlight during the day. Crawling on all fours, Devon attempted to get free of the loose soil and grasping claws of the skeletons, pulling themselves out of the ground all around him. His legs were nearly useless and kept sliding, only his arms had solid purchase still. The long tunic he wore today tried to hold him back and cut against his neck as he scrabbled to get to his knees.

River Dancer shot out with both hind legs at the rising skulls beside her, shattering them into powder. The remaining pieces scattered as the magic giving them unlife fled the lifeless corpses. She was up and wheeling upon the next pair in a breath, her teeth pulled an arm free from the shoulder even as claws raked her flank. Her squeal of pain jolted Devon and adrenaline poured strength into his limbs. He jumped from kneeling to standing all at once and swung his sword at the original skeleton he spotted.

It hissed at him and clacked its jaws menacingly even as his blade melted through the bones of its reaching forearms. The Blessing of Rhys made his blade cut through undead like a hot knife going through butter, but the thing was not incapacitated yet. It battered at him with its humerus bones, then went for his jugular with its teeth. Had he not gotten his sword up into a salute position as he got to his feet, its blade rising straight before his face, he would have been dead. Instead, the skull was neatly cleaved into two halves. The split halves fell upon his face, causing him to scream in fear even as the power that animated it left. It was the closest one had ever gotten to him. Heart racing, he pushed the inert form off of his chest onto the ground. The pieces of its skull had fallen to either side of him, carried forward by the momentum of its attack a mere moment before. From the leaf litter of the forest in front of him rose more and more skeletons, their moldering clothes and armor dropping off as they pulled themselves free of the worms and earth. Devon's stomach slowly dropped at the increasing number rising before him. Farther back, just left of the middle of his field of vision stood the clear forms of a flesh zombie and a skin zombie, the creations that only a greater undead or a very twisted necromancer would make, the kind that were done when the monster could take its time with the victim.

They were rare, by necessity. Most victims raised by a lich were zombies for bulk fighters and skeletons for swift shock troops. These others were experiments, pet projects, things done to impress others of their kind, or to prepare for a war, and here he was, alone. As he represented quite the target and prize, his odds looked worse by the second.

He couldn't survive this on his own.

Too many of the creatures moved to block his access to River Dancer even as he assessed the situation. He only had one chance. Giving a special, high-pitched whistle, he watched River Dancer's ears prick forward and shouted to her "Theovald!"

The sacred steeds were bred and raised to serve a single rider, it took five years for one to be trained up once a person joined one of the sacred orders. They usually answered to a single person only, but paladins who served together often could be familiar enough to a steed that they could be sent to find them in a desperate moment. Of course, the steeds were more likely to return to a familiar haven than a person, but either would work for Devon's purposes. "Hie!" he called and River Dancer whinnied, reared, and pivoted on her hind hooves to escape the grasping claws of the skeletons.

She galloped away, carrying Devon's hopes with her. Now he had to survive until help arrived, or die very slowly.

29
RIVER DANCER ALONE

Mirabelle and her mother were coming out of the clerk's office at the end of the street when Mirabelle saw River Dancer racing up, reins trailing dangerously behind. She knew something was wrong even before she saw the rents in her hide. Others in the town slowed as they noticed the familiar sacred steed, frantic and riderless. Shouts rang out as word spread quickly of a paladin in trouble. Using the clicks she had heard Devon use, Mirabelle tried to call River Dancer to her. The horse's ears flicked uncertainly, so Mirabelle offered her hand. "Let's get to the Temple, girl."

This seemed the right thing to say, River Dancer came up alongside her and let her mount. "Let father know something's happened to Devon," she called to her mother. "I'm going to rouse the paladins at the Temple, Rhys knows we have enough of them to do something, Hie-yah!" she called at the end, and River Dancer began cutting through the crowd with the skill of a trained sheepdog.

People started clearing a path for her, women raising their hands before their mouths, less aghast at her riding side-saddle than knowing that her fiancé might already be lost. Others were grabbing farm implements and weapons. Trouble this close by would undoubtedly hit them all soon. They would be prepared.

River Dancer showed none of her calm, placid nature now. As soon as they passed the corner of town, she ignored Mirabelle's touch on the reins and instead stretched out her neck and fairly flew across the ground. Cutting at an angle through the grassland, River Dancer chose a path leading up the slight hill towards the Temple.

It didn't take long for them to get noticed. The set up for the ceremony tomorrow had many at loose ends, so there were paladins among the temple laypeople and craftsmen going about their various tasks outside. Once they recognized her and her unusual rider, there were paladins running for the stables. Those out exercising their mounts came riding up. Among them was her brother.

"What happened?" Theovald asked her, wasting no words.

"She showed up at the far edge of town like this." Mirabelle gestured at the wounds in her flank. "She came in from the main road near the clerk's office. She let me mount her and ride her up here. Devon has to be in danger, go!" She would never normally think of shouting at such august figures like that, but they all knew the situation had to be dire for River Dancer to arrive alone.

Trinity trotted around River Dancer and confirmed Mirabelle's worst fears. "Those are skeleton claw marks, we need to get down there, now!" The three of them pounded away with another group of seven soon following. River Dancer pranced and toss her head excitedly. "Shh, no girl, we need to stay here. They'll bring him back." She wasn't sure the horse would listen to her, or even understand, but when Mirabelle tried the reins, she responded and headed toward the stables.

Securing the gate to a stall, Mirabelle left River Dancer in the care of the stable hands and dashed to the Temple proper to tell the Divines the news and to lend a hand in setting up a place to take the wounded. She held no illusions that all of them would return intact. She just hoped they would all return alive, especially Devon. The great door of the Temple of Rhys closed behind her with an echoing boom that sent fearful shivers up her spine.

30

UNHOLY NIGHT

Devon slashed at another oncoming fiend; the ground all around had become a treacherous morass of loose dirt and leaves hiding pits where the skeletons had lain. One misstep and he'd quickly join them in death, or worse be carried away to be flayed alive and then defleshed in the same fashion for as long as his body could hold out. Such acts fed the dark powers of liches. The accursed beings extended their unnatural lifespans by painfully draining the life force of others.

A thing like the bones of a snake joined with a fanged human head sped towards him, using the ribs like centipede legs. Horrified, he kicked it away and saw puffs of smoke rise where some gangrenous-looking venom dripped onto the leaves where it had been. His heart fluttered with fear, and his lungs burned as he forgot how to breathe. Too close, the things were too close, he thought.

His breath exploded out and instinct kicked in to draw a ragged one inward as he retreated a step. The distended, corpulent form of a skin zombie came closer and vomited up piles of dark soil into its hands. The neck sagged like melting snow from the lack, yet still it walked forward, heedless of the lack. A sickly greenish glow appeared from the skin zombie's hands as it dropped unholy earth upon something below it. Devon's eyes grew wide as a skeletal ox was revived from its place in the surrounding soil.

That wasn't right.

Skin zombies were supposed to be little more than dark magic batteries. They were a way to create an unholy bridge across sacred soil or to have dark energies available to draw on when a more powerful undead would be weak, such as during the day. This wasn't right.

Part of his mind tried to remain calm, to call up his training and sort things out logically. However, the gathering of so many undead drowned out the positive life force of his own body, making it a struggle to keep going. Death was a palpable miasma in the air. As the shadows grew longer, the skeletons became more cautious.

They wanted to take him alive.

Devon felt a sudden blow to the back of his head and saw stars. Falling forward onto all fours, he raised a hand to the wound and whispered the prayer to Rhys that granted healing. He could see again. There were the feet of the creature, right behind him. Swinging his sword out in a wide arc backward, he was rewarded with a hissing cry as the feet were separated from the rest of the creature's legs.

More surged from the front, seizing his arm and head. Bringing the sword back forward, he stabbed into the chest of the one seizing his skull. It fought for a moment, then stepped back, a blackened, burnt hole in its chest, but unperturbed for all that. The other pulled at an angle and slammed his exposed ribs against the ground. He gave a gasping cry at the bruising pain, and twisted helplessly at the end of his own captured wrist.

The one with the chest hole tried to assist, and Devon's sword struck the skull this time. It went down with a clatter and did not rise. That did not free him from the other's grasp. The flesh zombie, with its framework of wood and the skin zombie filled with cursed soil, both came into view.

He didn't intend to join them.

Devon shook from the effort, but twisted his body around through the leaf litter. Lying on his back, he struck with his free hand for all he was worth. The blade met the lower arm bones of the one pulling him, and a high-pitched keening came from the contact as the blade slowly burned through at an angle. At last the creature's hold faltered, its hand attached but dangling.

Devon scuttled backward, preparing to rise once more as his eyes met the glistening bits of coal sewn into place where the eye sockets would have been on the skin zombie. It flopped forward like a child moving the legs on a rag doll and leaned over towards him, its mouth spilling foul, poisoned earth as sound came from it. "Caught for the master..." it began, and Devon could see the flesh zombie beside it hefting a large rock to smash him with. Sweat stung his eyes and caused him to nearly miss the bright white and purple flash of light as the head came off the one and the arms off the other. It was all Devon could do to avoid the rock hitting him.

Now he could make out the sounds of horses all around, closing in on him. He saw Theovald himself take out the flesh golem with the help of Noble Heart. His steed stomped it into paste as soon as it went down under Theovald's blade. "Devon! Can you hear me?" Theovald called down to him.

Devon nodded his head from where he now crouched on all fours. Holding out his hand, he felt Theovald grasp it and pull him to his feet. After two failed attempts to get him into the saddle, Theovald had Noble Heart kneel for Devon and had his brother-in-arms lay over the rump. Trinity and Wayland crisscrossed in front of them, performing a complicated maneuver that confused the now simple-minded skeletons. They went from concerted efforts to all-out attacks, making them easy targets for the paladins and their steeds. Brilliant flashes erupted all around them as the blessed warriors of Rhys pummeled their undead foes. Despite his weariness, pain, and exhaustion, Devon's heart was gladdened at the sight.

He did his best to hold on as Theovald and Noble Heart picked their way through the trees and found the pathway back through. The sun touched his face here, orange warmth promising safety for a few moments more. Beside him, in the darkening woods, the blades of the paladins flashed like the tails of fireflies, illuminating the shining armor and welcome faces of his friends and comrades. Enervation took hold and Devon could no longer fight his weariness. Letting his head hang low, he closed his eyes and focused on just keeping in place. Theovald was cutting across fields to take them away from town on the most direct course to the temple. "Hang on, my friend, hang on," he murmured to Devon and Devon did his best to comply.

Arriving at the Temple, Theovald dismounted and helped Devon down. Without his help, Devon was sure he'd have wound up flat on his back on the ground. He couldn't help but cry out when Theovald tried to duck under the arm closest to his bruised ribs, and then immediately regretted it as Mirabelle appeared from the doorway of the Temple.

"Go to the other side," Devon whispered to Theovald, and tried to spare a smile to reassure Mirabelle but it quickly turned into a grimace as the slightly taller Theo went under his other arm to help carry him in. Bruises, cuts, and bumps that he didn't even know he had screamed in pain as he tried to walk.

It seemed it didn't matter to Mirabelle. "You're alive," she said softly, choking on the words as tears welled up in her beautiful blue eyes. Devon wondered if they were from joy or sorrow and if he needed to add them to his tally. But weariness fell over him again as full night descended and he barely said, "I am" before they got into the doorway and bustled down the hall to the cleansing chamber.

Usually this place was used for sacred ceremony preparations, but Theovald and the Divines laid him on a clean blanket and began removing his armor to assess his injuries. He didn't expect Mirabelle to stay, but she was soon pressed into service by the Divines to wash the dirt and sweat from his wounds. He hissed at each sore spot she hit and silently kicked himself each time as her brow furrowed deeper and deeper with worry.

At last Priestess Lila said, "Devon, you have cracked some of your ribs, I'm not surprised they are hurting. The slices from the weapons of the skeletons are dirty, but we will get them cleaned out quickly and use a disease-purging spell on you. Depending on how many others are injured, we will see if we can heal you magically tonight, or if you need to hold out until Rhys blesses us again come the dawn." Devon nodded carefully at her words. Speaking seemed to take too much energy.

Priest Magnus came up and Priestess Lila stepped aside so he could take her place. "I am more concerned about your spirit, Sir

Devon. You are suffering the spiritual damage of being around such dark creatures. Theovald let us know a rough estimate of their numbers and mentioned that there were... aberrations among them. Since we cannot know what form of malady they carried, at least not yet, it is best if someone watches over you until the blessings of dawn come and we can speak the prayers of matins over you. To that end, I'd like to ask Mirabelle and Theovald to share watch over you tonight. Their closeness to you will be the best aid to your weary spirit."

Mirabelle looked surprised at the request, but Theovald knew from experiences in the field what to expect. Both murmured assent. Priestess Lila returned to his side and kneeling down touched her cool fingers lightly to his forehead. Whispering the words of the purge disease spell granted by Rhys, he immediately felt better, as though his body stopped fighting something that he didn't even realize was there. He was still exhausted, but some form of tension left him and he felt less hot, although he didn't realize he even felt hot until he felt normal again.

Smiling briefly at him, Priestess Lila nodded once before heading away towards the chamber's exit. From far away, Devon could hear the faint boom of the Temple's main doorway closing. "So do you want to take first watch, or shall I?" asked Theovald to Mirabelle at last.

"I'll sit up with him first," Mirabelle answered. "Good, that will give me a chance to find out how the others faired and get their reports. We'll be able to see how quickly we can get your husband-to-be back on his feet for you," Theovald said to his sister.

She blushed at his choice of words. "I'm just glad you could save him, Theo."

Ruffling her hair he said, "What are brothers, and friends, for?" He looked straight at Devon at this last part. Devon spared a slight bow of his head in acknowledgement. Then Theovald was gone, and he was alone with Mirabelle.

"I'm glad you are alive, Devon," she said, taking his hand. He managed a tiny squeeze of hers in return. "I wasn't sure you would be after I saw what had happened to River Dancer." He tensed at the mention of his steed.

"Ri-ver?" he tried to say, his words halting and weak. Devon squeezed her hand tighter.

"She's fine, or at least mostly fine. She let me ride her back to the Temple, I set her up in the stalls outside. I'm sure they'll take good care of her." Devon sighed with relief and let his head fall back to the folded blanket that acted as a pillow. Holding Mirabelle's warm hand in his, he could almost hear her heartbeat, feel her steadying pulse helping to remind his own how to behave.

The fear field that most undead had to some degree or another could weaken the heart, others would interfere with the normal life functions of the living. Still others drained away all positive emotion and let despair fill the gaps inside in their wake. They kept going until you were ready to beg them to kill you just to get the pain to end.

Skeletons rarely caused much of an effect, but he'd never been around so many at once alone. It made him wonder if Kris and Barton had truly fallen to their blades or to the fear projected onto them. Either way, they wound up just as dead. He let out a softer sigh, his thoughts somber and weary. As his eyes slid shut, he felt the feather-light touch of Mirabelle's lips on his and his heart skipped a beat for a moment, then surged stronger.

He opened his eyes to see hers closed as her lips lifted and the kiss ended. "Mirabelle," he whispered, and his voice did not falter. "You think I don't understand what they are saying, but after the many nights I spent praying for your safe return, I do." Her eyes squeezed shut, the memory of pain written across her face. "I know what it's like to have an emptiness that fills up every corner of you until you don't think there is any of you left. But I also know that mine lifted when you returned. Let me lift yours from you now." Her hand traced a path through his damp hair, cradling his head as her lips touched his once more, no light touch now, but seeking, her mouth opening upon his to send a questing tongue through. Her other hand caught his up and so drawn into her kiss was he that he did not realize right away that she had laid it upon her breast. A jolt went through him then and sent shivers down him that made him tremble beneath her touch. She left off the dance of their tongues to move down his chin and kiss his neck. His hand fell away, and he groaned at her swift nips and kisses, desire welling up inside him, but he had not the energy to entertain it.

"What's all this?" Trinity called out as she arrived. Mirabelle sat back suddenly, leaving him blinking up at the centaur carrying Trenton who was gritting his teeth, his foot starting to swell.

The centaur's horse-brown eyes twinkled from out her weather-tanned skin, her black tail swishing side to side with amusement. "Oh, don't mind me, we centaurs have fewer reservations than you humans do. I certainly won't fault you for wanting to be together after such a harrowing event. I'm not so sure about Trenton here."

Trenton ground his teeth and said, "I'm really not in the mood to be listening to that. Besides, the others will be coming shortly to help heal us, then you can do whatever you want."

Devon tried to reply, but only succeeded in opening and closing his mouth a couple of times like a fish. That goaded Trenton into answering for him. "Oh for goodness sake, Devon, no one thinks you've been sampling ahead, but it's clear she isn't repulsed by you, either. We're going to both have quite a few visitors in a moment, since there weren't many other injuries. I got mine falling into a hole," he admitted ruefully. His light golden hair lay shading his stunning, ice-blue eyes. Trenton bit back a swear word as he dismounted and dropped to the floor, his foot failing him entirely. He inched backward, using his hands and his good leg so that he could get into a sitting position against the wall. "Devon, would you mind if I borrowed your bride-to-be to get this?" he asked, gesturing to his still swelling leg. "If the greave isn't removed soon, they will have to cut it off me, and Trinity isn't built for dealing with people lying on the ground."

Devon nodded and looked over to

Mirabelle to ask if she would be willing, but she was already moving to help. "Just take off everything from the poleyn to the solleret," Devon told her.

She paused, pushing loose strands of her dark bangs out of her eyes, "I'm sorry, I don't know what those things are."

Trenton shook his head, a rueful smirk on his face, "Don't worry about it, just take off everything from the knee to the foot if you can. It's getting painful, or more painful." Mirabelle worked at the various straps under Trenton's direction while Devon wondered what it would be like to come home to her and have her helping him out of his armor. What it would be like having an actual home again, not just a room at the various Temples along his route?

He realized it had been a long time since he could just observe Mirabelle going about her tasks, without being in the midst of them. His eyes drank in the sight of her ebony tresses, the gentle curve of her back, the strength in her shoulders and arms. Mirabelle was lovely; he knew it, but he had never allowed himself to see it before. It was nice to just observe her again, this time knowing she would be his bride.

"You're one lucky man," Wayland said as he came in, echoing Devon's thoughts.

"Yes, yes I am," he responded softly. He didn't feel nearly as exhausted anymore. Aside from all the aches and pains reporting in, he felt almost normal.

"I can hardly believe you survived as long as you did with some two score undead trying to cut you down," Wayland continued. Devon looked at him blankly for a moment and then realized he had been talking about the fight, not Mirabelle. Hopefully, he hadn't used up all his luck between the two.

More of the paladins assembled and lined up along the set of alcoves across from the sacred bathing pool. Devon had seen this before, he just hadn't been on the receiving end of it.

The Divinities followed, Priestess Lila speaking up first, "Well Victor-Paladin Devon, you gave us quite a scare, and scared up quite the prey out there. Magnus and I will take a small contingent with us tomorrow morning to discover what happened, but first let's get you sorted out. Great Victor Paladin Marsid, step forward." Marsid saluted and then placed one fist over his heart and made a slight bow to the Divinities before coming over to where Devon lay. As his field commander, he took a position at Devon's head. "Victor Paladin Catkin, step forward". This continued through Paladin Scarwrist and Great Victor Paladin Valdesh the Younger who took up position at his feet, the trainer who taught Marsid and watched over them all.

All at once they intoned the healing prayer, the power of Rhys flooded into him, stronger than he had ever felt before. It flowed in and washed through him from head to toe and then returned like a wave in a pool that touched the edge and raced back towards the center. He let out a slight sound, unable to keep up with the sensation of it as his wounds began closing all at once, his body growing hot around each wound site. He fought an internal battle to remain still, knowing he mustn't thrash, or he'd hurt someone or disrupt the healing.

The energy became a humming in his head, somewhere between a murmur and a distant song, and as it faded, he realized the hands of the others were gone. His body felt very warm, but no longer hot anywhere, and he didn't hurt at all. The relief was so complete, so sudden and total, his muscles were still clenching from the pain that had ceased to be.

Opening his eyes, he saw Marsid and Valdesh attending to Trenton's leg. Mirabelle knelt at Trenton's side, attentively observing the ritual and its effects. Devon tried slowly sitting up and felt nothing worse than a slight light-headedness as the remaining energies seemed to slosh about in response. Leaning against the wall, he saw Wayland and Scarwrist paying rapt attention to the second healing.

The prayer ended and Devon remembered River Dancer, "Wayland, what about my steed?"

Wayland looked over at him and said, "Don't worry about her, Trinity said she'd take care of her for you. She couldn't really help in here and given her nature she's careful and caring of our mounts." A speculative look came across Wayland's features that Devon definitely didn't want to ask about, but the Divines returned and Priest Magnus asked, "Devon, you've been healed physically, but we need to know if you and Mirabelle wish to continue with the ceremony tomorrow. There are still requirements you have to fulfill and we would all understand if you needed to delay it a day or two."

Glancing over at Mirabelle, he asked, "What is your desire?"

She leaned across and took his hand, saying in reply, "After all of this I would rather not let anything stop us. If you are prepared and able to continue, then I am."

Devon nodded in acknowledgment. Having seen far too up close and personal the terrors he faced and the risks, a small voice in him whispered that she would back out and run. That she would take a stand against all comers and pursue her objective regardless of what life threw at her was the spirit he saw in her and wanted in a wife. The more time he spent with Mirabelle, the less he could imagine anyone else in her place. She was the perfect woman for him.

"You heard my lady's choice, your Divinities, let it be according to her wishes."

Priestess Lila coughed into her hand at his wording choice. "As you say, Victor Paladin Devon. The hour grows late, you will need to begin your ablutions soon if you would keep vigil tonight. Mirabelle is welcome to purify herself, if it pleases her to do so. The rule is that the purification must be kept pure, this is not a Temple of Dido." Mirabelle blushed at her words and Devon dropped his gaze as they both realized the Priestess was warning them not to let their passions carry them away. "We'll begin preparations for your vigil in the main temple, Devon. If Mirabelle wishes any blessings, or to say any prayers of her own, we will attend to her in the vestibule. Should she need to return home, her brother Theovald will escort her."

Magnus added, "If either of you wish to eat before beginning, there is a late spread put out of breads, cheese, and cold summer sausage. The fighting disrupted the plans for the normal evening meal. Otherwise, wait until dawn, Devon." He said the last kindly enough, but Devon demurred.

"I think I shall forgo in favor of showing my gratitude to Rhys for His and Her intervention today." Magnus nodded, accepting Devon's choice to increase the difficulty of his vigil as a sacrifice to Rhys.

"And you, Mirabelle? You are not a lay member that you need do any specific rituals in advance, but if you have anything you would like to do to prepare for this sacred rite, you are welcome to assistance."

"I would like to purify myself," she said. "Very well, we will allow Devon to explain the process to you." Walking over to Trenton, Lila offered her hand and said, "Come Victor Paladin Trenton, you are healed and others need this space." A little smile played on her lips at Trenton's half-hearted complaints. The others trooped out after the Divinities, leaving Devon and Mirabelle alone.

31
THE PURIFICATION CHAMBER

Mirabelle turned suddenly shy once everyone else left, only able to bring herself to look at him from beneath lowered eyelashes, "What does this cleansing ritual entail, Devon?"

"Why don't I lead you through it?" he responded, rising. Taking her hand gently, he kept a steadying hand out for her as she stood. He led the way across the room to a large, pale birch wood cabinet. From this he removed a set of towels and initiate robes as she watched. He handed these to her and then procured a stoneware jar with a small dipping ladle in it from the back of a darkened shelf. Gesturing with his head, he motioned for her to lead the way to the pristine waters of the cleansing pool. So trying not to tremble, she did. How strange to be fearful of something that must be so ordinary to him! Yet if she made a mistake unknowingly, he might take it as a sign of ill fortune for their upcoming wedding, and the worry made her nervous.

"Do we just strip down and climb in?" Mirabelle asked, looking at the cut stone steps into the whiteness of the bottom of the large, circular pool.

"No," Devon replied shortly and took both sets of supplies from her to set them alongside the edge of the water. "First, we go this way." He laid his hands on her shoulders from behind and before she could be surprised, he steered her towards a second cabinet of darker oak. His sudden pushiness and rough handling confused her, but before she could turn to protest he released her and opened the other cabinet. Here he removed what appeared to be something made of plain tan sackcloth, but only one set. A handful of dried gourd slices went atop the pile. Then he took out a tall glass jar of some kind of crystals.

Mirabelle had no inkling of what they could be, so she waited for him to explain. "Come," was all he said as he shut the door, offering her nothing more than the simple command. Mirabelle breathed out her exasperation but held her temper in check. Devon rarely seemed to answer her well when she asked him questions, but perhaps she rushed him too much. She'd try waiting to see how he went about things for a change. She needed to understand him better if they lived together, which they would be doing tomorrow by nightfall! He walked over to the nearest alcove and she now noticed the low stool there and the long wooden wash bin before it. What in the world? "Wait here," he said, and set his collection of items down on the stool in the adjoining alcove. Then he left the room for several minutes. Mirabelle was beginning to think he was playing some kind of a horrible joke on her as she waited. Then he finally reappeared. "They've got it set, here," he sat her down before the cleansing trough and closed off a pipe leading out the back of the trough into the wall while he opened one a little higher that shunted into the trough itself. Steaming water soon gushed through the pipe that she had not even taken notice of, hidden by the shadows as it was. The water coming out was very hot and Mirabelle wondered if she was to bathe or be made into a soup with it.

"Do you want to test the water to see if it's all right?" he asked at last.

"I'm sure that will not be, Devon."

He smiled at that and said, "I'll bring some water to cool it down for you." He moved a flat-folded panel that lay beside the alcove and snagged a wooden pail. It was only after he moved it that Mirabelle realized similar ones were set on the left of each of the alcoves. Despite having been in the room for several minutes, she had missed all these details. They hadn't seemed important, but now she realized everything here was probably tied into the rituals that went on and resolved to spend less time listening to her inner fears and more time observing her surroundings.

Devon dipped some water from out the main pool and wiped the edge of the bucket with care so it would not drip before returning to her side. "It's considered good luck to add some blessed water to both parts of the cleansing, although some strive to endure as much heat as possible to purge all the physical impurities from the skin that they can." Mirabelle counted it a small blessing that she chose something that would be considered good fortune. She still wished he'd explain the steps in advance so she knew what to expect, but at least he finally seemed talkative again.

"I'm going to set the blind up for you. Strip down behind it, and you may soak in the tub or to use the bucket to douse yourself with water to get wet. The main pool is much cooler, so you will have to decide how warm you can stand to be before stepping into the other. This," at this he held up the strange crystals, "is a special ceremonial cleansing salt. It contains salt from the ocean and thus is blessed with the luck of Anjasa for beginning new journeys. There is also the oil of the olive, sacred to Quinn and Zsofia to grant wisdom on the path, and oil of lavender, blessed by Rhys to calm the spirit and drive off evil." Opening the jar he poured some into his hand and had her touch it. "You see? It's oily. So you won't feel dry after scrubbing your skin with this, but it is salt so it will scour everything away. Be careful when you rise up after rinsing it off, so you don't slip if you do the bottoms of your feet."

"Are you supposed to do them?" she asked.

Giving her a hint of a smile, he answered, "Yes." Mirabelle let out a heavy breath at the thought of falling after going through all this effort. Devon laughed at her consternation. "Don't worry, I'll be here. Just take it slow."

"Exactly where will you be?" she asked at last.

He rubbed the back of his neck, and wouldn't meet her eyes, "I'll be right next to you. I have to get ready, too, and I must be in my armor and at the main part of the Temple before midnight comes. We have some time, but don't take too long, okay?"

She looked at him askance, but only nodded as he set up the modesty barrier. He barely put up the first before placing a second between their two alcoves. She heard him setting up a third as she stripped down and wondered whether it was all part of the ritual or if Devon had suddenly become shy around her. What if he didn't want to see her naked form because it reminded him of what she did with Jarick and Lee?

That's stupid, she told herself. If he felt like that, he wouldn't be marrying you. His kisses alone say otherwise. A part of her still wondered why he didn't even want a chance to peek. She pushed that voice down and touched the water with a toe. When it didn't get scalded, she waded in. It turned out to still be warmer than she expected, and she bit back a hiss as she settled in.

Beside her, Devon called out, "You okay, Mirabelle?"

"Yes!" she called back and returned to soaking. She wondered how much time they had. Being indoors after everything that had happened today had caused her to lose track of time completely. Dunking her head in, she sputtered as she rose to the surface and reached for the salts. The first handful she barely got onto her skin before it dissolved into the water. The rustling next to her ceased, and she heard Devon running water into the next basin. She waited for him to finish before asking, "How do you use the salt? It seems to be dissolving on me."

"Oh, you have to get out and scrub yourself down with it. That's another reason for the bench. Sorry about that."

Ah, no wonder all the cautionary tales. Levering herself out, Mirabelle took the crystals and rubbed them on her skin. They seemed to bore into her and then melt away, leaving her feeling the gentle oil as she rubbed it on. Acting on a hunch, she tried rubbing the arm she had coated with the gourd scrub and it did a thorough job of it, taking off a lot more skin than she expected. It looked rather pink, but felt amazing.

Having the hang of it, she scrubbed every inch of herself, bottoms of the feet included, although she left some sensitive areas for last and just rubbed them with the salts and got back into the warm bath. Despite the warnings, she nearly slid, trying to get in before the bath salts made the surrounding sensation on her lower regions unbearable.

Sighing as she settled in, she could hear Devon chuckling from behind the screen.

"What's so funny?"

"Nothing, nothing," he said, ingeniously

"I thought paladins weren't supposed to lie," she said.

Now she heard him sigh, "Very well, as we are in the midst of a very sacred and holy ceremony that will determine how our future lives go together, I apologize for my deception. I was laughing at the sounds of your first experience with the purification chamber. It's rather nice, isn't it?"

She felt bad for chiding him, but this wasn't some lark they were on, it was serious. Perhaps it was like the rituals for the turning of the year. Their marital fortunes might hinge on their honesty with each other now. Did that mean she should admit her fears to him?

"I guess it is. You were right about the slipperiness of the oils." She didn't know how to ask him what she wanted to know, so she just blurted it out. "Devon, are you afraid to look at me naked?" she asked at last, desperately hoping no one was listening in.

Silence. A bit of splashing, then more silence. Mirabelle's heart sank to the bottom of the tub. She had to open her mouth and ruin everything. Just as she wondered if she should quietly leave, Devon responded. "No, Mirabelle, I am not. I suppose coming clean on one's thoughts and deeds are a part of the ritual. I fear I will appear over-eager. It is not seemly in a paladin to display such emotions in public, but when I'm close to you, I may restrain my actions, but I cannot hide the effect you have upon me. I don't want to frighten you away."

Frighten her? He was afraid she'd notice the stirrings of his body and flee from him? That explained how upset he became when he thought she had noticed his reaction to her when they rode out to see the house he was having built for them. It was hard to imagine Devon frightened of such mundane things. What sort of women had he been with? Shrinking virgins? Perhaps. He wasn't that much older, and his duties undoubtedly left him little time to pursue lustful past-times. All of this failed to answer her question.

"So... you don't look at me and think of what you'd seen?" she asked, her voice hesitant and bleak. The silence went on so long she thought he must not have heard her, but then he spoke.

"You mean the day in the market with those two men. No, Mirabelle, I rarely think on it at all." Mirabelle squeezed her eyes shut. Her heart wanted to leap and sink at the same time. He didn't despise her, but since she'd brought it all up the night before their wedding, now maybe he would! She sank lower in the tub, but she could still hear him. "You were a different person then, young. You're not the girl I met in the market running with thieves. You've changed. Instead of being moved by your passions, you are taking control of your life, making decisions that will direct the rest of it. Tomorrow, you and I will wed, and since you've reached your majority, you can take a different name if you choose. Who are you going to be, Mirabelle?"

Water sloshed over the lip as she realized he was right. Her majority had come and passed and with all the other things going on, she did not consider if she wanted to change her childhood name. "Do you want me to rename myself, Devon?" she asked.

"I will accept you no matter what you are called. You need only tell me and I shall accept your new name now and always."

He was no help there, but such a thing was always deeply personal. "My father called me sweet plum as a child, that's the name I'm leaving behind. Mirabelle is who I am and the name you came to love me by. I would rather stay that for you if the sound of it pleases you."

"In no way could you disappoint me, whatever name you chose. If Mirabelle is the name in your heart, then Mirabelle shall ever be the name upon my lips." Surprised again by the poet's soul that seemed to crop up in Devon from time to time, Mirabelle laid her head on her arms against the edge of the tub.

"So you don't despise me for what I've done? It won't haunt our marriage bed?" she asked, unable to leave it alone. "You won't look at my body and see them?" she finished, almost too quiet to hear.

She could hear Devon rising from the tub, water spattering against the cold stone.

Beneath the woven grasses of the modesty barrier, she could catch occasional glimpses of his toes as he did whatever he was doing. "Beloved, if the errors of our youth were to haunt us all of our lives, then many marriages would be ruined before they could begin. No, I do not hold your past against you. You barely knew of me and I had no claim upon you. These others will not be in our marriage bed, for we have yet to be in it ourselves." Mirabelle continued to watch his toes as he talked. They faced her way as he said, "As for your worries that I do not want to see you naked, you had best be prepared." The screen between them suddenly folded away, and she looked up to see him setting it aside neatly before facing her again. "Because I will help you with the next part, and I will see you naked, and you will see that I desire you. So let us put both of our fears to rest, shall we?"

Suddenly, having her head on her arms put her at a very different vantage point, and she turned over in the tub. Now she stared up at him, her body completely exposed, covered only by clear water as he gazed down upon her. His long, dark hair, slick with wetness, laid straight down with only a few strands dry enough to try and escape. His eyes traveled over her briefly and when they met hers, there was a hunger there that she had not seen before, a hunger that stole her breath away.

Without saying a word, he reached out a hand to her; she took it and stood up, trying not to stare at the very thin sackcloth tie pants he wore. A dark thatch bordered the rising fabric that seemed to show more than it hid. She realized what he meant now, her mind buzzing as he draped a soft towel against her skin and slowly led her to the clear waters of the true cleansing pool. What could possibly be left to cleanse after all this?

He held her up supportively under the arms, touching her only with the towel. As she set her foot in the water he drew the towel away and cool air raised gooseflesh over her skin even as she balked at the coldness of the pool before her. "Best to get in quickly," he said and stepping beside her, pulled her in with him. She shrieked and waded back towards the steps."

"You did that on purpose!" she gasped.

"Yes, I did," he replied, totally unrepentant, "and you cannot leave until the ritual is complete. Now either you may wash yourself with what is in the jar there, or I will wash you. It is up to you."

She looked at him in shock; he simply lay back against the far steps, grinning at her, if not evilly a bit hopefully. "I'm sure I can do it myself," she told him at last. Mostly because she was sure that if he began touching her she wouldn't be able to keep her word to the Divinities about not despoiling the place. For all the things she did with Jarick around the other thieves, bathing wasn't one of them. In fact, she had rarely been fully naked when she was with him. Here, with Devon's eyes upon her, she felt very self-conscious about bathing and he wasn't even touching her.

"Can you turn away while I do this?" she asked, subconsciously plaiting a braid into some strands of her hair.

Cocking his head to the side, he said simply, "I'm sure I cannot."

Fear switched to anger and exploded out of her, "Why ever not?!"

He frowned at her outburst, his eyes narrowing, and she started and backed up although he had not moved. Instead, he sighed and tipped his head back, his eyes closed. After several deep breaths he rose, his face composed, and strode through the waist-high water to her, although it was only thigh high on him she noted before she raised her gaze. She feared what his eyes would hold, but they were warm, not angry. Leaning down close to her ear, he rested a warm hand under her chin as he whispered, "Because I will not have you thinking I cannot bear the sight of you, wife, before we even have our first night together."

"I'm not your wife yet," she replied and then hated the words.

"That's true. Are you intending to have it remain so? Or are you my bride-to-be?" he asked gently. He pulled back to see her face and she could read the worry and fear on his.

"No," she breathed, "I am yours." She meant to say, 'your bride-to-be' but the words caught in her throat. It didn't matter. He smiled at last and leaned in to kiss her swiftly and deeply, leaving her trembling from more than cold when he broke it off and retreated to his former position.

"Good to know, wife. Now, you must finish the task at hand or I will be late, and I do not care to start such a serious thing as the rest of our lives together on the wrong foot." She tried to laugh, but it came out as a slight pant. Taking up the jar, she opened it to discover an unfamiliar and astringent, but clean odor arising from it.

"What is this?" she asked, wafting the scent towards her nose.

"It's a ceremonial hair wash made from tea myrtle, although it works all right on the body for certain problems. Just keep it away from your face and eyes; it will sting fiercely," Devon replied. He sat up suddenly, his arms no longer draped along the pool's edge but held before him. He rubbed his hands absently together and stared at the jar. "One more thing..."

Mirabelle paused, wary. Devon hemmed a bit before finally getting out, "This particular purification cleanser tends to be a bit... stimulating."

"Stimulating... how?" she had never found any soaps particularly "stimulating" outside of a pleasant scent.

"It feels on your body the way mint feels in your mouth. It's cooling and leaves a clean feeling, but it... tingles. I'm just warning you," the last coming out in a rush as he sat back again, his face looking concerned.

"You have to wash all your hair, don't you?" she realized.

"Yes. It is a purification ceremony. It was a touch shocking the first time I used it," he admitted.

"But I'm shorter than you, how do I...?" she began.

"Oh, you could stand on the steps. There is some railing there to help if you need it." He smiled helpfully at her, but she didn't feel reassured at all. So now she would lose even the mild screen of the water, and she was about to place something that even a man found stimulating near her most private of places? This had to be one of the weirdest 'cleansing ceremonies' she had ever heard of or experienced. A darker thought hit her.

Aghast she asked him, "Devon, did any of the clergy watch you when you first used it?"

He stared at her a moment and then burst out laughing. "No, no! I just had another paladin tell me. A trio of us were coming out of the field and one of the paladins with us just said to use it and got on with his own ablutions. I didn't get any warning. He had probably become so used to it he didn't think to mention it had any unusual effects. Don't worry, no one was spying on my fifteen-year-old self." His eyes crinkled with amusement, which she thought looked better on him than the worry. Might as well get on with it. She looked down dubiously at the small dab in her hand before hesitantly resting it against the dark hair of her mound. Perhaps talking to him would distract him from whatever this did to her.

"Wouldn't you have had to use it at your investiture ceremony?" she asked.

He chuckled at that, "You would expect so. I think they were out at the time; it didn't come up. So imagine my surprise the first time I came out of the field to this!"

And she did, it was even more cooling than the water around her legs below and it tingled in most unexpected ways. "Oh!" she gasped out, as the sensation grew more intense.

"See? I told you," he said, glancing away. But she could see his hands were gripping tightly to the sides of the pool and the coolness of the water was no longer enough to curtail his ardor.

Deciding she had this half of the requirement fulfilled, she stepped back into the pool and shivered as the mix of the cold water and the stimulating scrub left her body clean, but her thoughts were anything but. It had been a long time since she had done anything with a man, and this made her wish she could. She glanced at Devon, who was still studiously looking away.

He was handsome, she had to admit. His shoulders were broad, not as broad as her brother's but much more so than Jarick's. His long, dark hair was a deep brown that looked nearly as black as hers when wet. His mouth was small, compact, making him look sterner than intended sometimes, but the lips themselves were full. Somehow she had missed such little details until now. His body was tan from working on their new house in the sun, his arms a darker tan from days of riding. Though the healing was thorough, she could see a few pale scars on his sides where former wounds were left to heal naturally. Were they from before he took on his duties as a paladin or after? And from what she could make out beneath the water and from her spot in the tub earlier, she need not be concerned about any disfigurements or... small problems with the lower half of his body. Devon definitely had a man's proportions all the way through, and she wanted him, she realized. Right now when she couldn't have him.

Her breath quickened, and she turned away. A tingling in her lower regions arose that had nothing to do with the hair wash. Taking the jar, she dabbed a slightly larger amount into her hand to do her long hair. It always took more effort to clean than it seemed worth sometimes. With her back to Devon it went easier, and she soon had a good lather going. However, the tingling crept lower towards her brow causing her to gasp, fearful of the suds getting into her eye. She rinsed a hand quickly and placed it between, but wondered if dropping into the water would drive it in rather than out.

Clearly he heard her distress, for Devon asked, "What's wrong?"

"I think the suds are about to fall into my eye," she replied, her voice trembling out of worry and the tail end of desire.

"I'll help you," he replied and she could hear him wading out. She felt his arm beneath her shoulders and at the small of her back, "lean back." She did, and he cradled her against him with his right arm as he scooped handfuls of water with his left, rinsing it away and slowly lowering her backward until the cleanser left. She could feel her hair spreading out in a cloud and she lay at an angle over his arm that pushed her breasts high, her body floating lightly in the shallow pool. Of all the positions she might have thought she'd be in tonight, this was not on the list.

As the emergency passed, Devon notice as well. "Please stand," he said gruffly, choking on the words. She struggled to get her feet under her, which proved harder than expected in the shallow water. At last her knees touched the bottom, and she got to her feet, her hands brushing Devon's waist for support. He gave a strangled groan and tilted his head back away from her, his body frozen as if she were a poisonous snake.

"You need to go. Now. Finish your preparations," he spoke in a harsh whisper, "for I do not wish to break my vow to keep the sanctity of this place." Mirabelle could feel the heat coming off his skin and part of him brushed against her, rigid and reaching even as his hands were held stiffly at his sides. "Go. Now." There was either a droplet of water splashed on his face or a tear was tracing a thin track from his unblinking eye. His muscles rippled like those of a stallion as she looked at him, and she could feel his quick, shallow breaths. She backed away and climbed the steps out.

Using the towels as he suggested, she dried herself as quickly as she could, running her fingers through her hair to keep it from knotting. "There are brushes and combs in the oak cabinet," he said to her at last. Wearing one of the larger towels, she padded over to the cabinet and pulled it over. A short search turned up her choice of several. She returned to the edge of the pool and sat, brushing out her hair. Devon lay in the cool water, staring up at the ceiling. Mirabelle did not take it amiss, clear evidence of his desire for her still present in every line of his form. Reaching for her pile of clothes, she heard him call out, "Wait!" She paused and glanced over at him across the width of the pool. "There is a clean initiate's robe there. Put that on instead. You aren't supposed to wear soiled clothing after the ceremony. It's like deciding to go back to your old life." Well, she was glad he mentioned it. But the initiate's robe was rather large and voluminous. It seemed like an endless sheet and she couldn't make proper heads or tails of it.

"Here, let me help you," Devon said unexpectedly, and she heard him rise from the pool as she swam beneath the miles of cloth. With careful and deft hands, he soon had the hole for the head in place. She couldn't find it because an attached hood had pressed down over it, making it impossible to find from underneath. Devon guided her hands through the proper slots in the sides. His hands shook, but only a little, although there seemed to be far too many armholes in the garment for an ordinary human.

"Then what are these for," she asked, puzzled.

His voice sounded more like his normal baritone when he answered, "They are for a belt." He lifted a long cord and laced it through expertly, leaving her to tie it. "Now you are set. There are some sandals in a basket in the corner. You can put on a pair and carry your clothes out with you. The Divinities or any of the clergy can help you after that. You can get a blessing or Theovald can escort you home. It's no difficulty to drop the initiates robe off later."

"What are you going to do?" she asked.

"Me? I'm going to get back in the pool and try not to break my vows when I have to use that ceremonial hair wash. You are plenty stimulating to the senses, Mirabelle," he said with a rueful shake of his head. She walked to the door and turned to ask him another question, but it fell completely out of her mind as she caught the image of Devon stripping out of the barely helpful covering of thin burlap before wading back into the water.

No, he definitely had the body of an adult.

32
KEEPING VIGIL

Mirabelle's mind went numb, but her feet found their way unerringly to the chapel where she spent so much time. A kind laywoman invited her to sit in the vestibule as she crossed over to the quarters of the priest and priestess to let them know Mirabelle had arrived. Mirabelle squirmed uncomfortably in the slightly scratchy garment. There was little to be seen, but it didn't stop her from wishing for some small clothes under it. How did one stand it?

Priest Magnus and Priestess Lila returned shortly. "Greetings Mirabelle, shall we fetch your brother? I'm sure there are things you'd like to get done tonight before the wedding."

"Actually, what is it that Devon has to do?"

"Well, he shall kneel in the chapel his sword placed point down in a peace holder and recite prayers to Rhys until dawn. A few lay people will check on him to announce the hours and insure he does not sleep. Sleeping during a vigil is as serious as falling asleep during a night's watch as a guard. The vigils are to strengthen the mind and the spirit. Its difficulty is a sacrifice to the Divine. For Devon, it is an offering of strength and will to Rhys that the Divine may show favor upon his quest. In this case, to bless his marriage to you." Lila smiled kindly at

Mirabelle. "But it is something he must do alone. We, however, are at your service to aid you in any way we can to make the day blessed and bright."

"Then I would like to keep vigil as well. If my husband would perform such a sacrifice for me, then it is only fitting that I would do as much for him." Lila's mouth formed a delicate little "o," of surprise, and Magnus shook his head.

"I'm going to let you handle this one, Lila. I need to get some rest if one of us will check out the site tomorrow at first light. Goodnight, Priestess. Good night, Mirabelle," Magnus said and with a backward wave retreated into his quarters.

"Is it all right?" Mirabelle asked at last, realizing she might be interrupting others plans.

The priestess knelt down on one knee and clasped Mirabelle's hands in her own. "No, no, dear. You have every right to ask to perform a greater sacrifice to Rhys. I'm sure it will only strengthen the bond between you and Devon. He is deeply devoted to Rhys. You are very fortunate indeed to have someone as steady and dedicated as he is for a future husband." Lila looked about the room appraisingly and then rose, encouraging Mirabelle to stand.

"Here, we'll use this altar cloth for you to kneel upon. You probably aren't as familiar with the prayers for each hour of vigil as you aren't a trained laywoman. Instead, why don't we have you read the passages from the Book of Rhys? You've listened to them in ceremony, but they take on new meaning when read together. These are the very passages from which the prayers Devon will be reciting are made. This way you are echoing his efforts in a supportive manner. You would truly gain a deeper understanding of your husband-to-be by studying the words he carries in his heart. Will that suit you?" the Priestess asked her at last.

Mirabelle had not considered it before, but it made immense sense to her, to her now. "Yes, please," she in reply. Priestess Lila went out of the vestibule and returned shortly with a book. "If you need to use the necessary, do so now. It's over there." She pointed to a small door off the side of the chamber, just before a hallway to some darkened area. "Once you begin, all physical discomforts are to be born with grace as part of your trial."

"Oh yes, please," Mirabelle said. Until the priestess mentioned it, she didn't realize how much discomfort she was already in. The bathing had taken a long while, and she had had no opportunity for some time earlier. She had not gone since discovering River Dancer, she realized.

"I rather thought so. Go ahead, and upon your return I will have the proper starting chapter open for you." Mirabelle took very little time, the initiate's robe being more of a hazard to gather up, but the lack of small clothes making up for it. It seemed strange to be saying prayers in nothing but a shift, but probably represented something like coming unadorned before Rhys. The Divine was not impressed by wealth, only by what was in your heart.

Returning, she found Lila had opened the book on the chair Mirabelle had sat in earlier. Lila gave her a small smile and gestured for her to kneel upon the cloth before the book. "Are you prepared, Mirabelle? Is there anything else you need before we begin?"

"No, I'm ready."

The Priestess brought over a small cup of water. "Take a sip to cleanse your mouth before reciting the words you read in the book. These words are sacred to us and are the foundation of our faith. You, yourself, have seen the power of Rhys and his hand is surely upon your life. Here in this place, at this moment, you are seeking to be in his presence as a penitent. In these hours, consider your past and examine your conscience. You seek to eliminate one thing every hour that belongs in your past but is still haunting you. Ask forgiveness of Him in his form as the Smiter of Undead that he watch over your husband in the field."

Pointing to the book, Lila called her attention to an orange ribbon that marked the text that lay open. Priestess Lila took hold of the end of a purple one that marked a different section. Flipping to it, she said, "Next ask the Rhys in Her aspect as the Goddess of the Dawn for what blessings you desire upon your household as you begin this new life together. It is good and holy that you, as the female head of your house, ask this of Her, woman to woman. I believe it calls the blessings of that aspect strongly when a woman asks. So choose wisely. The first three hours are to purge that which you do not want from you. The last three hours will be to call in that which you desire."

Grasping a silver ribbon, she turned to a third section. "As we are well into Autumn, the night will probably run longer. This means your vigil will be longer, but we consider these hours those of bountiful blessing. You may ask for Rhys to watch over extended family, friends, or for any need or hope your heart may have. Remember that you may only ask for one thing each of the hours for Rhys the Warrior to cleave from your soul or for Rhys the Bringer of Hope to grace your life with. You are guaranteed three of each." She turned the book back to the spot with the orange ribbon.

Mirabelle watched her reach into a cabinet along the wall and draw out a small metal topped, flask. A clever handle allowed the Priestess to remove only a tiny amount of the oil from within it. Mirabelle had never been back in this area, nor seen where such ceremonial components were stored. She stared in rapt attention, her heart speeding up as Priestess Lila bent to touch the oil to her forehead, "Blessed be the followers of Rhys, Lady of the Dawn, Smiter of Undead, and Bringer of Hope. May you stand before Him/Her with a pure heart, pure mind, and pure body. May the blessings of Rhys pour forth like a river upon you, and may you be protected all the days of your life and your body and soul be protected after your death."

A small chill went up her spine as the words took on very real meaning. The Priestess stepped back from her and said, "Now the hour at the heart of the night has been reached, your vigil begins."

33

THANK RHYS FOR HORSES

"Time to get up," Theovald said to Devon, offering his hand, the faint hints of dawn were barely touching the stained glass windows around the chapel. Devon looked up at him blearily from his post. At least the first few hours weren't hard to get through. The sight of Mirabelle's breasts rising out of the water like those of a mermaid chased sleep right out of his head. However, those same images and others made it very hard for him to work on purifying his mind and spirit. After a good half candle-mark he gave up trying to clear the memory out and focused on his other deficiencies, leaving the issue for last, which seemed to work. He asked for Rhys' protection for Mirabelle for both when he was away and when he was near, then for any children they might have, and then for their extended family and friends, including this new town that would be his home, and lastly that he not disappoint his wife. It seemed a fair request for the bountiful hour.

Slapping his palm into his friend's hand, he gripped tightly as he rose, his legs leaden blocks that had lost feeling in them hours ago. Theovald kept his grip tight and levered a shoulder under Devon's arm. They had both done this for each other before, but it didn't get easier with age. Devon wondered how the older paladins like Valdesh the Younger and Marsid handled it. Dedication and training, probably.

"Thanks, Theo," he said at last, sheathing his sword and walking off the pins and needles stabbing his legs.

Theovald grinned at him, "Time for breakfast, old man!"

"Old man?" Devon scoffed, "I'm barely a year older than you."

"Ah, but you're getting married today, leaving the circle of us young bucks for that mysterious unknown called 'marriage'."

Devon punched him in the arm. "You're terrible, you know that?"

Theovald clicked his tongue and shrugged. "I learned everything I know from you."

Suddenly remembering Mirabelle's request, he halted in the hallway.

"Theo, could you do something for me?
You have a steady hand."

Theo slowed his steps, turning, "Now that one's just a plain set up."

"No! I'm serious. Mirabelle asked me to get my hair shorn even for today, about page length should do it."

"Ah, well, I guess you look like a shaggy goat. Let's go to my room, I think I have some shears in my gear there and you can shave as well." Theovald led the way, waving an arm for Devon to follow. "I'm still not touching that one."

It took little enough time for Devon to get shaved and for Theovald to find his shears. Grabbing the blanket from the bed, Theovald wrapped him up in it to keep any strands from getting into Devon's armor. Given how long the ceremony was, Devon appreciated the thoughtful effort. There was no way Devon could do anything about tickling, itching strands of hair when he stood before the altar, or later while he remained in armor. The very thought made him want to recheck everything.

Then Theovald started in on him, asking rather personal questions about how he and Mirabelle wound up together. Devon could only tell him the truth as far as he knew it.

Listening intently, his friend finally gave up and decided the matter was in Rhys' hands. Devon was thankful as Theovald had stopped halfway in the middle of cutting his hair to ask his questions.

At least his brother-in-arms had relented and finished the job at hand!

"There, you're done," Theovald proclaimed at last.

"So I don't look like a shaggy goat any more?" Devon asked, glancing into the mirror behind the water basin.

"No, now you just look like an old goat," Theovald quipped, ducking away from Devon's attempt to playfully shove him.

Carrying on their banter, they walked down the brightly lit corridor to the dining hall. The other paladins were seated in full gear, already digging in. However, today a few were serving as well.

"Here he is, 'bout time you made it, Rhys has nearly cleared the horizon. Much longer and it would be Anjasa's sun," Trenton called loudly, waving them over. Devon was grateful to see him in one piece after the harrowing events of yesterday.

"Look at my poor armor!" he lamented as they came up. A dent in the leg portion spoiled the perfect mirror shine, which was surely a crime to the vain Trenton. "I polished this thing for weeks and then you try to get your head taken off by undead. Is that any way to treat your wedding guests, Devon?"

Devon shook his head, but declined to answer. The events of the evening before were too raw for him to joke about. Instead, he began heaping his plate with egg pie, bacon, eel, and grilled vegetables. As soon as he lifted his fork, several mirabelle fruit rolled across the table from every direction, bouncing off his plate and going everywhere, much to the amusement of his fellows.

Devon rested his head on his hand, still shaking his head as he did so. "Really?" he asked.

"Now, now, no need to inundate him with fruit anymore, fellows, after today he can eat mirabelles in any season he wants," Trenton crowed. Most of the others laughed at the joke, only egging Trenton on. "I'm sure you are looking forward to having that sweet juice running down your chin."

"What?!" Devon asked, startled. He assumed the former comment was about nibbling on her skin, but Trenton's new one either got very rough or referred to an idea Devon had never considered. Did people do that? He bent his head back towards his food, but caught Theovald suddenly staring daggers at him. Devon hadn't even said it! Oh, in the name of Rhys, it was finally dawning on Theo that his best friend would deflower his little sister. If he weren't so hungry, Devon would have left before things could get worse.

"Now, now, enough of that," Valdesh the Younger said. "If you aren't going to offer helpful advice, just quiet down." For a moment Devon was grateful. Then Valdesh started in again with, "In the bedroom, women are like cattle or sheep, you have to lead them." He then launched into a harrowing comparison of the mating habits of field animals and those of men and women. Devon stopped chewing, his eyes wide with horror, fork sitting in the air utterly forgotten.

A loud cough interrupted. Excuse me, Valdesh, it's not like that anymore," Marsid said and followed it up with, "Devon, whatever you do, don't rush. The worst mistake a paladin can make is to forget all his training and speed to the finish. Make sure she has partaken of the pleasure of the moment before you do. And do what she tells you to do. This alone will save you much grief." This advice seemed sound, and he nodded with it until Marsid began how to tell if the woman was 'at her full' causing Devon to desperately reach for the cider on the table to wash down his food before he choked. He gulped loudly as he drank, trying to drown out what he was hearing. Setting the glass down, he saw Theovald still glaring at him, his face blacker than a thunderstorm. Hearing his sister get compared to cattle and trembling boughs were not conducive to building up feelings of good will.

"That's fine, everyone, I'm sure I've got it now," he announced at last, standing quickly enough to make the bench squeak against the floor and barking his knee against the top edge of the table. His plate was only a little less than half full, but he'd rather be hungry at this point than to have any more "advice" thrown at him. Thanking all of them as politely as he could, he tried to hasten out, but was halted at the exit by Priest Magus entering, dusting horsehair off of his robes.

"Ah, Devon, good. I have gone out with a pair of paladins and some local game trackers to assess what happened to you last night. I believe all of you would like to know," he announced to the room at large, his deep voice ringing out like a bell. There was a reason Magnus did most of the reading at the services.

Silence ruled the hall; you could hear the wind blowing through the leaves outside it was so quiet. "Paladin Trinity and Victor Paladin Catkin checked all the remains and insured that no more would rise. According to the tracker, and I concur with his findings, what we had was a lost caravan of settlers that perished in those woods some years before the founders of Riverfield discovered this place. Let us have a moment of silence for them." Magnus bowed his head, as did every paladin in the hall. Devon felt conspicuous standing up at the front instead of sitting with his brothers. Bowing his head, he prayed silently for the souls who came so far only to die chasing their dreams. He prayed as well for the loved ones who never knew their fates.

All too soon Magnus called their attention back, "I pledge to you, we will try to discover which caravan it was that we may contact their relatives and properly pray for their souls at our services. The other undead had discovered it and were harvesting it out of convenience rather than a larger plan, it appears. Some among them were more recent, though. Given their complexity, full reports will be passed up and double patrols will be sent out to insure no further activity escapes our notice. In the meantime, I have cleansed and consecrated the ground for a good mile all the way around. That includes your homestead, Victor Paladin Devon. I did not think you would mind," he said in a sardonic tone, but he added more seriously, "You need not fear to take your bride there. There will be nothing unholy that will approach that place for a mile in any direction for some time." That bit of news gladdened his heart. "Now then, I will not keep you fine soldiers of Rhys from your meals. Although there is one more thing to note, congratulations are due both Paladin Trinity and Paladin Scarwrist. The good Sirs Marsid and Valdesh the Younger have agreed that they have acquitted themselves well in a true field combat and will be given the proper recognition and honors before they return to the field." Applause rose, and the lizardman stood and bowed to Magnus and then Marsid and Valdesh before sitting back down.

Devon applauded and then ducked outside before the attention could get turned back to him. Leaning with his back against the wall outside, he sighed in relief, only to hear, "Hey there, Devon," as both Catlin and Trinity rounded the corner on him. "We thought we'd give you some real advice from a female's perspective." His face had to have gone pale, and he was grateful for the wall at his back to support him as the pair finished up their round of suggestions. He was certain his knees weren't up to the job, but he also cursed the wall because had it not been there, he wouldn't be pinned against it.

Finally, the pair moved off, having said their piece. And Devon was sure he hadn't expected position advice from a centaur when he finished his vigil this morning. Checking to make sure they were headed out to the fields, Devon slipped off to the stable to visit with the only one who wouldn't try to share any bedroom knowledge with him this morning, his horse.

34
THE MOST WORTHWHILE THINGS CAN BE THE HARDEST

Mirabelle rode out with Priest Magnus and paladins Trinity and Catkin. As she didn't have her own horse, Trinity generously offered to carry her. Having stood vigil, Mirabelle had far more sympathy for what the paladins went through, and upon hearing what she did, both Catkin and Trinity warmed up to her immensely.

However, Mirabelle was disturbed to hear what their mission entailed and how the battle occurred so very close to her new home. Devon had nearly died on their doorstep. Trinity broke off and carried Mirabelle up to her parents' house, suggesting she sneak in a couple hours of sleep if she could.

Sleep was the farthest thing from her mind upon realizing that her home might be next door to some undead charnel house. Learning what words like "excarnation" and "flayed" meant, and how close they were to applying to her soon-to-be-husband horrified her. Although she tried hard to keep her expression from showing it to the paladins, their casual discussion of it made her fear how common such things must be in their lives. She didn't want them thinking her weak, but how did they ride out every day knowing their enemies would do this to them if they were captured?

Probably by realizing if they didn't it would happen to their friends and loved ones. Her thoughts chased around in her head as she reached a hand to the door, only to find it opened on her instead with her father standing there.

"There you are. Your dressmaker is here and growing frantic. Your mother has been at that point since dinner last night with your brother, where you were conspicuous by your absence. I realize this is your day, but your brother is not a sufficient substitute for you when your mother is worried sick about you, your fiancé, and the safety of everyone on the guest list. Please get in here. This is no place for a man this close to the wedding." Mirabelle felt bad for her father, but by the end of his rant she started laughing and threw her arms around him.

"I love you, too, Dad. Sorry to worry you. I was pretty scared when I heard, too, and realized that I owed some serious prayers to Rhys last night for bringing Devon back alive. No one thinks he should have made it," she admitted aloud, her smile faltering and then a sudden hiccup turned into a sob. All at once she went from laughing to crying and sagged against her father, who did his bewildered best to keep her from falling.

"Ah, Mirabelle, daughter of mine, whatever am I to do with you? If your mother sees you like this she'll just start crying, too." He sighed and half carried her to the stump he used as a chair for working the grindstone in front of the house. "What do you think your mother and I think about every time Theo goes riding out? The same things you are thinking right now. You're sitting here telling me that Devon shouldn't be alive. Right?"

Between sobs, Mirabelle nodded vigorously. She had kept up a brave front in front of Priest Magnus and the paladins, but now that she was home she couldn't do it. She'd wind up one of those bawling brides that you are sure must get handed over to some sadistic monster, or who wanted to join a holy order and were told no by their family. She couldn't make Devon look bad today of all days. But that thought didn't help. Between it and the images of Devon getting torn apart by monsters, her brain was on overload and she couldn't stop it.

"Sweet Plum, look at me," her father commanded, his voice soft but compelling. Mirabelle fought against the crying jag to lift her head, tears pouring from her eyes. Her father sighed and took out a cloth handkerchief to wipe at them, but they kept coming. "You said yourself, by all appearances Devon shouldn't have lived through the attack, but that only shows he truly was meant to survive. Have a little more faith in Rhys. Nothing will happen to Devon ahead of whenever he is fated to join the Divine that he serves so well. I know none of this is easy on you, but sometimes, darling, the most worthwhile things are the hardest ones."

He pressed the cloth into her hand adding, "I don't know what is between the two of you; I didn't even realize you liked him until he failed to arrive back when he was expected, but I've never seen you as happy as you have been whenever he's near. As a man, I have to think that having someone as wonderful as you to come home to will only make him fight all the harder to survive when he's out in the field. So cheer up my little Sweet Plum. You're getting married today, and I believe the two of you will be very happy together. You compliment each other well. Just be patient with him. Military men aren't used to showing their emotions well. He'll come around in time. Now how about a hug? I've barely had time to see you these past few weeks and you're leaving our home for your own all at once. I'm going to miss you."

Her breath still hitching, she threw her arms around her father and hugged him tightly. She'd spent so much time with her mother and getting the preparations done, she didn't realize her father might be feeling left out. "I'll always love you, dad."

"And I you, Sugar Plum. Now go see your mother. She's at her wit's end."

Mirabelle hugged her mother right off the bat. Her mother looked poised to scold her, yet held off with her daughter looking distraught, face red and blotchy with tears. "What happened?" Daleen asked her instead.

Hugging her even tighter, Mirabelle said, "I love you, Mom."

"I love you, too, Mirabelle. Now what's wrong?" Daleen asked, extricating herself and holding her daughter at arms' length to study her.

"I found out that not only did Devon nearly die yesterday, but the monsters came from the woods right next to the home he has been building for us. I just couldn't keep pretending it doesn't bother me. It does. I'm afraid," she admitted.

"Ah, that is a lot to deal with the day before your wedding," so what happened to you last night?" Daleen asked, leading her over to a chair in the sitting room. Collette was already there, and whatever frustration she may have felt left her face as she heard Mirabelle's story.

"I stayed and prayed for him all night.

He kept vigil for me and our future, so I did the same for him. Rhys brought him back alive, I didn't want to fail to show gratitude in case...in case..." Mirabelle couldn't finish the thought and another sob escaped her though she tried to stifle the rest. Daleen went set a pot of water over the fire to boil, adding some ingredients for a soothing tea, Mirabelle knew. Collette moved her chair closer and sat patting her hand. Mirabelle didn't want to disappoint anyone, but the additional news this morning sent her sailing over the edge. She didn't know if she could do this, to cope with Devon going into danger for months on end. It was one thing to have it in your mind as an abstract, but to see it up close?

"Daughter, if you find you honestly do not feel safe going to that house, you may stay here. I'm sure your father and I can secure something small in town for you both. We won't let you come to harm if we can help it. You may be getting married, but you are still our daughter. Devon can likely find a buyer for the place and you can select a different location."

Her roiling emotions settled at her mother's words. She didn't have to go there if she didn't want to, Devon might be disappointed, but having been attacked so close by, he might not be as enamored of the locale either. "You're right. Thank you, Mom."

"That's what we're here for, darling. Now drink up." Taking the cup from her, she drank a good amount of the hot liquid, holding the mug in her hands afterward, and felt steadier for it. Daleen served a cup to Collette, and they sipped in amicable silence for a time.

Finally Daleen spoke again, "Mirabelle, despite any other issues you may have, I encourage you to go through with the wedding today. Since you accepted Devon's proposal, you've completely blossomed. Even before that, you became much more serious and reliable. I don't know why he has this effect on you, but he seems good for you, and I know he will be good to you." She sipped some of her own tea. When she continued, she stared into the cup and her voice was both deeper and softer. "There are always risks in life, darling, but some are worth it." Her words echoed those of her father, if said a bit differently. They thought she meant to call off the wedding. It hadn't crossed her mind until they brought it up, but she realized a small part of her wanted to run and hide in her old bedroom. Marrying Devon seemed too monumental a thing, a risk too great for her heart to survive.

Yet she wasn't a child anymore. Hiding away would be as much an illusion of safety as sticking her head under a blanket to keep monsters at bay in the dark. Loving Devon came with risks, yes, but weren't there rewards as well? The man set out to get them a home before their wedding and had it built in less than three weeks. He fought off a horde of undead and made it back to her side alive, and if she married him, the Temple of Rhys would always watch over her and their children no matter what.

Suddenly his pledges seemed far more valuable than the flowers and jewelry she once chided him about. "You're right. He told me if I married him that it meant our family, you and father as well as myself, would have more protection. We live on the edges of civilization, if we are going to face monsters, it's better to stand close to the monster slayers than to flee."

"Now that sounds like my Mirabelle," Daleen said and gave her a smile of encouragement.

"Do you want to see your dress now?" Collette cut in, "We have to get you ready soon if we are to make any final alterations and arrive on time."

Mirabelle nodded and stood up. "I'm ready."

35
AT THE CHAPEL IN THE GOWN OF AUTUMN FROST

The morning wore on and before long Devon took his place near the altar to await the processional. His armor remained spotless, unlike some others, since he didn't have it on when he fought the skeletons the night before. He silently thanked Rhys for the hundredth time for getting him out of there in one piece.

Priest Magnus and Priestess Lila looked resplendent in their white and gold garments with their purple stoles embroidered with the star violet bluets of Rhys.

Theovald stood on his right, just behind him a step, as his best man. His upset over 'the talk' given by the others at breakfast had finally dissipated and he stood proudly at Devon's side on the second most important day of his life. He had attended the most important day, that of Devon's investiture.

The aisle of the Temple was lined with paladins, prepared to salute the bride. Devon could see his family in a small section of pews up front with local townsfolk filling in behind. His parents looked pleased, although his cousins appeared to be taking bets. Devon kept his annoyance off of his face. He didn't want to know what they were speculating on.

He focused his attention on a pot of cut roses in the back,

surrounded by star violets. The roses represented Dido, the Goddess of Love and Life. He knew Theovald collected the star violets. They shouldn't even be blooming now; they were a spring flower. He wondered if they came from the grave of Sasha, Theovald's beloved. Could ghosts be blessed by Rhys? Were there undead who weren't inherently evil? Theovald's story suggested some level of goodness still, but a ghost was still a ghost and even he freely admitted that he came close to dying for this one.

However, Devon could not fault Theovald for a dedication to his beloved beyond death. Surely if he could protect Mirabelle from beyond, if he were to perish, he would do so. Suddenly the musicians struck up the precessional hymn. Priest Magnus and Priestess Lila led the way, their heavy garments blocking much of what lay behind them. They went around the altar and a blonde girl Devon didn't know scattered rose petals as they entered. Then Mirabelle's parents came together, taking up their places to his left, and as they moved away, the honor guard of paladins drew their swords and raised them to create a tunnel. He had only the barest glimpse of Mirabelle before the field of blades hid her from view. For once he did not care to be patient, but it was the moment he needed it most. Then she appeared and his breath caught in his throat.

Her dress appeared to be made up of frosted fall leaves. A set of violet star bluets was pinned near her shoulder and more decorated the edges of the long gloves on her wrists. The violet blues of the flowers were reflected in the elongated crystals set in silver that dangled from her ears. The same shades were picked up by her eyes, turning them from deep blue to a rich violet. A silver tiara made to look like the half sun of Rhys held mist-fine lace in place decorated with a cascade of bluets in sprays down either side of her face.

A stirring deep within his heart whispered to him at the sight. She looked like a bride who had been clothed by Rhys herself. There were no better omens he could ask for than what she chose. Gently wrapping his mailed hand around her gloved one, they turned together and placed their hands over the Book of Rhys as they prepared to hear Magnus intone the prayers.

"May Dido, Goddess of Love and Life, to grant you a long and loving life together. May Anjasa grant you the bounty of Spring. May Sigvarder keep truth upon your tongues that you may prosper together. May Zsofia and Quinn, in their great knowledge and wisdom, help you find your common interests that as you grow old together, you may always find joy in one another's company. When finally you leave this life, may Rhys guide you safely home." Now we shall have readings from the Book of Rhys."

He and Mirabelle stood for the entire ceremony and given his station it was very long. Occasionally he would squeeze Mirabelle's hand to see how she was holding up, and each time she squeezed back. He tried to keep his eyes forward on the Divinities, even though all he wanted to do was gaze upon the incredible beauty by his side. He couldn't believe she was here, that either of them were. He didn't deserve someone so brilliant, so shining, as if a star had fallen to the ground and taken human form.

At last the readings were over and cake and wine were brought out for them to share. "May you never grow hungry, nor ever thirst for as long as we are together," he said to her at last, holding one end of the plate brought out by Priestess Lila.

Mirabelle repeated the words back to him, holding her end of the plate in one hand. Together they each lifted a single small bite of cake and fed one another, showing their bond of trust. Priestess Lila took the cake away and replaced it with a chalice. Devon dropped a single gold coin into the liquid to honor Anjasa, then a single silver one for his dedication to Rhys. Linking arms with care first Devon then Mirabelle each swallowed a single sip from the cup, showing their choice to tie their lives and their fortunes together. Taking the cup away, Priestess Lila said, "You may now kiss your bride." Leaning in, he gave her but the softest and chastest of kisses. Mirabelle's eyes held confusion, but he turned her to face the cheers and applause of the assembled people.

Then the recessional song began, and he stepped out and felt her join him. Together they crossed beneath the blades of his brothers and sisters-in-arms to the waiting banquet outside. Valdesh the Younger gave his blessing and left out just after the presentation of arms to trade places with one of the town guards. No one wanted any trouble while the town was gathered up at the Temple. It would have pained Devon to have someone's house or store broken into during their ceremony.

It was nearly too cold for anything outdoors, but the weather so close to midday was pleasant and the number of insects to bother them were few. Sitting together at the head table, Devon introduced Mirabelle to his parents at last, and hers to his own. Then they all ate, the children of the Temple fetching dishes for them.

During the meal, Devon finally let his eyes drink in the sight of his bride. Mirabelle was truly his at last, and he was hers. Cries came for them to kiss and he could feel her surging to meet him. He laid his hand across her cheek and whispered in her ear, "Patience, my love." Then he kissed her lightly, pulling away sooner than either of them wanted. If he lost his control, there would be no end to the kiss. They were still in public and he had to fight against his desires, but soon, soon they would be alone.

36
CHASTE KISSES

Seeing Devon standing in the chapel's heart, his rich, dark brown hair resting lightly against his shining armor, he looked breath-taking. Mirabelle had to literally remind herself to breathe as she approached. The swords of the paladins rang out as they raised them in salute, lifting them high so that she passed under a bright, flashing archway. Emerging, she could see Devon's eyes filled with warmth and a softness that spoke more volumes of his feelings at this moment than words ever could. Her brother stood behind him, looking like the sun to Devon's shadow, his dark blonde hair shining like gold today. Mirabelle was glad Devon chose him as his best man, even if technically he shouldn't have. Should something happen to the groom, the best man was to take care of the bride. This ceremony would be the closest Theo would ever come to a wedding of his own with Sasha dead. Mirabelle spared a brief prayer for her and all those who could not be there today.

Then she was at Devon's side and the ceremony begun. She kept stealing glances at him, wondering at the chain of events that brought him to her. The words of her parents made sense now. She loved Devon and would fight for him; she had to understand that was exactly what he was doing for her. He was worth all the risk and potential heartache. Today he would be hers and she his for the rest of their days.

The prayers were intoned, and they shared the symbolic food and drink, Devon adroit even in the confining armor. Her mind raced ahead, correlating what such skills might lend to their wedding night. He was so calm, though, not the slightest tremor of nervousness. Mirabelle felt like she couldn't catch her breath when she gazed on him as their arms linked. She hardly heard it when Priestess Lila said, "You may now kiss your bride". She leaned against his armor, her head tilted up to receive his kiss, one that would set the world aflame surely, only to have his soft lips barely press down on hers and then linger hardly at all.

What happened? This was nothing like the kisses they shared beneath the willows or near their home. Surely he wasn't having second thoughts about her, but felt he couldn't back out? She had no time to find out as he lifted her hand and turned her to face the well-wishes of the crowd. Then the music struck up, and they were walking together beneath the blades and outside.

"That was well done, both of you," Valdesh said as he led the rest of the paladins out to where she and Devon stood. "May your future be all you hope it can be, and may the light of Rhys and the love of Dido guide you always." Mirabelle and Devon barely got to say their thanks before he headed towards the path to town and Devon led her away towards the banquet.

He settled her into her seat at the head table before taking his own. But then two strangers walked up to the head table and Devon's face lit up as he said, "Mirabelle, this is my mother, Kannitha and my father, Adelard. I'm so glad you made it in time," Devon said, rising to hug them both.

Mirabelle gently, if awkwardly, squeezed their hands in greeting. The dress Collette had created was amazing, but once up it was best to stay standing and once seated, it would take much sorting to rise again.

"It was a near thing, darling, the boatman we hired sprung a leak two days ago, and we lost an entire day of travel as he fixed it. I feared we'd miss the nuptials entirely!" Kannitha cried, flicking her fingers upward, showing it was in Fate's hands rather than theirs.

"I'm so glad you could be here. Anjasa must have had pity on you along the way," Devon replied, beaming at her. Mirabelle had never seen him so unguarded before.

"I have to say, you have a most beautiful bride, Devon. Your mother nearly had a fit that an invitation came for your wedding and she had never heard you write word one about her beforehand." Devon scratched the back of his head, looking shame-faced. "Well, it was a very brief engagement. The Temple is allowing me a grace period to get married before returning to the field. I sent the fastest courier I could, so you knew about it almost as soon as I did."

"It's not like you to be impulsive like that, Devon," his father said, his eyebrows knitting together, as he crossed his arms. He had the same strong shoulders as Devon, but walnut hair and grey-green eyes. Devon definitely took after his mother's dark brunette hair, nearly black where the shadows touched it. Her skin was paler than Mirabelle's olive, more like a cream that was made even paler still by the dark shade of her hair. A few freckles graced her brow. Both parents seemed to have a cowing effect on Devon, although neither raised their voices. Mirabelle could see how it looked from their point-of-view. She tried and rescue her new husband.

"It's not like that. He is best friends with my brother Theovald so has visited our family before on his rounds, but this time he decided that our family would be safer if we were tied closer together as we would have one or the other of them around most of the time that way. He explained the benefits of such a match before having to return to the field and offered me a proposal to consider while he was gone. When he returned, I accepted it. It was imminently practical."

His father seemed quite satisfied with the answer, but Devon was looking at her like she had been replaced with a changeling, and his mother was not mollified at all. "So are you saying you have no feelings for our son other than this practical agreement?"

"Well, I wouldn't say that. He's quite handsome, and we've become very fond of each other," Mirabelle realized she was addressing the ground and that she was blushing. That seemed to amuse Kannitha and eliminate her concerns.

"Oh, aren't you adorable? You're going to take good care of her, aren't you son?" she said, pinching Devon's cheeks.

"Yes, yes, mother!" he cried as he tried to ineffectually bat away her arms. The sight was so incongruous that Mirabelle couldn't help but laugh. She did her best to stifle it under a hastily grabbed napkin. So these people were Devon's parents? She could see a lot of him in them.

They chatted with them more during the meal, and her parents got to talk to him, but her brother seemed the most distant. Sometimes he would look over at her, but more often his eyes were unfocused, looking past her to the hill behind the town, close to their home where the cemetery lay. Mirabelle worried about him, but when she thought she would get up to speak to him, calls came for her and Devon to kiss.

She reached for Devon, more than willing to show that there was more between them than pledges and vows, but he held back from her again. Only a gentle kiss, longer than the first but still brief, did she wring from him with a whispered word on patience. It confused her and frankly, angered her. What was holding him back? Did he think that anyone here would look down upon him for showing some red-blooded affection? Or did he think they would whisper about her past if they showed off their true affections to the world?

Glancing around, she confirmed that none of her former companions from the thieves' guild showed up. Since most of the townsfolk did, given it was a huge event for the small town, she wondered what excuses they gave. She didn't expect Jarick, but Gemma didn't show up either, or even Storvald or Cory. Neither was Lee around, which did pleased her. Her skin crawled with the memory of his touch. She knew she probably shouldn't be thinking of them at all, today of all days, but she refused to be haunted by their memories anymore either.

Her time with them was one thing she gave up during her vigil. She planned to stop being hotheaded, but remembered that her spiritedness was something Devon said he liked about her. So she opted to be more cautious instead, to stop reacting before she understood the situation. If she were to be a shrewd haggler and a good head-of- household, she needed to think things through more and save the fire for when it was warranted. She also gave up her anger at Theovald. He grew up. It had to happen eventually, and it was time she did the same.

As for blessings, she asked Rhys to keep Devon safe, then her brother, and then her family. During the bonus hour, which felt like the longest of the night, she asked that she never shame her husband in word or deed. Devon had already seen the worst of her. It was time he saw the best, instead.

So instead of blowing up at him, she calmed her anger. Whatever his reasons, she would find out in private, and give him time to answer for a change. They'd come so far last night, she wasn't willing to let little fears settle in and ruin this day. When she stood to find Theovald, she discovered his chair was empty. She caught sight of her brother talking to her new husband over by the minstrels. His face looked serious, and he was making some complicated gestures with his hands while Devon nodded, looking just as serious as he leaned in to listen. She tried to walk over to them, but when Devon saw her rise, he loudly announced that they were leaving. It wasn't Mirabelle's plan to get going just yet, but they had not time to rehearse any of this together. The others gaily called farewell, and Trinity lead River Dancer over, her tack oiled and shining. Devon mounted first, and with Trinity's help they got her seated on River Dancer's rump comfortably behind Devon despite the many folds of the dress. A light click from Devon's tongue had them away, and Mirabelle watched the party and feast retreat, waving as they left, while growing nervous of what was next.

37

FIRST YOU MAKE BREAD

"Devon, should we really go to the homestead?" she asked now that they were alone.

His shoulders turned somewhat towards her, but she could not see his face as restrictive as his armor was. "It's safe now. Priest Magnus blessed it for a mile all around. Nothing unnatural can approach. If you don't feel safe, though, we could travel for our honeymoon instead. There are no restrictions on my time during my grace period, as long as I report in on time for my next round in two weeks. We must stop by the new house regardless as all our clothes and belongings have been sent over already."

Two weeks! "You'll be gone so soon?" she asked plaintively.

His shoulders twitched again, "I've already been on special leave for three, Mirabelle. I promise you, this one will be shorter. Only a couple of months and I will be home with you. Since it will be winter, they will probably allow me to just station here until spring."

"Then I'd rather not waste our limited time traveling. If you say the house is safe, then it must be true," she said, trying to sound decisive.

She felt Devon's hand on her knee. "It will be, beloved, I promise you. There are holy symbols of Rhys on both entrances. Nothing unholy will enter, even if they somehow got past Magnus' wards.

Should anything ever come, I will protect you. I promised you." His voice grew soft at the end, and she wished they were already there. As beautiful as her dress was, it didn't allow her to sit astride, and if they moved much faster than a walk, she'd fall off. Patience. Much too much of her time required the one thing she was worst at.

Finally, they arrived. It was only mid-afternoon; the sun sat fairly high in the sky for the lateness of the season. Nothing looked amiss or scary under the bright light, and the woods were a fair distance now that more timber had been harvested to make their fields. Still, she thought she'd make sure not to plant any fruit trees right up against its borders, just in case.

Devon got River Dancer settled in the single stall connected to the house while Mirabelle went inside. It was gorgeous. She had expected nothing other than boxes, really, and maybe a pallet made up on the floor. Instead, the interior was beautiful. Wood was laid in the fireplace, which was huge, with a small grilling area to the side and a long stone warming area in front. To the right stretched a mantle where she could set out dishes safely to cool. A rocking chair set near to that and a small wood table with four chairs stood opposite, the colors warm and inviting in contrast to the dark wood of the rocking chair. She wandered around in wonder; Devon had not shown her the interior. He had said that the masons needed to keep the site secure while the mortar set. He never mentioned that he built it based on her childhood daydreams. Did the man pay so much attention to what she said?

She wandered around, and it was all there, a loft room, the sitting area, there was even a screened off sun porch in the back which must have been Devon's own addition, but close to that was the lower bedroom, and in it a grandiose bed of carved wood, the headboard looking like the half- sun of Rhys and the canopy poles carved with the rose vines of Dido. Some vines looked so delicate they could have been real, just dried. A dresser stood across from it and a long hope chest at its foot. Upon the bed were pillows encased in pale linen with silver thread at the edge closest to the opening. A vast purple and white quilt done into the four-pointed star violet of Rhys, including the yellow center, completed it. She never dreamed such a thing existed, much less that it would grace her marriage bed.

Hearing the door latch, she returned to meet Devon as he arrived. "Devon, this place is beautiful," she said as he came in the door.

He gave her a wan smile and replied, "I'm glad you approve of it. I tried to have the builders include everything you asked for."

"You didn't have to do that, Devon," she said, fiddling with the fingers of her gloves as she removed them.

He stepped in close to her, raising his hand to touch her hair, "I did not do it out of obligation; I did it because I wanted to." Her heart fluttered as he stepped away, not wanting him to stop. "Wife, would you do me the honor of helping me remove my armor?"

Of course, that would have to happen first! "I'd be pleased to... husband," she answered, thrilled to say those words at last. Finally, she'd be his, and he'd be hers. All the desire she felt the night before came roaring back. She fought to keep her mind on the task as it danced with images of Devon's naked body entering the pool. The longer you remain distracted, the longer until you get to finally assuage these desires, she kept telling herself. Finally she got the shoulder straps loosened and Devon lifted away the breast and back plate sections. The vambraces gave her trouble until he showed her how to work the special catches on it. Once she freed his left arm, he went to work on the right and she tried to undo the straps on his lower legs.

There were a lot more catches and buckles than she expected. Mirabelle gained a new appreciation that knights, warriors, and paladins could get into and out of their armor so quickly. It was almost as bad as trying to get into a gown for a high ball! Soon, Devon was free of the last of it, placing it on a new armor stand near the door. His sword went next to it, hanging from a peg on the wall. He stretched and ran his fingers through his now shoulder- length hair. She doubted he realized how good he looked like that. Then again, maybe he did and was showing off for her. Now it would finally begin.

Except that it didn't.

Instead of finally coming to her and covering her in kisses, he lit the fire in the hearth. Well, that made sense. It would be cold tonight, and he'd want to check to make sure the flue was working. Perhaps they could lay some blankets out and cuddle in front of it later... after.

She gathered her skirts and settled as best she could in the rocking chair, determined to be patient. But next he dug around in the new jars and laid out a cutting board, dusted it with flour and began assembling ingredients. Mirabelle did not understand what this was about. "I'll be right back," he said. Pushing herself up and insuring she wouldn't trip on the hem of her gown, she went and looked. Yes, it looked like he was preparing dough, but for what?

She heard the pump running in the other room and Devon returned shirtless, with a bucket of water, his hair slicked down and wet. Well, maybe he had a plan after all! "I needed to get some water and after being in my armor in the sun all afternoon, I thought I would attempt to be more presentable."

"I don't mind," she answered.

"Oh, good," he replied and gave her a dazzling smile for a change. No, she minded less and less. But then he went back to making the dough. This had to be a first. She imagined trying to describe what to expect on a wedding night to her own kids. Well, when two people love each other very, very much first you make bread. Everything felt surreal. Was he teasing her? Was this some kind of test?

"Devon, what are you doing?" she asked. "Oh, I'm looking for the rolling pin so I can roll out this dough." Mirabelle squeezed her eyes shut and just rested her face in her hands. Once again, the man answered in the most obtuse fashion possible. She felt her anger start to flare, when her mind pressed forward the memory of her choosing to let go of her impatience and asking to never shame her husband. Oh, Rhys had a sense of humor all right. Well, Devon would explain eventually. Hopefully, before winter set in, but she would wait.

She began rocking to distract herself, wishing she had a book on hand. "You know, beloved, it's been a long day for me in my armor, I'm sure that dress must felt heavy by now. Wouldn't you like to change out of it?"

Oh, he was probably waiting for her to give him some indication that she was ready. "Yes, you're right, but I might need some help with these buttons in back." She stood, and he dusted the flour off his hands before attempting to undo the line of fine pearl drop buttons. She could feel his hands trembling and felt vindicated for her fumbling with his armor. Maybe now they could get the hammer to the anvil and get down to iron nails.

"You can probably hang that in the wardrobe in the bedroom on this floor. Your other clothes are in the hope chest. I wasn't sure how you wanted them arranged so I thought it best to leave it up to you," Devon said as he walked away from her and back to his bread. He placed the slightly bulky round into an iron skillet with a bit of oil. Utterly bewildered, Mirabelle stalked off to the bedroom. The carved roses were still beautiful, but they had little meaning if the two of them didn't consummate their marriage. She grumbled to herself as she threw open the hope chest. Maybe he was too tired after keeping vigil and entertaining all day? Before that, he nearly got killed in battle. Her motions slowed as she considered things from his point of view.

She was being selfish. She knew he wanted her, but if he didn't think he could stay awake, he might not want to consummate things and fail. It would look bad and be considered bad luck. "Oh, Devon," she whispered, glancing back towards the door to the bedroom. Her hand lit upon a very soft fabric and turning back, she held it up. It wasn't one of her things; it must be a gift, one for her wedding night. A silk chemise, with the thinnest of straps to hold it on, lay in her hand. The bosom was made of sheer lace done to look like roses, while beneath that the layer of silk fell in a long, straight line, pure as fresh snow and just as dazzling. Maybe he wasn't up to anything right now, but she could still treat him to a pleasant sight.

Putting away the 'gown of autumn frost', as Collette called it, she slipped on the silk chemise. Its cool, soft texture felt delicious against her skin. She felt desirable in it. Maybe that was enough for tonight. Returning, she took up her perch on the rocking chair. Devon seemed too engrossed in his baking project to notice.

He pulled out the pan, checked the contents, and to her further consternation, pulled out a block of hard cheese and began cutting slices. Was he still hungry? Wouldn't he have asked her for help if he was? Without turning around he grabbed an iron bread toaster, arranged the two items in it and held them towards the fire. Now this was going too far.

"Devon, why are you toasting bread and cheese? Aren't you interested in consummating our marriage? I mean, I can understand if you are exhausted, but wouldn't you rather spend your time kissing me instead of roasting bread?"

He turned to answer, did a double take, and nearly dropped the precious bread he spent so much time on. Turning back, he pulled the iron out and used a potholder to pull the melted cheese and browned bread from the poker and set the metal safely aside to cool. Carrying the slice to her, feeling the heat despite the cloth, he held it out to her on bended knee saying, "It's traditional among some of my Order for the husband to show his pledge to provide for the family by preparing the first meal for his bride on their wedding night. It's how a paladin shows his commitment to providing for his wife and their children all the days of his life. I thought you knew, that surely someone told you. I didn't think you wanted to wait for stew, so I made quick bread. I didn't mean for you to feel ignored. I apologize; I want you." His words came out in a rushed tangle, his eyes coursing over her as he spoke.

So that was it. As if all the ceremony they had already been through wasn't enough. Devon had to be half panicked now that no one had told her and they had sat here quietly for nearly a full hand span of the day waiting. Instead of saying anything at all, she leaned down and nibbled the very edge of the gift, then lifted it from his hands and set it on the ledge by the fireplace before wrapping her arms about his neck and kissing him soundly upon the lips.

He stood and drew her up with him, holding her tight against him, while she kissed him the whole time. Devon groaned against her hungry lips, legs buckling. He barely straightened under her onslaught. She could feel his desire stirring against her, and all at once he gathered her up and carried her across the threshold of their bedroom, far less tired than she gave him credit for.

38
A PERFECT CIRCLE

"Mirabelle, Mirabelle," she heard him whisper into her hair as he divested himself of the last of his clothing, then he slid her to the center of the bed and covered her smaller frame with his own. She let her hands run along the bare skin of his sides at last and heard him groan again at her touch. A fevered blush touched his cheeks as she met his gaze and he dipped his head down between her breasts, nuzzling and came up, as if for air, before kissing her neck with a hunger equal to her own.

Fire flooded through her limbs like the heat of the noonday sun. She wanted him like she never wanted a man in her life. How could he make her feel so much when they had done so little? Yet at the barest touch of his hand under her thigh, she arced up against him, his touch almost unbearable now that she could claim it at last. What would she do when it came to more than such light touching?

Her heart beat against the cage of her chest like a bird longing to fly free. Beneath her fingers, she could feel him doing the same. "Mirabelle," he whispered as he rose to look directly into her eyes, his own like dark forests that she lost herself in.

"Devon," she said back, unsure of anything anymore. Her times with Jarick did not prepare her for a moment like this. It emphasized that she never loved Jarick. She had tried to make herself believe that she did. He gave her some pleasure, but that was the difference. She loved Devon and because of that everything took on new dimensions. It was the difference of the colors of a forest at night and a forest come dawn. Devon was the morning sun rising in her life.

His hand reached between her legs and she clung tightly to him at even this barest foray. She saw him rub his fingers together, fascinated with the signs of her desire for him. "Are you prepared then, Mirabelle?" he asked at last. His very words sent a spasm of desire through her.

"I think so," she answered, wondering how she could bear to even wait any longer. In answer he slid the silk cloth up her body, his strong hands contrasting with the fabric as his palms followed the retreating cloth along her contours, his arms brushing against her raised nipples, sending shocks of sensation through her.

She marveled at how even his most inadvertent touch set her skin aflame, and as she gazed into his eyes, she could feel him positioning himself. Her breathing grew fast. At last, at last, her mind sang as he pushed into her, making them one.

Unbelievably, it hurt. Yes, he felt good, but she had not hurt like this since her first time with Jarick. Did the purification ritual cause this, or was it something else? Either way, it felt exactly like she was having her first time over again, but this time with the right man. The pain must have shown on her face because Devon murmured, "Are you all right?"

"Yes, yes, I'll be okay, just keep going," she replied, her eyes fluttering closed and her bosom lifted as he buried himself deeper within her. He began a rhythm, but it was so slow as to be excruciating. His was the tide at the beach, reaching farther each time, until it reached its highest point. She could feel every inch of him sliding against her, every moment, her body trembling, echoing the sensation like ripples in a pond. "Faster, Devon," she called, but he would not comply. Jarick always hurried, and she became accustomed to having to come quickly or not at all. Devon's deliberateness took her utterly by surprise, and her body trembled beneath him. A slow sensation, like a building wave not a sudden heat, filled her until it flowed out like the rolling white cap of a tall wave.

She felt like she was drowning in their lovemaking, yet it didn't end. Just as the incoming tide rose higher and higher, never fully retreating, her body remained in this warm pool of sensation, yet the surf within her built up again. The crest broke a second time, and she felt drunk on their love. She did not believe her body could withstand his gentle, steady attention much more. Never had a man taken his time with her. Perhaps this was the mark of a man over a boy, she thought, but Devon still was not done with her. He only asked, "Are you okay?" and at her assent, dove into her once more, causing her to cry out at the perfect feeling of them together.

Tossing her head back and forth on the pillow, she didn't believe she could survive much more and begged him, "Faster, Devon, please!" He paused, and gave a heavy sigh, but complied with her wishes. It was better, and so much more than she thought possible. A sheen of sweat covered them both and if her skin felt hot, then his did even more so, and his lips, ah, his very kisses seared her soul. When she came again, she cried out, wrapping her legs around him, unable to do more. She felt as if they were one, a perfect circle of him giving of himself, and she receiving. Mirabelle surrendered all of herself to the moment, to him, and was swept away, completely lost in this sea of love which they found themselves in together. Her heart knew his and when at last he came, she could barely recognize the sensation as separate from her own. He exploded inside her and bowed his head against her shoulder before his body collapsed upon hers.

She cradled his head and shoulders against her, as gentle now with him in the afterglow as he had been with her throughout. She kissed his damp brow and ran her fingers through his sweat slickened hair, amazed at his prowess.

At last his breathing slowed and his beautiful, strong body relaxed against hers. Turning sleepy eyes to her he said at last, "I hope I have acquitted myself adequately with you, my bride."

"You have," she whispered, "you have." Didn't he know?

39
WHEN TWO SOULS TOUCH

When she accepted his humble meal he was glad, but when she kissed him, he nearly came undone. Devon had been holding back and holding back for so long, it seemed almost painful to let even the barest hints of his need for her escape. He caught himself before either of them could fall over and took the risk out of the picture entirely. Sweeping her off her feet, he carried her to the bedroom and laid her upon the bed. His eyes raced over her body in the pale silk that hid nothing from him. Her form adorned the bedspread with the symbol of his Order, making her seem like a gift sent from Rhys himself. Perhaps she was.

Leaning in, he rested his cheek against her hair and murmured her name as he divested himself of what little clothing he still had on, unwilling to be separated from her even for so brief a time. Naked at last, he pressed his hands against the softness of her body to insure she was settled safely in the bed lest either of them fall off. He wanted to take no chances during his first time.

Placing himself ascendant above her, he was unprepared for her touch as her delicate hands ran down his sides in intimate ways that he had never experienced before. He groaned in unexpected delight and felt nearly feverish just from the touch of her hands upon him; he looked into her night ocean eyes and wondered how he could be so fortunate. Glancing down at her chest, he allowed himself to bury his face in their promised softness at last; they were all he imagined and more.

He nuzzled them, lightly kissing their sides through the cloth before raising his head, his cheeks burning with a new heat, one he had never allowed himself to feel until now. He gulped in cool air and began kissing her neck as she had done to his before under the serrated willows. His worries of what he should do faded as passion took hold; she reacted in much the same way he did. He crossed from one side to the other; kissing her all along the way. Breathing in her sweet scent, he felt intoxicated by it, by her, by finally being in the moment with his sweet Mirabelle.

He allowed his own hand to rove down the curve of her until it rested on the underside of her thigh. This brought her rising under him unexpectedly, her eyes closing and her breath escaping her in a gasp. Her fingers found his chest and rested there, so he paused until her eyes sought his and called her name softly, making sure she was all right and still with him. She answered with a single word, "Devon." His name never sounded sweeter than coming softly from her lips this way. He wanted to please her so much, his new bride who entrusted him with all of her. She gave him not just her body, but her future. He didn't want to fail her.

Lifting his hand up from her thigh, he brought it between her legs as he had been told to do by innumerable people's suggestions. He couldn't really feel much more than heat from her body, so great was the wetness there. Or did it just seem so to him? He lifted his fingers and marveled at the reaction she had to him. She wanted him as much as he desired her, it seemed, but he had to be sure. "Are you prepared then, Mirabelle?" he asked, searching her face for any signs of uncertainty or hesitation.

Instead, her body bucked beneath him and she quietly said, "I think so." Encouraged, he removed any barriers between them. He wanted to experience the fullness of her, not some entangling cloth, no matter how lovely. Lifting the garment free, he felt her skin hot beneath his touch and then her taut nipples grazed the delicate skin beneath his arms as he freed her from the cloth, causing an answering squeeze in his loins. Ah, Mirabelle, what is it in you that can draw such from me?

Nervously, he grasped his swollen rod and laid the tip against her soft folds, moving it up and down until he believed he had discovered her center and hoped he was right. At last he pushed in against her folds and felt them part for him. He tried to enter slowly but still heard her hiss slightly, as if in pain. Her face read the same. "Are you all right?" he asked quietly, holding still lest he actually cause her the least suffering. "Yes, yes," she answered back swiftly, "I'll be okay, just keep going." This wasn't the same thing as not being in pain, but the others had mentioned that it could be painful for a woman the first few times. He wondered why they tolerated it at all then, but as he slowly slid himself deep within her warmth she rose again, her bared breasts dancing before him as her eyes fluttered closed with a look that echoed more of pleasure than pain. Satisfied, he moved within her, slowly, carefully both to keep from hurting her and to keep himself from 'coming to his full' first. For all that he had tried to ignore all his fellow paladins' advice, it came back to him anyway, and being new to the experience, he listened to their words. Well, the most helpful sounding parts.

Mirabelle clung to him and her body shivered and twitched as if striving to match him. He didn't expect this and could not tell if she was arriving at her own culmination or not. All of it felt good to him, so he did his best not to be overwhelmed by the experience of being one with her at last. He just plunged on with a slow, steady pace.

"Faster, Devon," she called out, startling him, but if he hurried, he would surely not last, and he feared to hurt her. Instead, he kept his even pace and felt her thrash beneath him, making it harder and harder to focus.

Unsure of what she was experiencing, he paused mid-stroke to ask, "Are you okay?"

"Yes," she answered and reassured he took up his pace once more, sliding in swifter and harder than he intended at first, causing her to cry out. Her head thrashed back and forth on the pillow beneath her and he grew concerned. However, she only called out, pleadingly,

"Faster Devon, please!" He stopped instead, wondering what to do. Marsid's words continued on in his head, "Do what she tells you to do."

He sighed heavily. Surely he wouldn't last long this way, but since Mirabelle asked it of him, he must do his best to try to fulfill her wishes.

Leaning in low, like a horse preparing to run full out, he quickened his pace, his body sweating with exertion. He kissed her mouth then, feeling the pressure building up within him. Suddenly she stopped striving, stopped trying to match him, but wrapped her legs around his back. Her body pulsed against him, and she sighed with such a soft, sweet sound that he felt one with her at last. In the midst of that moment, he felt a greater love washing through him, the call of the Divine, as he lay joined with his wife. Time seemed to slow, to stop, and he could feel all of Mirabelle's hopes and fears within himself and his own moving to rest in her. He knew they could survive anything if they took up each other's burdens instead of their own, and with the revelation came release. He fell back into his body, into time. Empty of all strength, he bowed his head against her shoulder, and then collapsed fully upon her, unable to even disentangle himself from her.

She turned slightly, and cradled his body gently against hers, her lips a tender blessing upon his brow. Her fingers traced cooling furrows into his hair and he hoped he had made her happy. His eyes felt heavy, but he needed to know. "I hope I have acquitted myself adequately with you, my bride."

"You have," she whispered, "you have." He would have drifted off right there, but

Mirabelle spoke again. "Devon, I have to confess, I've felt nothing like that in my life. I don't even have a word for it, what we shared is so different from anything I've ever known, I have to know if you felt it, too."

He considered the event and knew at last what must concern her so. "Yes, beloved, I believe so."

"Then what word describes all of that?" she asked earnestly. He realized there would be no rest unless he explained it as best he could.

"That, my dear Mirabelle, is ecstasy. I felt the same thing when I first felt called to serve Rhys. It's how I know when I've made the right decision about something important, but without all the physical exertion we went through just now."

"It's when we mortals experience Divine Love. I didn't expect it to happen to us. I've heard of it happening between two people who deeply love each other. It's the closest two souls can come to touching while veiled in a body of flesh, so I'm glad to know you experienced it. Perhaps now you understand why I am so committed to my calling. How could I not be, knowing so deeply and fully that it is what I have been sent here to do?" Devon gathered up one of her delicate olive hands into his tanned one and gazed lovingly into her eyes.

"Well, I hope it means more than that this time," Mirabelle answered, testing the feel of her fingers wrapped in his. "I hope that it is a good omen for our future."

Smiling, Devon gathered her up into his arms, saying, "As do I."

As they drifted off to sleep together, Devon held Mirabelle close. He kept her body gently sheltered from the cool air of evening within the warm, protective circle of his arms. Looking down upon his bride tenderly, Devon marveled that Mirabelle had entrusted him with the most precious treasure she owned: her heart. In return, he would give her the most sanctified gift he had, that which formed the very foundation of a paladin's honor: steadfast commitment and love. He would keep her gift safe, enfolded within his heart of hearts where no storm could assail it and no thieves take it. Kissing her softly, he closed his eyes at last, blessed in ways he never dreamed possible with a helpmate he never hoped to find, one that he could wake up to every morning with renewed joy.

GLOSSARY

- Adelard-Devon's father who lives in Riverfield.
- Adelle Maron-fashion designer who shows her work off at the Winter's Night Ball, but likes to live in the country for inspiration and to get away from the gossiping and jockeying done at Court. She intimidates people with her proud and commanding presence.
- Alarick-Mirabelle's father. He is a farmer and orchard owner who, along with his wife Daleen, decided to plant some of the more uncommon crops to sell to the nobles in the cities. That is why they have the small, highly fragrant plums his daughter was named for and the tiny champagne-style grapes that can be nibbled off the stem while reclining.
- Ali-Priestess of Dido known for her cheeriness.
- Anjasa-one of the Four Siblings. Anjasa is the goddess of the full sun and luck. She protects waterways and guides lost travelers. Her temples are often lighthouses on or near water.
- Aubrin-Great Victor Paladin of Sigvarder.
- Bailey-Member of the Riverfield Thieves Guild. Large guy running to fat. He's baby-faced so he winds up looking like a

GLOSSARY

giant toddler. Likes to throw his weight around and bully when allowed. Talks big, but he's actually a coward when someone challenges him with intent.
- Bard-one of the Four Siblings. He is the god of musicians, storytellers, and bards. As such, his symbol is found at the hearths of inns rather than in formal temples dedicated to him.
- Battleforge-A mountain town that was attacked by a full-scale undead army. Theovald barely survived that event, not all he was with were as fortunate. As dawn rose, the ghost of his fiancée drove off the wraiths waiting in the shadows where the light coming down the mountain hadn't reached that were going to attack him. He's been struggling with the burden of that vision ever since.
- Caseus-Father of Sasha. He is a dairy farmer who raises sheep and goats and produces cheeses to sell.
- Casimir-Victor Paladin of Sigvarder. Was at Battleforge with Theovald during the attack by the undead.
- Catkin-Victor Paladin of Rhys. Her sacred steed, Dayspring, is one of the fastest so she is often sent with messages. She has dark hair and pale skin. She's not from Riverfield. Fond of Theovald.
- Collette-Adelle Maron's first-rank apprentice. She has good instincts and has been longing for a chance to show off her skills.
- Cory-Member of the Riverfield Thieves Guild. Goes by the code name of Corby. He is a young boy on the edge of his teen years. His ability to look sweet and innocent is a boon to the group.
- Cyrano-Great Victor Paladin of Sigvarder. Instructor of the salle.
- Daleen-Mirabelle's mother. Farmer and orchard owner with her husband Alarick, she has a history with Adelle Maron that allows her to stand on equal footing with the intimidating woman.

GLOSSARY

- Darveed-Mage-for-Hire and part-time detective often in service to the Temple of Sigvarder in Sanctuary.
- Dayspring-Catkin's blood bay sacred steed. Known for her sleek lines and speed. When the Paladins of Rhys need a message out fast, Catkin and Dayspring are often chosen.
- Devin-Victor Paladin of Rhys partnered with the sacred steed River Dancer. He has dark hair and brown eyes.
- Dido-Goddess of Life and Love she is the bride of Rhys.
- Divinity-An alternate generic term for a Priest or Priesstess.
- Duskdale-A city further north than Mistvale. Site of a recent attack by undead. It only has a shrine, not a full temple at it.
- Edmond-merchant in Sanctuary.
- Enkairos-the name of the world where the stories take place.
- Field, The-this is the secret sacred ground where all the paladin's mounts are born. When they are summoned or sent, that is where they go or pass through. Only those born there can travel with them. That is why most paladins can't, however, the breeders and handlers from The Field, can.
- Glassglow-Paladin of Rhys. One of the first Lizardmen paladins. He has a mottled pattern of blues and greens on his skin, light blue bands on his stomach like the underbelly of some snakes, and hints of yellow near the horny growths on his head. His forked tongue is blue at the base that goes into purple then black at the tip. His goal is to help save his people from continuing to be thralls in the service of other beings like dragons or liches.
- Geffrey-owner and innkeeper at The Silver Rushes Inn in Riverfield.
- Gemma-Member of the Riverfield Thieves Guild. Her code name is Gem. Gemma has a large, soft, curvy body with fiery brown eyes and dark brown hair. She is motivated by greed and a desire for fine things she can't afford on her own, but she can be sympathetic and thoughtful of others.

GLOSSARY

- Hanalie-seamstress and mother of three in Riverfield. Married to Hubert the Tanner.
- Happy Story-Young server at the Temple of Rhys in Riverfield. Children are given hopeful childhood names that they can change as they come of age as adults.
- Heathsrow-Frontier town farther out than Riverfield known for its stone buildings and sheep farming. Has a temple dedicated to Dido at it. It lies about 14 miles from Riverfield.
- Heidrune-blade and utensil seller in Riverfield and mother of four. Married to Vance the blacksmith.
- Honey Flower-Young server at the Temple of Rhys in Riverfield. She has blonde hair and green eyes. Still very young.
- Hubert-Tanner in Riverfield. Married to Hanalie and father of three.
- Jarick-Current leader of the Riverfield Thieves Guild. Goes by the code name "Black Jack". Has red hair, freckles, and bigger dreams and talk than he has skill. More interested in power and what people can do for him than actually leading them.
- Jeweled Cities-rich trade cities along the coast of the Azure Sea.
- Kannitha-Devon's mother. Dark brunette hair that is nearly black where the shadows touch it. It makes her skin look paler than it actually is. She has a few freckles on her brow. Devon takes after her in hair color and gentleness.
- Kelesandra-Goddess of the Mountain Elves. She governs prosperity, abundance, life, death, and the hunt. Known as "Goddess of the Hunt" by the elves.
- Kosh-Former head of the Riverfield Thieves Guild before getting caught and sent to Wyvern's Gate Prison.
- Laguna-A major port town that has some waterways for streets in portions of it. It lies west of Mistvale and Duskdale. This is where Devon and his family are from.
- Lee-Member of the Riverfield Thieves Guild. He is Jarick's

GLOSSARY

second-in-command and goes by the code name . Has very yellow teeth and not known for having the best hygiene. Lee is a follower looking for scraps from the table of those above him.

- Leonessa-head of the guard in Riverfield.
- Lila-Priestess of Rhys stationed in the temple in Riverfield. She has a quirky sense of humor, but is always ready to aid the members of her order and community. She is well-skilled in cleric powers and uses her humor to counter her serious presence.
- Little Mercy-Young server at the Temple of Rhys in Riverfield. She is a little girl, full of giggles and not old enough to be fully coordinated yet. Many of the children who serve are orphans. Serving at a Temple insures they have a safe upbringing and will learn to read and write so they will have skills useful in the outside world if they choose it when they become adults.
- Masquerade Ball-A ball to honor Dido's return from her time as Lido, Goddess of Sorrow and Death. Since it is drawn from the apocrypha of Rhy's taking on a female form to woo back Dido, it isn't officially honored by the Temple of Rhys, but it is by the Temple of Dido. For many, it is a chance for singles to find romance and for couples to honor the importance of romance in their relationships. It is a day dedicated specifically to courtship rather than sex. It is also one of the biggest social events of the year and one where elaborate costumes are shown off.
- Magnus-Priest of Rhys stationed in the temple in Riverfield. He has dark hair, a moustache, and a short, trimmed beard. His deep voice can be heard clearly and loudly in a crowd or in the back pews of the Temple. It rings out like the tolling of a bell. Cheerful and often easy to talk to, he is a skilled cleric and a good listener.
- Mandy-A childhood friend of Mirabelle who lives in town in Riverfield.
- Marsid-Victor Paladin of Rhys and trainer

GLOSSARY

- Melandra-Mage that Theovald held in his arms as she bled to keep the wards up against the invading undead at Battleforge. She died as dawn arrived, but placed the scales of both a blue dragon and a red dragon on her tongue before she passed. The legend is that those who are given a scale freely by a dragon may make a single wish. The price for the dragon is that the scale will never grow back. If one swallows a such a scale, it is said they will come back as a dragon in their next life.
- Mitch-Member of the Riverfield Thieves Guild. Goes by "Springer" as his code name. He is handsome with dark hair, cool grey eyes and flawless skin. He dresses well, has a very precise style, and real skills. Shows no real interest in Mirabelle or Gemma.
- Mirabelle-Sister of Theovald and daughter of Alarick and Daleen. Member of the Thieves Guild with the codename of Mirror. She got her mother's dark hair, but has a more fiery temperament than either of her parents. Loves stories of the wider world of Enkairos.
- Mistguard-a city north of Riverfield. Lies between Riverfield and Duskdale.
- Mizzel-Resident of one of the outlying farms near Riverfield close to the woods. He died from cutting his leg with an axe while chopping wood. Bled out before those trying to help him could get him to a temple for healing.
- Naga-A mysterious race of half-snake, half-humans that live among the Eastern Islands.
- Necessary, The-when someone says they need to use the necessary, it means "the restroom".
- Noble Heart-Sir Theovald's gelding. He's not fond of the noise of crowds in towns. Not one to stay on task when not in battle. If Theovald isn't paying attention when they are riding, Noble Heart will look for a nice pasture or go back to a temple to graze in. When undead are around, he grows very alert and will try to warn the people or horses around

him that there is danger. He is very on point and responsive to commands when in battle.
- Old Man Truant-a farmer from Riverfield who died from a widow maker branch falling on him on his property.
- Orla-younger serving girl at The Silver Rushes Inn in Riverfield.
- Paladin is someone who is a dedicated servant of a God/Goddess in the military branch arm of a religion here. Has not seen battle. Victor Paladins are those who have been tested in the fires of battle. Great Victor Paladins are major generals who have survived many battles and are considered to have a certain mastery of tactics and diplomacy. They are usually older and are retired from the field.
- Pazel Wormwood-Riverfield's apothecary. His family is known for a string of shops from Riverfield to the capitol city of Sanctuary. Theirs is the first "chain" store. The Wormwood family's claim to fame is that you can find the same items and same quality at all their shops. Pazel added a soda counter to his as the town liked to make ice cream annually before the last of the ice cut from the nearby waterways melted come summer.
- Raymond-Cemetery caretaker who takes over in Duskdale after the uprising in Paladin's Honor.
- Red Sunrise-Young server at the Temple of Rhys in Riverfield. He has dark red hair, a freckled face, and doesn't like to study much. He does try, but is unrepentant that he isn't big on it. Jaunty and active, he's actually quite likeable. He keeps being warned by Priest Magnus that if he doesn't study harder his adult name will be Rock.
- Rhys (female form)-Rhys is the goddess called "Lady of the Dawn, "She of the Hearth Fire", and "Bringer of Hope". Most honor Rhys' male form as he conquers the undead. However, Rhys the goddess is form Rhys took to court the goddess Dido when she went into despair. She is the

warmth of hearth and home and has granted mana from her hand to her people before.
- Rhys (male form)-(Pronounced as "Rise" but in some regions it's "Reese" due to language shift) The husband of Dido, Rhys is the "God of the Dawn" and "Enemy of the Undead" and "God of Innocence". It isn't the naivety of not knowing but the innocence of knowing what is bad and choosing what is good.
- River Dancer-sacred mount paired with Sir Devon. She is mostly motivated by food, has a placid temperament, and doesn't spook easily. She's smarter than an average horse, but not as smart as a person. She can recognize places she's been and horses she's known. She can recognize danger and will try to communicate the risk to her partner/rider. Will stand fast and listen well to commands when in battle.
- Riverfield-Home of Theovald and Mirabelle it used to be the farthest edge of the frontier settlements before Heathsrow was built.
- Sacred Mounts-Specially bred horses that serve as the mounts of paladins. They are smarter than normal horses, but how smart does vary between individuals. It takes years for them to be bred and trained, so a paladin who gains one takes good care of the steed. They are also born in The Field, a special area within the capitol city of Sanctuary from which they can be summoned or sent to aid their paladin rider. Because of their nature, they are not allowed to be housed with normal horses. All of them are battle trained and can be dangerous to by-standers if they feel threatened or dislike someone. Their partnered paladins have to keep watch over them as well as get watched over by them.
- Sanctuary-Capitol city where the heads of the orders of paladins are located.
- Sanctum-the town center of Sanctuary where all the orders of paladins meet and sort out religious problems as well as helping with some secular ones.

GLOSSARY

- Serafina-noble girl at court in Sanctuary.
- Silver Rushes Inn-Tavern with food and beds for travelers in Riverfield. It doesn't see many travelers as yet, so the innkeeper tries to keep the local tradesmen happy with decent meals and drink. The name implies the ambition of the owner to make the "silver rush in".
- Sonya-crowned ruler in Sanctuary.
- Storm-Victor Paladin of Rhys. His sacred mount was killed in a nasty fracas in the East. It was worse than the events at either Battleforge and Duskdale. His replacement mount had been bred, but she was a yearling during Paladin's Honor and it takes at least 2 years of training to prepare one for field work so as he said, "It's still my own feet or a standard horse for now."
- Storvald-Member of the Riverfield Thieves Guild. Goes by the codename of Stork. He is tall and ungainly-looking, but is actually quite dexterous. He acts as a lookout to spot potential marks and signal if one of the members has been spotted.
- Scarwrist-Victor Paladin of Rhys. One of the first Lizardmen to become a paladin. He was present at the Battle of Duskdale.
- Sigvarder-one of the Four Siblings. Eldest child of Rhys and Dido, Sigvarder is the "God of Justice" and "Judge of the Dead". His symbol is the azure dragon and the silver crescent moon. The azure dragon represents the frozen lands where the blue dragons live and the crisp clarity that comes with the cold. Justice is meant to be clear, and cold, not favoring one side or another nor being muddle-headed. The crescent moon represents inevitability. "All things must end" is one of the phrases commonly used by his followers. They also point out that "All things begin anew again." Just as autumn turns into winter, winter turns into spring. People can find new hope and new opportunities if they let go of the past and mourning in their season and seek what good lies on the path ahead. The followers of Sigvarder often pass

people on to Anjasa's luck and journey phase when they've reached that point.
- Silverlight-Sir Trenton's steed. Smart, playful and vain. Full of vim and vigor, Silverlight imitates Trenton's attitude a lot, often to Trenton's dismay. Gets VERY serious when the chips are down. Playful and a bit of a prankster, otherwise. He's smarter than anyone knows.
- Taryn-Mother of Sasha and a resident of Riverfield. She is a dairy farmer and raises goats and sheep. Known for selling cheese, milk, and cream locally.
- Tatyana/Tatiana-one of the Four Siblings. Goddess of ocean waters, skilled trades, and crafting. Tatyana was formerly a minor deity of the ocean. After the First Cataclysm, her island drifted to the frozen northern waters and she wound up mostly forgotten during the interim. Upon being rediscovered, she was invited to be a part of the family of Rhys and Dido. Her found family includes Anjasa who had familial ties to her in the past. However, the relationship shifted so they are now siblings.
- Temple of Knowledge-the vast library stronghold in the Great Desert created when the Storm King used the last of his being to destroy a predatory lich. Dedicated to Quinn and Zsofia, it waited a hundred years after the Second Cataclysm to open its doors to outsiders. Craftsmen and researchers strive to be accepted for study in their great halls to learn of lost arts, techniques, and knowledge. In return, they leave record of the new skills and lore they discover. The place is so vast, the librarians of it were able to form a conclave that lasted through the Second Cataclysm.
- Theovald-Mirabelle's brother and Victor Paladin of Rhys, partnered with the sacred steed Noble Heart. He was born in Riverfield and engaged to a childhood friend named Sasha. A vampire came to their town and took Sasha away. Theovald, untrained, got lucky in a fight and killed it. That kept Sasha from turning into a vampire, but she died from

the blood loss instead. After mourning her greatly, he joined the Order of Rhys to fight undead so that no one else had to go through what he faced.
- Trenton-Victor Paladin of Rhys, partnered with Silverlight. Both of them are known for their vanity.
- Trinity-The first centaur to become a paladin of Rhys.
- Valdesh the Elder-Great Victor Paladin of Rhys stationed in Sanctuary and Valdesh the Younger's father. He sits on the paladin councils and the city councils.
- Valdesh the Younger-Great Victor Paladin of Rhys stationed in Riverfield and the one who trained Marsid.
- Vance-the blacksmith in Riverfield. Married to Heidrune, father of four.
- Vivienne-one of the court fashion designers in Sanctuary.
- Wayland-Paladin of Rhys. He's a little more on the devious end.
- Winter's Night Ball-a huge social event at Winter Solstice in the capital of Sanctuary. The best seamstresses in the land show off their skills by having their dresses on display at the event. Nobles who like the look of the pieces place their orders for unique outfits for the rest of the year or for specific special events like Dido's Masquerade.
- Wynn-legendary matriarch of the Wynn line from the days of the First Cataclysm.
- Wynnimar-Great Victor Paladin of Sigvarder. Descendent of Wynn.
- Quinn-Sage God of Enkairos. Married to Zsofia. They are "The Grandparents" and "Guardians of all Knowledge and Wisdom". They are honored by most of the orders in some form, but their main followers are in the vast, hidden libraries that were created after the Catacylsm of the Gods. Their symbol is the half-moon with the white quill and the black ink bottle. Quinn represents the quill. However, rarely is one spoken of without the other of their pair.
- Zsofia-Crone Goddess of Enkairos. Married to Quinn. They are "The Grandparents" and "Guardians of all Knowledge

GLOSSARY

and Wisdom". Their symbol is the half-moon with the white quill and the black ink bottle. Zsofia represents the ink. When the First Cataclysm occurred, their followers were inspired to build strongholds in remote regions where they could safely house the remaining knowledge of the land. These library-temples were locked down during the pillaging of the liches. They opened up after a century and are considered exotic places to study and become masters of one's craft.

BESTIARY

- Brownie-Helpful house spirits that look like brown-skinned, furry people. They can be diminutive enough to sit on a pot hook or nearly as large as an ordinary person. They tend to abide with a family and work at night. They do not like to be seen. While helpful to their family of choice, they can be mischievous and even turn to hindering them if they don't give their house spirit the proper due. While milk or cream is usually given to them, bread and cream is also acceptable. Woe betide the person who dares try to harm the family of a brownie in their own house.
- Centaurs-Upper torso of a human attached to the four-legged body of a horse, centaurs are uncommon to see in Enkairos. They tend to keep more to themselves in their own society, but have been known to lure away youths and maidens on occasion to join them.
- Dragons-Winged, scaled, intelligent, giant reptiles dragons come in a number of varieties. Blue ones live in the cold wastes of the north or on mountain tops and can freeze people with their breath. Red ones like volcanos and breathe fire. Not all varieties have been recorded and categorized.
- Eel-A type of fish with a long, modified tail. Popular as a food for those who live near waterways that have them.
- Elf/Elves-The elves of Enkairos are often called "mountain

GLOSSARY

elves" as they live on an isolated piece of land by the ocean and are only seen off of it rarely. They have pointed ears, sharp eyesight, and a deft way of walking through nature as to leave little or no path.
- Fairy, Diminutive-These are the tiny humanoid magical beings that float around on butterfly or moth-like wings.
- Fairy, Trooping-Considered to be related to the elves, the trooping fairies are known of in lore as making pilgrimages twice a year, but they have not been seen by humans since the First Catacylsm.
- Griffin-Half eagle and half lion, griffins are fond of eating horses and known for lining their nests with gold. These are two traits that bring them into conflict with humans.
- Lamia-An all-female race of shape-changing humanoids. They are said to mate with human men and then kill them. Little is known about them.
- Lich-One of the greatest scourges of the land, liches were once human. Through necromantic magic, they keep their husk-like bodies going to continue learning the dark magics that allow the dead to be raised and turned into undead. They are masterminds that build up the numbers of humans and other races to experiment upon and to play war games with. They have become the greatest threat since the dark gods were locked away beyond the Outer Dark.
- Lizardmen-A scaled, reptilian humanoid, lizardmen live in swamps and often have simple lifestyles. They are usually considered evil, but most of their attacks on humans and other intelligent races are not by their own choice.
- Razmorah-A strange, insect-like monster inhabiting mountain passes. It is somewhat like a giant centipede crossed with a finned lobster. It doesn't seem to need a lot of water and has some amount of telepathy.
- Skeleton Warrior-The fleshless bones of some poor person or creature given a pseudo-life via necromantic magic. They serve the one that created them and attack tirelessly. Only

GLOSSARY

when the pieces are too damaged to link back together do they collapse, or if the spell is broken.
- Sprite-The more elemental type of diminutive fairies with dragonfly wings and great speed.
- Zombie-A shambling, rotting corpse that has a powerful bite and grasp despite its decrepit-looking frame. They can cause diseases, including the slow transformation of a person into another zombie who gets bitten by one.
- Zombie, Flesh-Created by taking the muscles off a person and attaching them to a wooden frame, flesh zombies act as shock troops that may not hold up well, but tire living opponents with their numbers. They were created by a lich who wanted to make the people he transformed into troops stretch farther.
- Zombie, Skin-These are the skins of intelligent beings that were removed in a single piece, brought to unlife, and then filled with unholy soil. They act as a mana battery for casting magic or doing necromantic rituals, but they can also empty themselves out to create a safe pathway across lands that have been blessed or made holy.
- Zombie, Snake (a.k.a. Skeletal Snake, Snake Skeleton)-Other creatures can be used by liches and other necromancers to make undead. The Zombie Snake or Skeletal Snake looks like an animated set of snake bones, but they have a gangrenous-looking acid venom. They often cause fear just from seeing them, but their unnatural movements increase that in those who watch the hypnotic pattern. Their bite can lead to a swift, but painful death.
- Unicorn-A divine creature that used to serve as a messenger to the gods. A hide as white as moonlight, a spiraling horn upon its forehead, they look like a horse with cloven toed hooves like those of a goat and a tail more like that of a lion. They tend to have more of a wild creature's muscle and whipcord look rather than that of a fat, happy pony. They retain the power to heal wounds with their horn and purify drinking water of poisons by touching it with their horn. It

is also able to pierce anything with it, although they may not always be able to extract it. While sometimes hunted for their power, those who kill one find to their dismay that the power does not reside in the horn, but rather in the abilities of the living creature. Just as the hands of a surgeon aren't any good without the healer attached, the same is true of unicorns. Some still try to experiment with it as an alchemical ingredient, although others believe those who hunt and kill such creatures are cursed. They appear to be intelligent, but are not known to communicate with humankind. Some regard this as proof.

- Werewolf-Cursed humans who turn into wolves. Some have the curse in their bloodlines, others acquire it by being bitten. Most are considered evil for many werewolves commit terrible atrocities while in their bestial state. If some are able to live peaceably within society, they keep their condition very quiet.
- Wraith-A type of undead that appears as a dark half-cloaked person with nearly skeletal, overlong fingers. The cloaks cover the face so there is nothing to see but shadow and they become formless rags below the waist. Floating through the air at night, they are able to chill people with their touch and seem to delight in paralyzing one limb at a time and then slowly draining the heat or life out of people. When they can't reach someone, they can create a field of despair around them that drains the positive emotions from their victims until they throw open their defenses and beg to die. They can't be harmed by ordinary physical weapons like swords or arrows. Magic and fire are the most well-known ways to combat them.

CPSIA information can be obtained
at www.ICGtesting.com
Printed in the USA
JSHW020148260522
26346JS00003B/5

9 781735 895659